Black Heart Auctions

SELLING INNOCENCE

JAYCE CARTER

Selling Innocence
ISBN # 978-1-80250-568-9
©Copyright Jayce Carter 2023
Cover Art by Kelly Martin ©Copyright September 2023
Interior text design by Claire Siemaszkiewicz
Totally Bound Publishing

The Omega's Alphas
Owned by the Alphas
Shared by the Alphas
Saved by the Alphas
Protected by Her Alphas
Caught by Her Alphas
Tamed by the Alphas
Claimed by the Alphas
Exposed by Her Alphas
Trained by the Alphas
Reclaimed by Her Alphas

Ready or Not
Fake It 'til You Make It
Opposites Attract
Third Time Lucky
Enemies Closer

Grave Concerns
Grave Robbing and Other Hobbies
Hell Raising and Other Pastimes
Saving the World and Other Bad Ideas

Dark Sanctuary
Bound by Fear
Trapped by Doubt
Buried by Despair

Nemesis
The Corpse Princess
The Resurrected Queen

Larkwood Academy
Silenced
Whispers
Screaming

The Devil's Luck
A Devil of a Time
Devil May Care
Run Like the Devil
The Devil's Due

Black Heart Auctions
Selling Innocence

Collections
Sun, Sea and Sinful Delights
Secret Santa: To Catch a Fox
Cupid's Academy: Stolen
Hot Bite: Summer Trips and Other Reasons to Get Naked

SELLING
INNOCENCE

Dedication

To my sister Jaymie — my rock

Chapter One

Kenz

Someone once told me the only cages that hold us are the ones we make ourselves. The idiot who said that clearly hadn't ever found himself locked up in an actual cage like *this*.

People walked past, glancing in as if I were some exhibit in a zoo instead of a flesh-and-blood woman. Some paused, leering or looking on with pity, but none stopped long enough to make me think they'd help.

A gag in my mouth kept me silent, and the cuffs on my wrists hooked together behind me, which meant escape on my own didn't seem all that probable.

Nem would have found a way...

I cursed myself yet again for not being my older sister, for not being as tough or as smart as the others in my life. They would have never let themselves get abducted, but I wasn't them.

I never lived up to the people around me, did I?

Whispers drifted to me, from the faceless people who walked by. Due to the light at the far wall, shadow bathed their faces and kept me from recognizing anyone.

She's so pretty.

A little old for my taste.

Might be worth some fun if she doesn't go for too much.

I wanted to shake my head, to tell them to screw off, but instead, I only trembled. Their words hit home, reminding me of *exactly* where I was, of how I'd gotten here.

I was at some sort of auction, and I was nothing more than merchandise here. The people who walked by were customers, people who had come to buy whatever illegal goods were put up for sale.

In addition to myself, I'd spotted paintings, jewelry, even a white tiger with the prettiest black stripes I'd ever seen. This was a place where people could buy anything — including me.

I sighed and rested against the bars at the back of the cage, trying to drown out the noise that surrounded me. How had everything changed so fast? How had I ended up here when my life had been so predictable just yesterday?

I just want to go back to yesterday…

* * * *

Yesterday

"Yes, Colton, I know!" The phone rested between my ear and my shoulder as I rushed through my room.

"You say you know, but the last time I visited, you weren't using your window locks." Colton's voice held the same annoyance it usually did. It was the sound that would send most smart people running, but I'd grown up with that voice.

"You don't understand. This is *Florida*, and it gets hot and muggy! I have to crack the windows."

"We'll have a better air conditioner set up, then."

"I don't need that. I just need to open the windows at night to let the cool air in."

"And when you let in perverts along with the cool air?"

"Well, at least I'll have a man over then." I let out a little squeak of happiness when I spotted my sketchbook, tucked under a sweater. I really needed to learn to organize better, but I'd never been good at it. Now that I didn't have people hired to do the job, I'd had to recognize how bad I was at it.

"You are more than welcome to have men over," Colton said. "Of course, I hope they aren't men you care about, since dead men don't make it to second dates."

I rolled my eyes, glad he remained safely on the other side of the country so he couldn't see it.

"Don't roll your eyes."

This time I stuck my tongue out, wondering just how I had lived so long with such overprotective worriers in my life.

"Now, if you don't listen and keep the windows closed and locked, I'll have cameras put in."

"You will not," I argued for what had to have been the millionth time. Having them see how I came and left was bad enough, but the idea of them actually *watching* me every moment I was home went way too far.

A scuffle on the other side of the phone happened before a smoother voice spoke, one who could convince almost anyone to do almost anything. "Do you have a boyfriend, Kenz?"

"No, Dane, I don't."

He let out a long sigh as if relieved. "Good. Now, have you gone to the doctor recently? Aren't you due for a checkup?"

"I had a checkup two months ago!"

"Her red blood cells were low," Bray called from behind, telling me Dane had put me on speaker. "She should go back to see if the iron pills resolved it."

I nearly asked how Bray knew that but shut my mouth before I did. Bray was a tech genius. He could find *anything* if he wanted to. My medical records and test results would have proven no challenge for him.

It drew my gaze to the pill bottle on the counter, the one that had gotten delivered to me the day after my appointment, the proof that they'd been involved from that point.

"I set up an appointment for her to see her diabetes specialist," Bray added on. "It will be in three weeks."

"She won't answer our calls anymore if you do this," Rune muttered, and I could almost see him shaking his head at the others. "Leave her be."

"She's leaving her windows open!" Colten argued back. "And there have been break-ins around there. She's in a nice apartment, but that doesn't mean she should ignore her own safety."

"Enough." Nem's voice cut through the chatter of the others, and again I found myself jealous. It took only one word from my sister for her to take control, even of men like those four. The noise on the phone changed again, making me suspect she'd taken the cell and turned off speakerphone. "I'm sorry," she said softly. "You know how they are."

"Yeah, I know." I tossed my sketchbook into my bag, checking to ensure my insulin pen was safely tucked inside, then surveyed the room once more for anything else I might need. "Look, I've got to get to class."

"Okay, Kenz. Have a good day. I'll call again in a few days." Just when I'd thought I might get off easy, Nem's voice floated back through the line. "Make sure you bring your pepper spray."

I glanced at the pink pepper spray that hung beside my front door, one of the ten that I had because each time any of them visited me, they always brought more.

And it wasn't *just* the pepper spray. I also had stun guns, Tasers, blades of all sorts and a 9mm in a safe in my closet. Normal people brought candles or sweet treats as gifts, but not my family. They brought weapons with them each time.

"Got it. I'll talk to you later." I hung up the call and tossed my phone into my bag with the rest of my things. At the door, I glanced at the pepper spray, then shook my head.

I didn't need it, and I refused to live in fear just because my family was paranoid. I locked the door behind me, then rushed off for school.

* * * *

I sipped my coffee, the elevator taking *forever* to get where it was headed. Then again, I had a feeling that was less about the speed of the elevator and more about just how my day had been thrown off by the call earlier.

The light over the doors lit up at floor three, and I let out a loud sigh. Of course, the time I was busy, someone else had to get on. The elevator slowed then stopped at that floor. The doors slid open, and a man got on along with me.

I had a moment of wishing I'd brought my pepper spray.

The man was tall and lean, but he had a physique I knew well. After growing up surrounded by killers and fighters, I could tell the difference between a body crafted in a gym versus one built by hard work and violence.

He had short black hair, long on the top but shaved tight on the sides and stunningly golden eyes. He said nothing as he got on but placed himself in the back corner of the elevator. Again, it set off warning bells in my head—it was something I'd seen the Quad do enough times to prevent anyone from sneaking up on them.

He didn't look my way, but I still felt as if he studied me. He wore a pair of slacks and a dark gray button-up shirt, the sleeves undone and rolled up to his forearms. He certainly didn't look like a student here.

I narrowed my eyes, wondering for a moment if Nem had lost her mind and hired a bodyguard for me. She'd threatened it enough times, but maybe she'd finally gone ahead?

If she had, she had another think coming. This man didn't come close to blending in anywhere.

The elevator shuddered to a hard stop, causing me to lose my footing. I stumbled forward, sure I would end up face first against the floor.

Before I hit the ground, however, someone strong and hard caught me. I jerked my gaze up to find the man there, having moved so quickly and silently that it startled me, reminding me that I had no idea who he was beyond identifying him as dangerous.

"Thanks," I whispered before pulling myself back together and stranding straight.

The man nodded and took a step backward.

"These elevators are always stopping." A nervous little laugh escaped me. "When I first got here, I never took the elevator because it scared me, but now? I guess dying in a fiery crash is better than walking up all those flights of stairs."

I cringed at my own words, the ones that escaped me in a rambling mess.

Worse, the man didn't even *try* to respond. He turned his golden eyes to me, as if to acknowledge that he'd heard me, but he said nothing back.

I pressed my lips together instead of saying anything else and digging myself any deeper. Thankfully, the elevator shuddered to life again and started its crawl toward my floor. When it reached there, I hurried off with one more soft *thanks* to the mystery man before I escaped the humiliation.

Attendants packed the room by the time I arrived, but at least all the people meant I didn't have to worry about anyone noticing how late I'd gotten there.

Of course, the full room confused me. The art department at my college hosted many artist meet-and-greets like this. They said that speaking to working artists was the best way to learn and gather information, so they'd host such events a few times a month. My professors always offered extra credit to go, and I sure needed that, so I always came.

However, it was usually just a few people and one artist questioning their decisions in life as they spoke to a mostly empty room.

This time, though, we had standing room only.

"Ms. Fox," Grisham Oreando, my student advisor, said as he walked up to me.

"It's still weird that you call me that while not letting me call you Mr. Oreando," I pointed out and took a sip of my coffee.

"I dislike that name. It feels too distant. However, it's a matter of basic manners to call a girl by her last name." He offered me a familiar smile, the one that made us almost feel like friends rather than him just being my advisor.

"Why's it so busy? Did Professor Calling offer extra credit or something?" She had made her lectures nearly impossible to pass, and she rarely offered extra credit. It was the only reason I could think that so many students would show, especially because I swore I spotted a few who never bothered coming to classes.

"You didn't hear? Vance Moore is here."

I twisted to cast a look of pure disbelief toward him. "Vance Moore? Are you kidding?"

"I am not. He rarely does these things, but I hear he was in town and contacted the school at the last minute to see if they might want him to speak."

"I guess that explains all the girls here. They probably just want to get a glimpse of that playboy. I mean, is there a model he hasn't bedded?"

Grisham chuckled softly. "I don't disagree. However, if you want your extra credit, you should go sign in officially."

"Fine," I muttered. "I'll go sign in then leave before I end up squished by the hordes of girls." I offered a wave to Grisham before heading toward the back, where the table with the sign-in sheet sat. I didn't expect to learn anything from some playboy artist who cared more about getting his paintbrush wet than actually drawing, but the day would be a waste if I didn't at least sign in.

I set my coffee down beside the clipboard and exchanged it for a pen on a chain connected to the clipboard. Once I'd scrawled my name there and checked the professors whose classes I was taking, I picked my cup back up again and turned.

Only to find a wide chest before me, so close that I nearly ran right into him. I jerked backward, avoiding touching him, but I didn't come out unscathed. The lid to my drink popped off and coffee spilled over the rim.

I hissed as the hot liquid touched my hand. More splashed onto my shirt, but that had more time to cool.

"Sorry," the man muttered in a clipped tone as though *I'd* been at fault, then turned and walked off.

It left me staring at his back, glaring at the idiot. He'd stood close enough to me that he could have played the part of a train molester, but he acted as if it had been *my* fault?

He was tall and broad, with dark, neatly cut hair, which was the extent of what I could identify from the back. *Well, he has a nice ass, too.*

I grabbed a napkin and patted it against my shirt— not that it helped. It was like trying to soak up ocean waves with a handkerchief.

"Are you okay?" The masculine voice was almost lyrical. It sounded far too pretty for someone male and drew me to turn.

The face that stared back at me made me freeze in place.

Why was it that seeing celebrities in person felt so weird? I'd seen Vance Moore on TV plenty of times, in magazines and on internet sites. I could pick him out of a line-up with ease.

However, having him staring down at me with those familiar bright blue eyes rooted my feet in place, making me suddenly understand why so many women had come.

He pulled his lips into a smile, one that hinted at mischief. It reminded me that he'd asked if I was okay, and I had entirely missed that.

"Yeah," I said, rushing the answer out as if to cover up my previous distraction. "No use in crying over spilled coffee, huh?"

His gaze dropped down my front as he lifted one of his blond eyebrows. He lowered his voice so it didn't carry. "You know, you should consider changing."

At that, I finally looked down to realize that, yeah, the coffee had managed to turn my previously cute white shirt entirely see through. It showed off the lace bra I had on, like the world's worst wet T-shirt contest. "Just great," I muttered, wishing I'd brought a jacket or something.

Vance slid off his jacket and draped it over my shoulders, the action smooth enough to tell me he'd done it plenty of times before. "Come on. I always bring some extra items when I'm speaking. They gave me a ready room just down the hallway."

"No, it's fine." I tried to remove the coat, afraid to get it dirty. A man as rich as Vance no doubt had clothing worth a small fortune. I didn't want to risk ruining the nice coat. "I'll just go back to my apartment."

"I insist." Vance placed his arm around me to halt my objections and guided me back, toward the exit at the far end of the room. "I couldn't in good conscience let a girl wander around with her shirt see-through. If someone attacked you, I'd never forgive myself. Please?"

It was the 'please' that got me. No one asked me anything in my life. Instead, people dictated to me, told me where I would go, what I would do. Sure, he was being pushy, but the please made it impossible to resist.

"Fine," I muttered, giving in. I'd just have to keep my wits about me, because Vance was the exact sort of man I didn't need interfering in my life.

* * * *

"Here." Vance dug a shirt out of a black rolling suitcase. The cotton was so soft in my hands that I struggled to not rub my cheek against it when he tossed it to me.

"I really can't take this." The idea of being indebted to anyone didn't sit well, but the thought of getting any closer to Vance was beyond a bad idea. A relationship with anyone wasn't smart for me, but someone with as much money and fame as Vance would only end up putting me in danger.

Him, too.

Still, Vance flashed me a smile I'd seen so many times from him in interviews. There it was, the face that had made the world fall in love with him. It made my stomach shift, that old cliched feelings of butterflies I knew better than to trust. He'd used that smile, that face to get him a place in the world.

Despite the fact he hadn't released any new art in five years, as far as I knew, he'd managed to stay the It-Boy of the art world because of his charm, his money and his good looks. He wore a long-sleeve black turtleneck along with a pair of gloves that covered his hands. I thought back to the interviews I'd watched.

Did he always wear them? I couldn't recall a time when he hadn't. Maybe it was some weird artist quirk?

"I insist," he pressed. "This is just a T-shirt. It's no big deal and it's the least I can do. Come on, change. There are wipes on the table over there in case you need to clean off the coffee. Take them into the dressing room right there, and I'll keep an eye on the door since there's no lock."

My ability to say no had dwindled to nothing, so, defeated, I grabbed the wipes and went into the dressing room at the back. It had a curtain for privacy, and I pulled that closed. Red skin showed where the coffee had hit me, and I used the wipes to clean the sticky area. Once I'd done the best job possible at that moment, I pulled on the shirt he'd handed me.

It was baggy on me, of course, but something about the soft cotton made me want to snuggle up in front of a fireplace and drink hot cocoa. It was like a piece of comfort sewn into the form of clothing. A faded image sat on the front, so old that I couldn't make sense of it beyond strips of colors.

Was this shirt important to him? If so, why would he let me use it? If it wasn't, why would he have had it for so long?

Or maybe it was one of those things that was made to appear old while actually just being trendy.

I bundled my old shirt and stepped out, finding Vance there with a sketchbook open and in his arm. He seemed fully focused on whatever he held, a seriousness in his expression I hadn't seen from him before.

It drew me in, made my feet pause as I just watched.

At least, it did until I realized that he didn't hold just any sketchbook. That was *my* sketchbook.

"Hey!" I rushed over to snatch the book away, indignation swelling inside my chest at the fact he would go into my bag and take my private things.

Vance didn't hand the book back, instead twisting and holding it out of my reach. "You're not bad," he said, his tone different from it had been before.

"Give that back! It's not yours."

"What year are you?" He flipped through my book, effortlessly avoiding my attempts to swipe it back each time I tried.

"First year." I crossed my arms, giving up. I wasn't getting that back until he decided. Trying to fight him over it wouldn't get me what I wanted, so why try? I'd only end up looking foolish.

"So you're smart? Good to know. Dumb, vapid girls are fun for a while, but they get boring fast." He shut the book, then handed it over. "You have nice lines, but make sure you focus on your perspective. You forward fill your pictures too much and ignore the background—it's a pretty common shortcoming of newer artists."

I stormed over to my bag, then shoved my book back inside with enough force that a tiny ripping sound suggested I'd torn the lining. *Just great.* "I didn't ask you for your opinion."

"Smart people accept good advice whether it's asked for or not." He smirked, his expression losing the luster it had before. Out there, he'd played the part of gentleman, but here?

He reminded me of a lion, lazy and arrogant and so sure of his own superiority. His blond hair appeared more yellow because of the fluorescent lights, and his blue eyes were almost shockingly bright. A five-o'clock shadow covered his cheeks, the presence of it enough to make him look a little less boyish than he would otherwise. One of his eyebrows was slightly higher than the other, as though he always had that one cocked up just a bit.

"Polite people don't go through another's things."

"Polite?" Vance waved that off as though unimportant. "Politeness is something for boring people. It's a set of rules I have no intention of following—and I'd suggest you do the same. So, I've given you advice and my favorite shirt. I think that earns me your name at least, doesn't it?"

I gave him the sort of look I'd learned from Rune, one meant to encourage him in no uncertain terms to back the hell off. I'd never really mastered the look, but I could only hope it gave him some pause. "That feels like another one of those politeness things, and since you don't believe in them, I think I'll follow your lead. I'll have the shirt cleaned and left with the receptionist for the art department tomorrow."

"No need."

"I thought you said it was your favorite?"

"It is, but why don't you keep it until I come get it back from you?"

"I don't plan to see you again."

"We'll see," Vance said with a laugh, the sound far too confident for my liking.

Instead of arguing anymore — it didn't seem that would get me anywhere — I left the room, slamming the door behind me.

This day was just getting weirder and weirder, wasn't it?

* * * *

"Where are you?" Jarrod's voice on my phone was hardly a surprise and neither was the way he went straight for the heart of the matter, forgoing any small talk.

"I'm busy."

"I didn't ask if you were busy. I asked *where* you were." His question came out as a warning, as though to challenge me to just try lying to him. Then again, Jarrod never asked a question he didn't already know the answer to, and he knew damned near everything.

I gasped as I was struck by a hundred and twenty pounds of teeth and fur. Because I'd been focused on the call rather than my surroundings, I hadn't even braced myself for it and ended up sprawled out on the linoleum floor.

"Kenz?" Panic bled into Jarrod's voice just as a long, hot tongue dragged across my face.

I pushed the overly excited mastiff puppy off me then scrambled to my feet, managing to save the phone before one of the retrievers took it and ran off. "Sorry, dropped the phone," I said, worried that he was already getting on a plane from just that moment.

The man really was that paranoid. Despite not having much of what I'd called a fatherly influence in most of my life, Jarrod — my sister Nem's biological father — had taken that role for me as well. He liked to show up unannounced, usually with food and money, then leave just as quickly. It felt like always having a shadow ready to swoop in should I need it.

"What was that?"

"Just an overeager man who doesn't know his own strength."

Silence met me, and I had to remind myself just who I was talking to.

"It was a dog. Well, he's a little over a year, so he's more of a puppy."

"So you're finally going to admit to getting a job?" Which meant Jarrod knew damned well that I was working part-time. It shouldn't have shocked me — it was pretty stupid for me to ever think I could hide something like that from him.

It made me sigh, feeling like a kid who thought I'd gotten away with something only to find out the adults had just been humoring me. "I didn't lie or anything."

"No, you aren't the type to lie. Of course, you learned the talent of misdirection very well."

"How long have you known?"

"Since you interviewed. Your boss called around to your references, and because I set those up, I was contacted."

"I'm surprised you didn't stop me."

"Your boss and coworkers all had clean backgrounds, so I saw no reason to intervene. Well, other than Riley. Riley has a habit of piling up traffic infractions and parking tickets. Don't get into a car with her."

I went about filling the water bowls at the doggy-daycare and boarding place I worked, pups following along behind me and fighting for my attention. I couldn't shake my unhappiness at Jarrod knowing.

Which, of course, he picked up on even through the phone. "You're upset?"

I laughed softly. That was so Jarrod—smart and observant enough to tell I was unhappy but bad enough with feelings to not understand why.

"I'm fine," I said.

"No, you aren't. What's wrong?"

"I just thought this place was my secret."

"I only know because I'm looking out for you. Nem and her idiots are the same."

"Yeah, I know." I sat on the edge of the barrier that kept the dogs in the center area, letting my heels strike the wall as I swung my feet. "It's just... I don't really get a lot of time to myself, where I don't feel like I'm under a microscope."

"But that is one reason you moved, why you live across the country. How could you still feel watched so far away?"

"Because you all are *still* looking over my shoulder! Nem picked out my apartment, Bray goes over my transcripts and medical records, Rune keeps sending self-defense teachers to my house, Colton threatened a new resident in the building until they left because he claimed the man 'didn't look like a good person,' and Dane had someone *drug test me* in secret one time! I'm supposed to be living my own life, but I can't go more than a day or two without you all intervening. I thought that this job was the one place in my life where I didn't answer to anyone, that I got on my own and that I controlled myself." My shoulders drooped. "I guess I was wrong about that, huh?"

Jarrod said nothing at first. In fact, it took so long that I thought for a moment he'd hung up. "We just worry," he said.

And just like that, I felt like the bad guy. I remembered what happened to my mother, to everything Jarrod and Nem and the Quad had seen happen. It wasn't like I was someone capable of protecting myself much, so could I really blame them for worrying about me?

"I know," I said, hating that I had no good answer for what to do from here. "I know you worry, that you don't want anything to happen to me. It's just hard to live like that. I thought when I moved I'd finally get to make my own choices, but it isn't like that at all. I still feel trapped. I want you all to trust me, to let me make my own mistakes. Sometimes I think about just running away, about trying to disappear and become anyone else, someone normal who doesn't have to deal with this all."

It was a stupid idea, of course, but I finally admitted it to him. I didn't think I'd ever actually try it—it wouldn't work even if I did because running from Jarrod or the Quad would take a skillset much bigger than my own—but the temptation was there.

He sighed, the sound making me feel even guiltier. "I'll talk to Nem for you. What if I got them off your back a bit? Nothing can change them entirely, but maybe I could get them to give you some space?"

I snorted at that idea. Jarrod was impressive, sure, but I doubted even *he* could manage something like that. It would take a miracle to get Nem or the Quad to loosen their grip on me, even a little.

A bell chimed to signal a customer had arrived, and never had I been so thankful for one. "Look, I'm sorry. I'm just stressed, but I have a customer. I'll talk to you later, okay?"

"Sure. We'll talk later." Jarrod hung up, but I couldn't shake the hurt in his voice.

I slid the phone into my pocket before hopping over the short wall and heading for the front lobby. The daycare was small enough that we didn't have a regular receptionist. It meant a lot of running back and forth, but I didn't mind that.

Staying busy made the time go by faster. I didn't make much money here, but it had never been about money. I had all I could use and more — a leftover from my parents' estate since Nem had refused to take a penny of that. Instead, it was all about my own independence.

I stopped short when I crossed from the back into the lobby and spotted the customer.

He was beyond lovely, taking me entirely by surprise. His hair was dyed red, but because it was shorter, it didn't look nearly as unnatural as Nem's. Dark eyes peered at me, and he wore a hoodie sweater that made him look like another college student. He wasn't that tall, his body lean, but none of that mattered. A sheen on his lips caught the lights, and when he smiled, I wondered if I should hold on to the wall to keep myself upright.

No man should be that pretty.

I said nothing, distracted by his good looks, and finally he let out a soft chuckle. "Is this Paws and Pause Boarding?"

You're at work you stupid floozy – get your head in the game!

I nodded, leaving the door to the back cracked open so I could hear if the dogs started snapping at one another. "Yes. Sorry. I was in the back and didn't hear you right away. How can I help you?"

He walked up and stuck his hand out, a friendly smile on those perfect pink lips. "My name is Char. I heard this place is fantastic, and I wanted to check it out."

"Wonderful. Are you looking for daycare or boarding?"

"Boarding. I go on a lot of trips. I was having someone stop in at my house to check on him, but I didn't like leaving my dog alone the rest of the time. I thought he might do better at a place like this, where he gets attention all day."

I nodded, then moved past him to the reception desk. From the top drawer, I pulled out a flyer that had our prices, rules and information. "Here's all the basics. We don't have a wait list right now, but if you're taking vacations right around the holidays, we do fill up. I'd suggest securing a spot early. What kind of dog do you have?"

"An Australian Shepherd," Char said. "He's a sweetheart but he's always on the go!"

I laughed at the exasperation on Char's face. I knew that feeling, having taken care of a few Aussies in my time already. "They are a handful. The nice thing is that we don't just take care of the animals – we also will do daily training lessons to keep them engaged. In fact, most clients can't believe how much better behaved their dogs are when they get back."

"That sounds perfect. Do you do the training?"

"I do some, but I'm just a part-timer here. Mostly, I help out. We have a great trainer on staff who creates all the plans. You can meet him before you make up your mind, too, and create a list of what you'd like him to work on."

Char took the flyer from me, only glancing at it for a moment before looking at me again. And wow, his eyes should be illegal. They looked darker than they were because of the red in his hair, like they could drag a person into them.

Worse, he had that, 'I really care,' vibe that made a girl feel safe and happy. I'd lived most of my life around killers, around men who could keep me safe but rarely understood a thing about feelings. Char, though?

He made me feel like I could tell him anything and he'd take my hand in his and assure me I'd make it through.

And boy was that tempting...

"Maybe we could get some coffee?" he asked, the words coming out slightly shy as though he didn't usually ask girls out.

The temptation hit me first. In fact, my mouth had already opened to tell him when I got off before my brain caught up.

Romance was so not in the cards for me — not now and probably not ever. No matter how the idea of spending a day with a man like this excited me, it just wasn't the sort of thing I could have. The thought of having to lie through my teeth the entire time — even about something as simple as my name or age — stole all the thrill from it.

So I closed my mouth and shook my head. "Sorry, but I'm not interested in dating."

"No?" He asked as if my rejection interested him more. "Well, how about I leave you my card and you can call me if you change your mind?" He pulled a business card from his wallet, then set it on the counter.

He didn't hand it to me, probably because he knew I could turn it down if he did. Instead, he left it there, making it my choice what to do with it. "I'll look this over and call you guys when I'm ready for my next trip. If you don't call me, at least I can see you then, huh?"

"Yeah, sure." I made certain my voice didn't give him any hint of desire, to make sure I gave him nothing to latch onto.

He turned and left after that, the barking of the dogs reminding me that I had a job to do.

What was it with today? Was it just the day when the universe wanted to show me hot men I couldn't have?

Fate did seem to have a vicious sense of humor...

* * * *

I cracked my window after turning off the alarm sensor. I could almost *feel* Colton grinding his teeth as he got a notification about the sensor even from across the country.

Funny enough, however, I didn't get a call. Maybe Nem told him to leave it be? I was on the ninth floor, which meant the odds of anyone managing to get inside from there were next to zero.

And really, if they managed it, they'd earned it.

The cool breeze from outside felt wonderful, reminding me of how stuffy the apartment could get.

Sure, I could close all the windows and run the AC, but that was different from a lovely breeze.

I settled into my bed, stretching out and trying to ease my muscles. I loved working with the dogs, but it took its toll on me. I had small scratches and bruises on my legs from the overly excitable pups, but I wouldn't trade it for anything.

Sometimes it felt like those dogs were the only thing I had in my life that was honest. I didn't have to pretend to be someone else around them, didn't have to worry about what they wanted from me, didn't have to play a part. Instead, I got to just exist, which wasn't something I'd had much of in my life.

Sleep came quickly to me, aided by the long day and cool breeze. I dreamed of my father — my real dad — and last time I'd seen him. Most of my dreams were from that night — the fear, the questions, the pain from the bullet he'd fired at me.

I woke with a gasp, bolting upright in bed, my hands flying to my side as if I still had the wound. I pulled up my shirt to check, but it was the same healed scar it had been for months now.

Would I ever manage a full night's sleep without waking up like this? Without a nightmare yanking me awake?

An odd sound drew my gaze toward the door to my room. It took a moment for my brain to sort through it, to identify it.

Footsteps.

Could it be the Quad? Maybe Jarrod had decided our earlier conversation needed a more immediate solution? Or maybe Colton wanted to prove a point about the window? I wouldn't put it past any of them, and they weren't the sort of people to knock or the kind that a locked door would keep out.

I got out of bed, straightening my nightgown. None of us needed the embarrassment of them catching a glimpse of something they shouldn't.

"You know, normal people knock." I walked into the hallway, ready to give whoever it was a piece of my mind.

Except, instead of any of the men I expected, I found six men in black masks standing in my living room. They all turned their faces my way, drawn by my question. My gaze went to their weapons, a history of being around such things making me take note of them without delay or thought.

Finally, my brain snapped into motion and I turned, ready to rush back to my room, to lock the door and go for the gun in the safe. *Why didn't I grab it to start with?* Because I hadn't really thought I'd be in danger. No matter how dangerous I knew the world was, how much violence I'd seen, I never thought it would find me here. Or maybe it was better to say I refused to consider it might find me here.

I didn't make it more than two steps before a large hand caught my arm, yanking me to a stop. A rag covered my mouth and nose, and the slightly sweet scent of chloroform filled my senses.

I had no chance to do anything before darkness took me.

* * * *

Present

I blinked back the tears, refusing to let myself cry. *Not a chance.*

Doing so would prove that I was the little kid people saw me as, the spoiled girl with no brain or backbone of her own.

Instead, I reminded myself that Nem and the others were always overprotective. They'd looked out for me my entire life, no matter how much I'd fought against it. Now that I actually needed them, I had no reason to believe they wouldn't come.

I missed my life from yesterday, but if there was one thing I'd learned well, it was how fast life could change. From one day to the next, a person could lose everything and gain something entirely different in its place.

The only real goal was to get to tomorrow, to stay alive long enough for everything to settle, to hope things got better.

A new man walked up, dressed in a well-made suit, an air of power radiating off him. It was easy to tell who was in control usually, and there was little doubt that this man was. "You're awake in time," he said.

I dropped my gaze, fear eating away at me, unable to bring myself to look directly at him. His dark eyes intimidated me too much, and I feared doing something to make him mad.

"You are going to have a very difficult time if you're this weak." He continued to speak as though it wasn't one-sided, as though we were having any normal conversation. "Do you know why I avoid selling certain things here? Because I dislike seeing them harmed after purchase. Things bought should be well cared for. It is why I rarely allow animals sold for meat or fighting purposes. Many people bought here go on to still have good lives, but you? You seem far too delicate to survive whatever comes next. I hope you prove me wrong, however."

The echoing of steps had me lifting my gaze to find the man walking away, his back to me as though I were no longer of any importance to him.

"You're up," a man in a nice suit, but nothing like the one the boss had just been wearing, said before clicking the locks off the wheels under my cage. He started to push the cage, the action knocking me backward and into the bars. Since my hands were still bound behind me, I couldn't brace myself. "Wonder how much you'll go for. We don't get many women sold, and most of the ones we do get are a lot prettier than you. Then again, having someone you can do anything you want to? That usually fetches a pretty high price." His chuckle was dark, as though he imagined every humiliation and depravity that could befall me with absolute glee.

What an asshole.

Bright lights blinded me for a moment, and murmurs from a crowd filled the silence. The cage came to an abrupt stop and I forced myself to my feet, the action difficult because of the way they had bound my hands behind me still. The higher position, however, let me look out as my eyes adjusted.

I was on a huge stage, as if this were some play, and every seat before me was filled. Booths lined the space as well, up above the regular seating, but they remained dark so I couldn't see into them.

"Now, our special item for the evening. A twenty-one-year-old female. She has a clean bill of health other than a well-controlled diagnosis of type one diabetes, comes from a wealthy family with access to a trust fund, and is entirely unbroken. We will start the bidding at five hundred thousand dollars."

I fought against the way my body shook and reminded myself of the plan.

Just survive long enough for someone to save you...

Chapter Two

Kenz

I'd been to auctions before, mostly charity ones when my father had dragged me there to show me off. Those had been loud with plenty of alcohol flowing.

This was *nothing* like those. An auctioneer stood beside me, speaking into a microphone that echoed out through the large auditorium, but no one yelled back. Instead, a screen above our heads showed numbers and a dollar amount, and the auctioneer would announce that amount — the new winning bid.

It didn't feel nearly as hectic as the previous ones, somehow more refined. What a ridiculous thing to think, given they were auctioning off *people*.

"The current bid is five million. We will be closing the auction if no one bids come up in the next ten seconds." He started to count down, each number feeling like another strike to me.

My life is worth five million?

I almost wanted to laugh at the idea of that. Since Nem had given me all of Dad's estate, I had access to so much more than that. If only I could buy myself.

The gag in my mouth ensured that even if I wanted to try something like that, I had no chance.

"Three, two, one—" The auctioneer paused, his eyes widening when a new number popped up on the screen. *Ten Million. #3529.* "It seems we had a last-minute bid," he said, seeming to gain his footing again.

Why did that shock him, though?

The auctioneer started the countdown again, the numbers coming slower than they had before. This time, when he reached one, nothing changed. He swallowed hard, the action impossible to see from the audience, before flashing a bright, fake smile. "The merchandise goes to number three-five-two-nine for ten million dollars! That concludes our auction tonight. Congratulations to our winners. Please wait in your spot and an accounts manager will come to handle payment, and your merchandise will be delivered to the address you provided once the funds have cleared. For all others, feel free to enjoy the refreshments in the main room."

The curtain for the stage drew shut, hiding us from the view of the audience.

"What the fuck was that?" the auctioneer snapped before turning toward the side and gesturing for someone standing there to come closer. "How did that happen?"

"I don't know."

"I thought this item was settled to go to four-six-five? Did that change?"

The other man shook his head, his eyes wide as though he knew this would fall right on his head. "No.

It was supposed to shut off when four-six-five bid five million."

The auctioneer turned his gaze on me, his eyes narrowed into a clear threat.

"Well, haven't you turned into quite the problem?"

I backed away, but when I pressed against the bars, I had nowhere else to go.

"What should we do?" the other man asked.

"We can't change the winner—it would ruin our credibility and the boss would realize something was wrong. Turn the merchandise over to the winners but contact the other client and let them know that a mistake occurred. We can try to smooth things over and possibly connect the two clients to make their own deal as well." The auctioneer rubbed his temples as though this had turned into a difficult day for him.

Which I might have laughed at if I were braver. I was pretty sure I was having a far worse day, after all.

The auctioneer tsked softly, as though I were a nuisance for him, then turned his back on me. He spoke once more to the other man, waving his hand dismissively. "Get her ready and send her out. We will deal with the rest later."

"Yes, sir."

Which meant I really had gotten sold like property, and I was getting turned over to whoever had just paid ten million dollars to own me.

This wasn't going to go well...

* * * *

My wrists ached from the cuffs. I'd tried not to move too much, not to pull at them or irritate my skin anymore, but their tightness meant they chafed no matter what.

The car hit a bump as it turned, the momentum toppling me to the side. I fell against a solid body, but I couldn't see because of the blindfold that now covered my eyes.

Strong hands shoved me back upright as though I were just property. It was how everyone had treated me thus far. None of the people I'd dealt with had been unkind or rough. It felt like people working at a store, where they didn't want to harm the merchandise but didn't see it as important, either.

The car slowed, and I held my breath as I waited to see if this was it. We'd stopped many times, but none had been the final destination. This time, however, the engine turned off.

My stomach rolled, and I swallowed to keep everything down. I wasn't Nem, I wasn't tough, but I only had to hold on a little longer. There was nothing Nem and the Quad couldn't do if they were motivated, and they'd be motivated to find me.

Just keep your head down and your mouth shut.

I had to bide my time—that was all.

Doors opened and the car shifted as bodies left. The person to my side got out of the car, then a hand wrapped around my arm and guided me out. They didn't yank me, didn't make me trip and fall. *Don't want to bruise the merchandise.*

No one spoke, which put me on higher alert. If they'd laughed and joked, I might have been able to relax more. Instead, I had faceless, nameless bodies around me, people guiding me but seeing no reason to actually acknowledge me, to speak to me like a person.

"Watch the step," the man holding my arm said, but even with the warning, I caught the ledge and almost toppled forward. The man's grasp on my arm kept me from landing on the ground, but it also jerked my arms, the cuffs biting into my skin.

I hissed but said nothing, even when wetness dripped down my fingers, telling me the cuffs had cut me.

A knocking happened, then a long, silent moment. Finally, new voices. They felt familiar, but I couldn't place them. Maybe I'd just heard too many voices lately, was too on edge and looking for anything I could identify?

"Thanks," the voice said.

"Sign here, please, to authorize the official transfer of goods," another man said. A familiar scratching of pencil against paper happened, then a hand pressed against my back to force me a few steps forward.

"Nice doing business with you," the man who spoke said, then took my arm and guided me farther in that same direction.

I jumped when the door closed, when it slammed and startled me.

A tremble started through me, one I couldn't control. Everything suddenly felt real, as if it had been some bad nightmare but now I couldn't wake up.

I'd been sold to a stranger. People didn't *buy* humans for anything good. No one bought a person because they wanted to shower them with affection and love.

The shaking worsened, even as I forced myself to walk, to not pull at the hand that guided me, to not make any problems.

Be a good girl. Do what you're supposed to.

The rules I'd lived my life by echoed in my head.

If I just focused on doing what I was supposed to, the rest would take care of itself, right?

Still, I shook so hard that my teeth chattered. This energy raced through me, filling me, as if it might vibrate me apart until I shattered into a million pieces.

"You got her?" another voice asked, another man.

"Yeah. Handover was easy."

"She hurt?"

"Doesn't seem to be. Shaking like a leaf, though."

"Not a shock there."

Hands touched my face, making me flinch away. If I'd been thinking, I wouldn't have done that, but I couldn't help it. My entire body remained strung tight, on alert, just waiting to react to danger.

Someone grabbed my chin, the grip tight. I squeezed my eyes closed, tensing, ready to get hit. Instead, they pulled the blindfold away.

I didn't open my eyes right away, fear keeping them shut. I felt like a kid who was afraid, hiding under the bed, thinking that if I didn't see the threat, it couldn't hurt me.

I knew better than that, but finding the bravery to open my eyes seemed impossible.

A soft snort to my left, a sound that came out like mocking, finally made me risk opening my eyes.

And when I did, I froze. I'd thought the voices were familiar, but I sure had never expected *this.*

To my side, the man who had escorted me from the front door, was Vance Moore, the artist. Also in the room was the man from the elevator and the one who had run into me, causing me to spill my coffee. Finally, sitting on a sofa, staring at me was Char, the man who had come into my work and asked me out.

I rushed toward Char, my feet moving so fast I nearly tripped. "Char? What's going on?" I recalled the sweet way he'd spoken to me, the safety I'd felt when he'd smiled at me.

I had no idea what was happening, but I knew he was the only person in that room I could trust.

I stopped just in front of him, staring down and into those dark eyes of his. Except, he didn't smile. That kindness I'd felt from him was absent, as though it had never been there at all.

He moved his gaze to the others dismissively, as if I held no importance at all. "So what are we supposed to do with her now?"

"If she runs off, she'll just end up picked up again." The man who had spilled the coffee crossed his arms.

"We can just lock her up, can't we?" Char asked.

"I'll watch her," Vance said, his tone the same as he'd used before, like a sensual promise. He sounded as though he could already see me naked and he had already gotten himself halfway to satisfied. Worse, he made me believe he could deliver on those promises. "My bed is cold here since you all don't want me to bring women back. I could use a nice warmer."

I took a step away from Vance, putting extra distance between us.

The man from the elevator still said nothing, his gaze unnerving in its intensity. He simply watched, as if he gathered and stored each piece of information.

"Let Vance deal with her, then," Char said.

I opened my eyes wide and looked up at Char again. "What? No, please! Just tell me what you want and I can give it to you—just let me go, please." I blinked quickly, my eyes burning with tears I refused to let fall. Char had seemed nice before, caring, so I pleaded with him.

Char looked at me again, then rose and caught my chin between his fingers, grasping tightly. "You think I care? You think where you sleep or what happens to you matters to me at all? You're a fool, then, and I suggest you stay out of my way."

As soon as he released me, I jerked my gaze away. I couldn't stand looking at him, seeing how different he was. It reminded me of Dane, of the times I'd watched him slip into a different role.

Except, Dane was *Dane*. This man seemed hollow, empty, as if the only emotions he knew were the fake ones he wore when needed.

And I'd fallen for that ploy entirely...

"She can't stay with Vance," the man who had spilled my coffee said. "We need her help, and I don't think she'll be useful after a night with Vance."

"You wound me," Vance said, though his expression didn't appear all that hurt.

"It's late," the man said again. "We'll go over the rules tomorrow and work out a plan. For tonight? Tor, you watch her."

The gazes of the other men shifted to the one from the elevator, the silent one with the golden eyes. *So he's Tor, huh?*

"Why does he get to have all the fun?" Vance asked with a pout.

"Because Tor won't do anything questionable."

"Boring," Vance muttered. "But fine. I'm going to bed." He didn't wait before walking out as though the entire conversation hadn't mattered.

Char followed without a word to any of us.

"I'm Hayden," the man who had spilled my coffee said. He grasped my shoulder, then turned me so my back faced him. When he touched the cuffs, I held in a pained breath, my wrists feeling raw. Just as quickly, however, there was a click and the metal fell away. He picked up a small black bag from the top of the table and brought it over to me. "There are insulin pens in here along with a reader. They're the same brand you were using before, according to the auction house. If there's a problem, just let Tor know."

I took the bag from him, ignoring my own fear. Things like the management of my diabetes took precedence over my own worries, and just holding the bag made me more secure.

"I'm going to suggest, for your own good, that you don't cause any problems. Get some sleep—I'm sure you need it. If you cause trouble, though, I have no problem locking you up," Hayden said.

I nodded, even if it wasn't a question, too scared to even consider arguing with him. He seemed to take that as what he needed, because he nodded once at Tor then left as well.

I turned back toward the only man left, the silent one who unnerved me.

I don't know if this is better or worse...

Chapter Three

Tor

How did I end up in this mess?

I sighed as I looked at the frightened girl in my room, the way she trembled, the red that lined her eyes. Amazingly, she hadn't cried yet, but that had to be out of sheer stubbornness.

And I did mean *girl*. She was twenty-one according to all her records, but she didn't seem much older than a teenager. Then again, from her history, it seemed she'd lived off her daddy's money. She was a trust fund baby who had never had to do anything herself.

I should hate that, but a part of me wanted her to keep that. I wanted her to go back to her perfect little life without having any idea of the uglier sides of the world. I hated when *anyone* lost their innocence. It was something that should be protected at all costs.

I opened the door to the bathroom, then gestured for her to use it. She eyed it suspiciously, but when her gaze fell to the bag in her arms, she seemed to give in.

Her medical condition concerned me. I understood how taxing such things could be, recalled my own struggles with health. I didn't envy her the ongoing struggle, but at least it seemed she was used to it. Her medical records suggested that she kept a close eye on her numbers, that she managed her condition well. We had ensured that we had the same brand and type of both a continuous reader and the insulin pens that she'd used previously, making the transition easier.

After around ten minutes, Mackenzie returned from the bathroom, the bag still in her arms like a shield. Then again, I felt that way about my weapons. I never felt safe or whole without them. However, her pose displayed the damage to her wrists.

They were badly bruised, and one side had cuts, as well. Whoever had put them on had done so too tightly, and no doubt pulling her by her arm had added pressure.

I couldn't just leave her like this.

She brought her wrists forward, glancing down at the damage as if noticing it for the first time. I expected her to lose her shit, to start crying, to beg me to let her go. When a person saw their own blood, it tended to get them willing to give in. It reminded them of their own mortality, of all the other things they could suffer.

Except, Kenz didn't do that. She didn't cry, didn't give the marks more than a cursory glance before dismissing them and looking at me again. "Your name is Tor, right?"

I nodded as I went over to the large on suite bathroom, grabbing the first-aid kit from a cabinet. When I returned to the room, she was right where I'd left her.

Part of me had wondered if she'd bolt the moment I had my back turned, but it seemed she wasn't the fleeing type. Was it because she was afraid of what we might to do her if she tried?

Smart girl. Or, perhaps it was better to say it helped me. It was easier to deal with people who fell into line.

I didn't enjoy her fear, but it simplified my life.

I held up the first-aid kit.

Kenz looked at it, then shook her head. "I'm not hurt."

I pointed at her wrists.

She tucked them behind her, as if that erased that I'd seen them. Then again, why would she trust me? Especially when she was hurt?

Whether I understood her reasoning or not changed nothing. She was under my care, and I took that seriously. I doubted she'd trust me, that she'd agree to let me help her on her own, which meant pushing.

I tossed the first-aid kit on the bed and pointed to the foot of it. Kenz swallowed hard, then shook her head again.

Too bad. I caught her arm, careful not to yank her hard, but pulled her over so she sat on the bed. I had a feeling one reason it went so easily was that her legs wouldn't hold her much longer on their own. She still held the bag of her insulin like a lifeline.

I crouched in front of her, close enough to discourage her from causing a fuss, and flipped open the lid of the first-aid kit. I took out and tore open a wipe, then caught her forearm to hold her still. The shaking went on, but I held her securely as I cleaned the blood away.

Blood didn't bother me, not in my line of work, but a tightness in my chest said I didn't care for it here. Then again, I'd never enjoyed seeing innocents die needlessly, and this girl struck me as damned innocent.

I put antibacterial spray on the wound, ignoring her hiss at the sting. A bandage finished off the treatment, since I couldn't do much about bruises or the other minor scrapes. I repeated the actions on the other wrist, allowing her to switch which arm held her bag.

I tossed the trash away and put the kit back in the bathroom when I'd finished. After washing my hands, I returned to find the girl had still yet to move. She stared at her wrists as though it would help her understand something. I could almost see how she went back over the past few days, over everything that had happened, no doubt wondering if there wasn't something she could have done differently, something to change this all.

I'd seen people make that face so many times — often just before they met their end at my hands. People liked to think they could control things, change them, but that wasn't reality. Everything was chaos, and we could only try to survive it.

I locked the windows, ensuring they wouldn't budge, that the alarms were all in place. We had a state-of-the-art security system at the house, and given the sort of men we were, the enemies we'd made through our lives, we always made sure to set it. I slept light, but that didn't mean I should make things easier for her.

Not that she struck me as the sort of girl to run. That took courage, and Mackenzie reminded me more of a wet kitten than a threat.

I snapped my fingers to bring her gaze to mine, gestured at the bed, then turned the switch off, bathing the room in darkness.

Enough light poured in from the mostly full moon outside to still see in the room. Kenz didn't move right away, and I wondered if she'd fall apart now.

Everyone fell apart in situations like this. They lost the nerve they'd cobbled together within themselves and shattered beneath the pressure. Darkness and quiet weighed heavily and caused the cracks to appear quicker, people's minds giving in to their worst worries.

However, Kenz didn't do that. She breathed in deeply, then crawled beneath the blankets of my bed. Her form shook, but her breath didn't catch.

I took a seat in the large armchair beside the door. I'd spent countless nights in places a lot worse than this. I could catch a few hours no matter the location.

Sleep was vital, and people like me either learned to sleep anywhere or we ended up dead.

Her breathing evened out, and within about an hour, soft snores echoed in the room. A smile tugged at my lips, the sensation so strange that my cheeks ached slightly.

I let my eyes slide closed, lulled to sleep by the rhythmic sound of her snoring. Who knew it could be this relaxing?

* * * *

Kenz

A shower made me feel as though not everything in my life had changed. Why could water do that? Like some baptism that washed away the troubles and fears and made me human again.

A note on the side table when I'd woken had told me to feel free to shower when I rose, then to come out to the living room when finished.

My glucose reader showed the time was nearly noon. The device connected to the sensor I'd placed on the back of my arm already, tracking my levels and set to alert should they go too high or too low. My old reader was the same type, but had connected via Bluetooth to my phone. They had probably picked a stand-alone reader to keep me from having access to a phone.

That reminded me of my place, didn't it?

Without a blow dryer, I settled for towel drying my hair, then doing a French braid to keep it out of my face.

However, after cleaning up, I realized that I had nothing to put on. The clothing they'd put me in for the auction — a sweet-looking white nightgown — sat in a crumpled pile on the floor like a coiled snake.

I couldn't bring myself to even touch it, as though it would pull me back into that mess if I neared it.

However, going out in a towel was also probably a bad idea. I could almost hear the Quad in my head, telling me not to parade meat in front of hungry dogs. The night had passed without Tor touching me, but the last thing I wanted was to risk a problem.

I left the steam-filled bathroom, then opened what I assumed was the closet door. There weren't rows of clothing here, nothing like my own closet. Instead, he had a few simple outfits, most of which were repeats, as though he found a shirt he liked and bought it in white, black and gray. Shoes sat lined on the floor, everything in its place.

This is the closet of a psycho.

Anyone who had their ties perfectly rolled couldn't be normal.

I took one of the large button-up shirts. Tor hadn't struck me as the overly angry type, so I didn't think he'd get too mad over me borrowing a shirt. I picked a black one to reduce the risks of me staining it and because black hid more.

Buttoning it reminded me just how large the man was, when the tails of the shirt reached just above my knees. I wore shorts *far* shorter than this.

I didn't want to risk any up-skirt issues, though, so I also took a pair of his boxers. I would have preferred a nice pair of baggy pajama bottoms, but I didn't see anything like that.

Was he a sleeping naked sort of man?

Given he hasn't said a word to me, I doubt he'll answer even if I ask.

Of course, asking people if they slept naked wasn't the sort of question people were supposed to ask.

The boxers sagged on my hips, but they'd work better than nothing. A glance in the mirror made me laugh.

I looked like a kid playing dress-up. At least no one could claim I was using my feminine wiles to get my way, not dressed like this.

After wasting as much time as I could, I ventured into the hallway. I half-expected to find Tor there, leaning against the wall. I'd woken a few times during the night, and each time, when I'd rolled over and glanced toward the door, I'd found him seated in the chair, his golden eyes locked on me.

Had he stayed up the whole night or did he just sleep so lightly that any movement from me woke him?

I sighed, wishing the note had included directions. From what little I'd seen last night, this house was huge.

I tried to recall the night before, the direction we'd gone, but I'd mostly stared at the floor, too afraid to look directly at Tor or to do anything wrong.

Still, as I searched my memories, I was pretty sure we'd gone left down a long hallway with closed doors.

Large houses weren't new to me, didn't make me uncomfortable. I didn't prefer that, but I at least was used to it.

I passed by lots of closed doors, the house oddly silent.

When I'd lived in places of this size, we always had people around. We had cooks, cleaners, security and staff, all waiting to rush in with anything we might have needed.

It made me slightly less comfortable, the entire house feeling abandoned.

Then again, if it was abandoned, I'd be free, right?

Just as that thought hit me, a door opened, and a familiar man stepped into the hallway in front of me.

Char's hair was wet, making the red darker and more burgundy. A drop of water ran down his neck, soaking into the neckline of his plain black T-shirt. He narrowed his eyes when he spotted me, forcing me to stop short. "Are you trying to escape?"

I shook my head, grasping the front of the shirt I wore, bunching it in my hands to keep from shaking.

"Then why are you wandering around without an escort?"

"There was a note telling me to come to the living room," I said.

"You aren't anywhere near the living room."

"Well, no one drew me a map."

He lifted one of his dark eyebrows. Was that his natural hair color? *Does it matter?*

Char clicked his tongue, then jerked his head in the direction I'd come from. "Follow me."

"You're going to help me?"

"I'm going to help myself. If you get turned around anymore, you'll never make it to the living room, and that'll waste my time. Let's go." Char walked past me as though I were nothing but a nuisance to him.

It made me feel like I had back home, back before Nem had returned. How often had my father done the same? Treated me like I was just a bother he was forced to deal with? Other than the Quad, the security had done the same. The boarding schools my father had paid had treated me no differently.

I was just a problem for everyone.

Even Nem and the others…

They all had to do so much to watch over me, and even if they never acted like it were a problem, it didn't make me feel any better.

Just once, I wanted to stand on my own. I didn't want other people hiding things from me, thinking I needed to be protected.

However, a lifetime of trying so hard to do well, to get noticed for being good kept me silent as I followed him, swallowing down everything I wanted to say.

Instead, I took notice of the house's layout. Most mansions were set up in a fairly standard way, with the ground floor for public spaces and entertaining and the upper floors for living. With houses as large as this one, they didn't put all the bedrooms together. They were made for different extended families to stay together, thus were made up of wings.

Which meant I must have wandered into the wing Char used rather than finding my way to the stairs?

And of *all* the people I could have ended up around, it had to be *him?*

He confused me more than anyone else, the difference between how he'd behaved before striking from how he acted now. Dane had taught me to catch lies, to spot masks, and I wasn't horrible at reading people, so how had he tricked me so well?

Because you wanted him to be that other person.

"Stop sighing," Char snapped.

"Sorry — I'll try not to breathe."

He snorted. "Sounds like a plan."

The insults that swirled in my head were *all* Dane's. He'd taught me that swearing was an art, that to do it well, a person needed to mix both vulgar and non-vulgar words. I'd gotten pretty good at it, but I kept them to myself.

Pissing off Char any more than my mere existence seemed to wouldn't help me a bit.

Finally, we reached the stairs. From there, I peered around at the open space and layout. A set of stairs went to the next floor up, and this one opened in two directions. I hadn't reached the stairs again, which meant the two wings must connect elsewhere, too.

Did that mean Hayden and Vance lived on the third floor?

"Hurry up," Char said, already halfway down the staircase.

I grasped the railing and rushed down, having to grab the waist of the boxers part way down when they started to slip. *Still worth it to wear them.*

I stayed a few steps behind Char until we reached the living room, the space the same as when I'd been here the night before.

At least, I thought it was. The truth was that I'd been so flustered I didn't recall much about it. The room was huge, lined with large windows that opened to a backyard with a deck. Toward the other direction was a large double door that had to be the front of the house. That side lacked windows — a smart safety measure to ensure privacy.

I caught a glimpse of a kitchen with white marble countertops and stainless-steel appliances to the side, though it was set pretty far back and surrounded by cabinets. It all confirmed that this space was made for visitors and company. In fact, it felt so familiar that a part of me wondered if I'd been here before.

No, it just looks like every other mansion my father rented.

"So we're all up?" Hayden walked in, a bowl in his hands.

"Aren't you quite the tease?" Vance's voice came from just behind me, close enough that his breath warmed the nape of my neck. "Wearing men's clothing like that? You surely know what that does to a man..."

My cheeks heated but I stayed still, unwilling to address his stupidity. Vance seemed the sort of man who enjoyed the game more than the prize. The last thing I needed was to interest him any farther by playing hard to get.

"Knock it off," Hayden said before handing me the bowl he held, then pressed my arm as he gestured toward the couch.

"You need to have more fun." Vance's voice held a pout though he didn't follow me.

Did that mean Hayden was in charge?

"I have plenty of fun." The deadpan delivery of those words from Hayden made me fight a smile, thinking back on the Quad, on Bray and Colton who were masters of that dry humor.

And as soon as I thought about them, a pain in my chest made me admit just how much I missed them. They were difficult and caused me more than a few problems, but they were also some of the only family I had.

I took the seat, then peered down at my bowl. Scrambled eggs with mushrooms and cheese. I was beyond thrilled not to find something sugary where I had to worry or avoid it to start with. The first bite showed they were perfectly cooked and seasoned.

Tor walked in and glanced at me then Hayden. He pressed his lips together, then left the room for a moment. When he returned, he had a second bowl of food and handed it to Hayden.

Did Hayden give me his own bowl, then?

I opened my mouth to thank him but shut it just as quickly. Drawing attention would probably only make him mad, or he might mock me, making it clear that he wasn't doing it for me.

Instead, I ate quietly as the others took their seats. Char had coffee, Hayden and Tor ate, and Vance had made some sort of green breakfast smoothie that he drank out of a mason jar with a straw.

No one spoke at first, and each passing second drew the tension tighter. It almost felt like a family breakfast, but we *weren't* family. They were men who had bought me like a piece of property and me? I was the unlucky girl who'd found herself in a cage.

And I still had *no* idea why. If they knew who I was, they'd have said my real name at the auction, wouldn't they? That was my main selling point—my blood, my family history.

When the silence got to me, when I couldn't sit there and stare at an empty bowl any longer, I blurted out the words in my head. "Why did you buy me?"

Hayden spoke without missing a beat. Had he been waiting for me to break first? "Because someone else was after you, someone we're looking for. I won't hide this from you because it involves you. We aren't in the habit of buying women, Mackenzie."

"Kenz." At his look, I whispered the rest. "No one calls me Mackenzie—it's just Kenz."

Hayden nodded. "Kenz. We're searching for someone. That person attends the auctions on occasion, but they returned from overseas when the list of items up for sale came out. It told us there was something important there they wanted. That person bid on you immediately, so we bought you out from under them."

"Is that why I saw you all before the auction?"

"Yeah. We could rule out most of the items, but you were the wild card, the thing we didn't recognize. We wanted to see if what it was about you he might want, but honestly? After meeting you I didn't figure you were what they were after."

"Then why would they want me?"

"We don't know. Not knowing doesn't change that it's true, though. Now that we have you, we can find out why they want you and use it as leverage to draw them out."

"Leverage? You mean bait, don't you?"

"Leverage," Char pipped in. "Leverage implies we'll trade you for what we want, and I've got no problem with that."

Again, he reminded me that he was an absolute douche.

I ignored him, since his statement didn't help that much. Instead, I focused on Hayden who actually told me things. "So, who is this person?"

"His name is Lorien Hatchett, but he has plenty of aliases. He's the last surviving son of the Hatchett family, but he doesn't do much to run it right now, leaving that to his mother. He keeps a low profile, never appearing in public, living under another name that we don't know. He's known for his work as a hired killer. This is the first time I've seen him change his plans for something—he even canceled a contract he'd taken to come back—which says that you're extremely important to him. Given you don't fit what normally goes up for sale, he probably hired the inhouse finders at the auction to pick you up, then he went so far as to bribe the auction house to ensure he won."

I frowned. "Then how did you win?"

Vance snorted as if he found my question adorable. "Lorien isn't the only one with connections. I grease palms better than he does, so here you are."

And is here really any better?

These men hadn't done anything to me yet, but that didn't make them trustworthy. I recalled how often people had cozied up to me in my life, people who had betrayed me just as quickly.

I frowned as I tried to work out everything they'd said to me, to make sense of it all. "If he has that much power, why would he go through an auction like that? Even if he bribed them to win, what would the point be instead of just abducting me himself?"

Char sighed as though annoyed with how little I knew. "There's a reason people go to this auction — the protection. Everything bought at that auction comes with security guaranteed for as long as the buyer owns it. The auction house will get involved if anyone tries to steal an item purchased there. That is built into the fees the auction house charges. They don't protect it directly, but by reputation. Not many people want to tangle with the auction house, because they are *brutal* to people who cross them. I hear those who try to steal things bought from an auction are rarely ever seen again. Rumor has it that they've recovered everything that was ever stolen after an auction. By buying you from them, he both ensured he could keep you and that his hands were kept clean."

"So what are you going to do with me?" I asked, forcing myself to face that head-on. I was at their mercy, and I had no idea what any of this meant in a practical way.

Hayden didn't answer at first. Finally, he sighed. "We can't let you go, not right now. First of all, if we did, Lorien would just pick you up. He's done this much to get you—he won't give up now. We could get the auction house involved, since you're guaranteed ours, but then they might realize we were cheating as well. They're just as likely to target us as him. Basically, you've got no real choice but to stay with us."

I could go home…

If I returned to Nem, to the Quad, they could keep me safe. However, that would mean admitting I couldn't cut it on my own. It would mean going back to that pretty but confining cage they'd set up for me.

Somehow, even the thought of this danger wasn't enough for me to do that.

Also, I still didn't understand this Lorien or what he wanted, how dangerous he might be. I couldn't ask Nem to take that risk, to throw her into this mess.

Getting back to Nem would mean either telling these men who I really was—*talk about a bad idea*—or trying to escape, which didn't seem all that possible right now. It meant that wasn't much of an option. *Guess that means they're right—I don't have another choice.*

"Will anyone be looking for you if you don't go back to your place?" Hayden asked.

The answer was yes, at least eventually. Given Jarrod's promise, Nem and the Quad *should* give me a little time, but at some point, they'd come looking. Saying that would only cause me trouble, though, so I shook my head. "My parents are gone."

"No lawyers or anything keeping a close eye?"

Skirting the truth was never easy, but given my poor lying skills, I did the best I could. "I have lawyers, but they won't notice if I don't go home."

Hayden nodded. "Good. We don't want things getting complicated because someone tries to rescue you without understanding the situation."

"So I'm supposed to just stay here?"

"We paid ten million for you," Char reminded me. "I suggest you start pulling your weight to make that worth it."

I flinched, scooting farther away from Char on the couch.

"Stop scaring her," Hayden snapped. "And yes, for now, you'll stay here where we can keep an eye on you. If you have to go anywhere, you'll go with a guard. We'll get another room set up for you today, so you can have your own space. Once we figure out why he wants you, we can use that to draw him out."

"And if you manage that? If you get what you want? What happens to me, then?"

Hayden shrugged. "We let you go back to your life. We don't want to own a person. When we get what we want, you're free."

"And Lorien?"

"This doesn't end in any way other than his brains spilled all over the concrete."

So much for thinking Hayden is the nice one...

Chapter Four

Hayden

"Why are you staring at me like that?" Kenz's question made me realize that I had, in fact, been staring.

"I'm guarding you, aren't I? That means I have to watch you."

She pressed her lips together, the action seeming to hold back whatever else she'd wanted to say. Her having things in her head that she didn't share annoyed me.

It made me continue speaking when I otherwise wouldn't have. "You look around like you're checking for danger."

"Doesn't everyone do that?"

"No. I've guarded a lot of people over the years, and most who need guarding have no idea what threats are out there. They live perfect lives, and my job has always been to make sure they don't need to know about the risks."

She glanced at me, her expression tentative, the face of someone smart enough to think things through. "So you do bodyguard work?"

I nodded as we walked, her matching my pace. We had no reason to lie to her — when this was over, she could tell her story to anyone she wanted. We wouldn't be around to worry about it. "Yeah. I spent time in the military but decided I liked protection work. I did work on my own at first, then started my own security firm. Most people who hire me — rich folks — don't have any idea about the dangers around them. You look around like you do, though. You check down each alleyway, you take note of people who pass by. You aren't paranoid, but you notice. Those are skills taught to professionals."

Kenz shrugged before she wrapped her arms around herself. She still wore Tor's button-up shirt, but we'd traded his boxers for a pair of Char's pajama pants. They were still loose, but since Char was the smallest of us, she'd been able to pull the waist tight enough to make them work.

Not that Char hadn't complained. Then again, after five years of dealing with him, I was used to his complaining. It drifted into background noise anymore.

"Maybe I'm just careful."

"In my experience, rich spoiled princesses aren't careful. If you don't want to tell me who taught you — I won't push it. Don't think that I can't spot a lie from you, though. If I had to guess, I'd say it was a bodyguard you had before."

Her gaze dropped to the sidewalk just after a wave of sadness slid over her delicate features. It tightened my chest, made me want to reassure her.

I shook away that feeling. It was just a holdover from my work as a bodyguard, from my desire to take care of a client. It wasn't just my job to keep them alive—I had to care for their wellbeing also. That attention to detail was probably why I'd done so well, why my company was considered one of the best in the country.

However, she wasn't a client. She was a tool, and I needed to remember that.

"I'm surprised you're taking me to the store," she said as though to fill the quiet and break the tension from before.

"You need things. You'll be with us for a while, so we can't have you walking around in borrowed clothing."

"I figured you'd make a list because it was too dangerous to take me out. Aren't you worried we'll get caught? Or that I'll run?" The corner of her mouth tucked up, a sign that the girl had a mischievous side to her.

"We're about two towns over from where you were picked up and where we live, so I doubt anyone here would be looking for you. As far as you running away? You don't strike me as the type brave enough to run."

"You're right about that..." Her voice trailed off, but what I had meant as a joke seemed to hit a sore spot for her.

Instead of pressing the topic, I moved on. "A list works for small things, but you need clothing. It'd be a bigger headache for me to have to pick that out, and it would be better for you to try it all on." I rubbed my hand against the side of my neck as I admitted the last part. "I don't have the most experience with women, so I couldn't even guess at everything you need or what might fit. I could have sent Vance, but who knows what you'd get if I did that."

She laughed, the sound lyrical and sweet. It was the first time I'd seen her laugh. "Heavens forbid he was left to his own devices. I'd probably just get lingerie and sex toys."

Her words were so frank that I inhaled saliva, the action causing a coughing fit. I hit my fist against my chest to try to regulate my breathing as Kenz patted my back.

Which threw me for another loop. People didn't just touch me—certainly not ones after I'd bought them. This was either a sign of Kenz being stupid or simply far too trusting.

I had a bad feeling it was the second one…

"Sorry," I said once I caught my breath.

"You can't be that shocked by my joke."

"Young girls didn't speak like that in *my* day."

"Your day? You don't look that old."

"I'm forty-three—old enough to see you as a young girl."

She chuckled again as though *I* were the adorable kid. "Well, I'm sorry for shortening your life then, given you don't have a lot of years left."

"You're surprisingly mouthy for someone in your position," I pointed out. "Most people would be a lot more afraid."

"I guess I'm less afraid of you now that I see mentioning sex toys will cause you to choke. Besides, danger isn't that new a thing for me." She went to tuck her hands into her pockets, but it was like she'd just remembered she wasn't wearing anything with pockets. Her cheeks reddened and she crossed her arms instead.

"People like you don't usually get comfortable with danger. They don't get used to anything uncomfortable. Money makes it so you don't have to."

"Yeah, well, maybe you don't know me as well as you think."

"No? I don't go into any job or mission without knowing everything I can about it. As soon as we heard about you, I did my research. Mackenzie Fox, age twenty-one, a first-year fine arts major. You lived in Washington with your father, Harold Fox, when you weren't in boarding school until he passed away last year. You have a trust fund with roughly ten million in it, but it appears well run and you don't overspend, so I expect that amount will grow due to investments. No major health issues beyond diabetes and no legal trouble. How am I doing?"

She swallowed hard. Nervous? Did she just not care for how much I knew? It had to make her feel at a disadvantage.

Though, at the same time, I knew my comment was just petty. *Grow up, Hayden.*

It was strange, because usually, I read people well enough. However, now, dealing with this young girl who should have been so easy to categorize and figure out, I kept getting confused.

Just who is this girl?

Kenz

Having a shadow while I shopped was far from new. I'd spent most of my life having people follow me for my own safety. It had either been bodyguards or people associated with my schools. It was only once I'd come to Florida that I'd started to do things on my own.

It meant having Hayden with me felt normal. In fact, I had to give him credit.

I'd had good bodyguards and bad ones, ones who were so distracted I wondered what good they were and others who remained so close that they stepped on my heels.

Hayden knew the line between those and walked it as though the most natural thing in the world for him. He checked the dressing room prior to me entering, then remained outside with his back toward the door until I'd finished. He remained close enough to intervene if needed but otherwise remained out of my way. If he wasn't a criminal who had bought me at a black-market auction, I might have considered hiring him in the future.

"Do you have shampoo?" I asked.

"Of course we do. Unless you think we don't bathe?"

"Men like to use that six in one nonsense. That dries my hair out," I explained.

"In that case, pick whatever you want to use. Vance probably has something fancy, but…"

I snickered at his meaning and completed the thought for him. "But I probably don't want to get naked in his bathroom?"

"Exactly." Hayden walked down the shampoo aisle with me, saying nothing as I picked out shampoo, conditioner and lotion.

Lines between his eyebrows made me pause. "What?"

"I thought you'd complain about shopping at a supermarket. I've protected a few celebrities, and they're usually far pickier about the products they use and where they get them."

"I'm not that picky. I could have even made do with the six-in-one nonsense if I had to, but I prefer to have something that works. Plus, I don't really want to smell like sandalwood or motorcycle grease or whatever men smell like."

Hayden's lips spread into a smile, but as quickly as it appeared, he wiped it away. It made me laugh, reminded me of the times when Bray had done the same. Sometimes, there was nothing more fun than amusing someone who really didn't want to be amused. It surprised me, too, how comfortable I felt with him.

I'd already picked out clothing, underwear, a new purse, lotions and washes and all that necessary stuff. I'd picked up some strips and a regular glucose reader as a back-up, along with a few snacks that could be tucked into my purse.

Which left one last thing.

I headed down two aisles, Hayden remaining to my left, his gaze moving smoothly around the store, taking note of any threat. His competence calmed me enough that I didn't feel the need to do it as well.

I peered at the boxes on the shelves, searching for what I needed.

When Hayden noticed where we were, at the products on the shelf, his eyes widened.

"I can go wait over there." He gestured toward the end of the aisle.

I put on my most innocent expression. "Why? Someone could attack me here."

"I think you can handle this part on your own, don't you?"

"They're tampons, Hayden, not assassins. You don't need to run away."

He snorted softly as he rubbed the back of his neck. His tan skin hid it, but I'd bet if he were paler, his ears would have been red. "I'm not running. I'm just offering you some privacy."

"I didn't ask for privacy, and I don't think it's for me at all. You're supposed to be some tough bodyguard, right? Periods can't make you that nervous. How will you protect me during one whole week a month?"

"You're enjoying yourself *far* too much right now." He'd dropped his tone as if to threaten me, to remind me of my place, but it only made me giggle.

It felt impossible to fear someone this freaked out by some rolled cotton.

"You really don't have much experience with women, do you?"

"I already told you I didn't. Now, can you get what you need so we can go? People are staring."

I glanced to the opposite end of the aisle to find that he was right. Two women kept glancing our way.

Why? Did we look like we were dating? Or maybe because of the age difference, they thought him an older relative? Did it really matter?

"Fine," I said and reached toward the top shelf for what I needed. I went to my tiptoes, but even still, it was too far.

A hand appeared by mine, brushing against me, as Hayden grabbed the box for me. *Impressive. I thought he'd be worried they might bite if he got too close.* He tossed the box into the basket, then held his arm out toward the register. "If humiliation hour is over, are you finished?"

Even though he was clearly finished, he waited. I got the sense that if I wanted or needed anything else, he'd have suffered through the trip. However, I'd gathered all the necessary things for around a month.

I just had to hope that we could wrap this all up by then, because I didn't want to spend the rest of my life getting bossed around by these four.

Chapter Five

Kenz

I stirred the food in the pan, swaying my hips as I worked. I hadn't cooked much before, back when I'd lived in those big houses with staff or at the boarding schools. However, upon moving out on my own, I'd found I enjoyed it.

It felt like I was an adult, like I was actually taking care of myself as I made food to sustain myself.

"There is something damn pretty about a woman cooking. Also, you look more comfortable in the kitchen than I'd expected."

I tensed at Vance's voice, wondering just what game he played at now. He set off alarms in my head each time he spoke, and I'd learned to listen to those. He was too smooth, and with him, I constantly felt like I danced to his tune.

Vance hopped onto the kitchen island as he watched me. At least him being contained there made me feel more confident that he wasn't going to do anything weird.

Probably.

"I like cooking," I admitted.

"Yeah? I never learned."

"Is that why you were drinking a smoothie?"

"I can manage a blender, at least."

"How have you gotten to your age and not learned?"

Vance gestured at himself with a smirk. "You know my last name's Moore. I've got the sort of money that means I never had to learn."

His words made me pause. It made us seem similar, which I hadn't expected. Then again, we'd both grown up rich, right?

It was one of the reasons the great playboy artist Vance Moore was so well known. He was a talented artist, sure, but that wasn't the only reason for his success. He'd come from serious money, already had a well-known name. As the youngest son of a family of politicians, he'd been the bad boy, the mess-up, the womanizer while the rest of his family settled down and got serious.

I thought back to Nem, to how much she'd accomplished and how horribly I'd fallen short.

Guess we're a lot alike...

Except, unlike me, Vance didn't seem bothered by his place as the second-best offspring. Instead, he embraced it. I wish I could do that.

"I didn't cook much at first either," I said. "I had chefs, and they never let me into the kitchen."

Vance chuckled, his shoes tapping against the cabinet doors as he swung his feet. "I remember making cookies one time when I was six. The second I went to open the oven, Taylor, our house manager, walked in and had a heart attack. He was so worried that a precious Moore child might burn themselves." Even though he laughed, the sound didn't strike me as joyous or happy.

I understood that stifling feeling. People always thought the other side was better, that others had no problems. We showed that wasn't true at all.

No matter how great a person's life looked from the outside, they still had problems.

"Careful!" A shock of pain went through my wrist a moment before I found myself yanked backward. I dropped the spatula, which bounced against the tile floor.

Vance pulled me quickly to the sink, then turned the cold water on full. He put the small red burn on my wrist under cold running water in the sink. I yanked at the surprise, but Vance held me still.

Which brought him right up against me. His gaze was hard as he stared at the mark, his eyes empty.

The expression threw me.

I'd seen Vance snarky, arrogant, seductive, but never like this. It was as though he saw something terrible, some bottomless pit that threatened to pull him into its depths.

"Vance?" I asked, whispering his name because the moment felt too charged.

"You should protect your hands," he answered as though he hadn't heard me, his voice thin and pained. "They're all you have, at the end of the day. Artists should always protect them."

"I'm okay." I wasn't sure what else to say, the moment so thick that I struggled to breathe in at all. "It's just a tiny burn."

Vance swallowed hard, then yanked his hand away from me. That hand and the black gloves were drenched, along with the sleeve of his shirt. It turned the light gray fabric dark.

"Your food's burning," he said, his gaze still locked on my wrist.

That brought me back to the moment, to what I was doing. Sure enough, when I spun around, smoke escaped the pan as the chicken turned a not-so-appetizing black. I rushed over and turned the burner off, then moved the pan to an empty spot to cool.

So much for lunch...

I turned, ready to make a joke to Vance about how I should have left the cooking to the chefs, it seemed, but I found myself alone.

He'd left?

Something uncomfortable sat in my stomach, a feeling I couldn't identify. Pity? Concern? I didn't know, but it dug deep and gnawed at me, like a sad tune I couldn't get out of my head.

That empty expression of his wasn't one I expected to ever see on Vance's face, but I hadn't imagined it.

I was pretty sure I'd glimpsed something he'd never wanted to share, and I had no idea what to do about that.

Don't risk getting any closer to these men than you have to. You know where this life leads – to an early death.

* * * *

Char

I dropped down, my hands pressing into the grass beneath me as I lowered myself into a push up then popped back to my feet.

Burpees sucked, but they worked. While Hayden and Vance preferred body building in a gym, I'd never been a fan. Body-weight exercises offered far more advantages.

Strength, flexibility and balance. Plus, a physique like theirs made blending in far harder. It served me better to have a more average build that hid easily beneath clothing.

Sweat had soaked through my shirt, making the fabric cling to me, but I wasn't done. *Just one more set.* I used to hate when trainers would tell me that, especially because I knew it was a fucking lie when they did so. Now, however, I used that trick. I told myself one more when I knew I had at least an hour left before I'd call it a night.

Training mattered, though, and it was often the only thing standing between success and failure, between life and death in my world.

Not to mention it was a great way to burn off the excess energy that ran through me.

We were *so* close.

Five years of struggling, of establishing ourselves, of failing to locate Lorien and we *finally* had a lead.

All because of that girl.

I refused to even use her name. What did her name matter? She was a tool, just someone to get us closer to our ultimate goal.

Why did Lorien want her? What would happen to her? Those were questions for better men than me. All I cared about was paying Lorien back for what he'd done, for everything he'd stolen from me. If that girl had to pony up part of the tab, well, life sucked for us all.

"You're going to run yourself into the ground." Hayden's voice made me look up just as I lowered myself into the pushup.

The asshole managed to sneak around far too well. Only Tor was better, but Tor also never spoke, which meant he could do it without anyone noticing.

I blended into crowds, but I wasn't nearly as silent as the two of them.

"I'm almost done," I said before popping back up to my feet, then running my forearm across my eyebrow, catching the sweat before it dripped into my eyes.

"You always say that then push yourself too hard. We're getting close, so don't risk what we need to do because you wear yourself out." Hayden held out a water bottle to me.

I almost refused it. Hayden's habit of acting like the father of our little group annoyed me. I was more of a working on my own sort of person. Groups only invited problems and betrayal.

I'd always been a believer that two people can keep a secret, so long as one of them is dead.

However, Lorien was too big a fish for any of us to catch on our own. This little family Hayden wanted to make would serve its purpose, but I was out the moment we finished this.

And I had no idea what *out* would look like.

It honestly didn't matter. As long as I did what I needed to do, as long as Lorien paid, I didn't care about a second past then. It was just darkness, just formless night, something I couldn't even try to turn into a future.

"Do you really think she can help?" I asked to change the subject as I took the water bottle.

"Well, Lorien wants her. Since we've had her, he's been reaching out to every contact he has looking for her. The auction house called to set up a meeting, too."

I twisted the lid from the bottle and gulped down half the water. "He works fast, huh?"

"I still don't get why he wants her, though."

"Maybe he met her before? Became infatuated?" I couldn't imagine that, especially not after meeting the girl. She was pretty, in a naïve and innocent sort of way, but she was just some rich kid. She wasn't a supermodel, didn't have any discernible talents as far as I could tell.

Still, people had weird tastes.

"Maybe, but he's methodical about his work. I can't imagine him randomly seeing her and going through all this trouble."

Yeah, that's pretty unlikely.

"She's keeping things from us," I admitted.

"Can you blame her? As far as she knows, we're just some men who bought her from an auction. That doesn't earn a lot of trust."

I shook my head after taking another drink. "It's more than that. Come on, you're smart enough to notice. She should be falling apart right now. She should be crying and flinching and begging us to let her go. Instead, she's going shopping with you and cooking meals and talking to us way too easily. She isn't nearly as afraid as normal people would be in her place."

"So you don't trust her because she's braver than you think she should be?"

"Experience toughens people up. From what's on paper, that girl's lived a perfect life. She was spoiled by her rich daddy until he died. She lived off her millions, only deciding to go to school for art, probably for shits and giggles. A girl like that should cower at the sight of us, but she doesn't. It means she's seen things worse than us, that she's spent time around things scarier than us, and that's what worries me."

Hayden sighed as he sat on a chair on the deck. "People's lives aren't as perfect as you like to think. Money doesn't fix all problems. Just because she seems like she's had it easy doesn't mean she has." He stared off into the distance, shadows in his eyes reminding me that we each had our own past.

We'd come together out of pain and rage, had kept anything personal beyond that terrible night to ourselves, but moments like this reminded me we had our own scars.

"Just keep an eye on her," I warned. "Pretty faces have a habit of making people stupid."

"I didn't think you cared what happened to me." Hayden's humor, as usual, was bone dry.

"I still need you to finish this. If you want to walk into her trap? Feel free, just don't ruin my chance of revenge while you're at it. I won't let *anything* get in my way when it comes to Lorien."

"Well, that sounds like a threat."

"It's a warning. I'll remove any obstacle, and that includes you or that girl. There's no price too high, nothing I'm unwilling to do, not if it puts Lorien in a deep damn hole."

Hayden stared at me so long it made me shift in my spot. I lived my life in the shadows, being whoever I had to at any moment, which was why when his sharp gaze dug into me, I wanted to plaster a smile on and fall to one of my many disguises, to hide anything real.

Except, Hayden was way too smart to fall for that. He'd seen me at my worst already.

"You know, if you live for nothing but revenge, you'll end up in the ground, too."

"Fine with me," I said before tossing back the empty bottle and dropping to do another burpee. "I don't have any problem digging two graves."

Chapter Six

Kenz

One week down…

I rubbed my eyes as I lay flat on grass in the backyard, staring up at the sky. Dampness soaked into the back of my shirt, and despite the warmth of the night, a chill ran through me.

A week of living here, of dealing with these men, of abandoning my old life and pacing through this property. Other than my outing to the store, I'd been stuck within these walls. It reminded me again how lonely a house full of people could be.

How many times had I lived around others? So many staff members, so many underlings who worked for my father coming in and out of my homes, but they'd lacked warmth or a sense of family.

I thought I'd gotten past that.

No, that's not true. Even after moving out here, my life hadn't filled up any. I was too afraid of outing myself, of trusting anyone, so I never let any person close. I made *friends* at school, but they never came over to my place, we never met up outside of campus. Talking to them had exhausted me as I kept my lies in order, as I feared what might happen to them if I slipped up, so I'd maintained my distance.

At least my apartment had been quiet and empty, since I found far more comfort in that than in the noise of a house where no one gave a damn about me.

Cloth struck my face, obscuring my view. I moved it, realizing it was a cotton throw blanket, light enough to use in the summer. I glanced toward the house to find Tor sitting at the edge of the raised deck, watching me, his golden eyes seeming to glow even in the darkness.

"Thanks." I shifted the blanket over me. It didn't help with the chill — the cause of that sat far deeper — but it still made me feel calmer.

Tor said nothing, but thus far, he hadn't. He'd watched over me a few times — everyone took turns — but even then, he'd stayed silent. He attended meetings with the other men, but he always remained on the sidelines, watching.

"Can you not talk?" I brought my gaze from him and back to the sky, to the open darkness, the bright white spots that shone down.

Something struck the ground beside me, and I frowned as I twisted to pick it up.

A phone?

It had no password and opened with a press of the button, a symbol at the top showing an unread text message.

A few clicks later, and it came up.

I can speak, but it hurts and is difficult, so I usually don't.

I glanced up to find him staring back at me. Was he waiting for a response? Was this his attempt at conversation?

I'd certainly had stranger ones.

"I'm sorry. Were you born that way?"

He shook his head, then his fingers flew across the screen of the phone in his hand. His quickness said he usually communicated this way.

I had thyroid cancer as a kid. The surgery to remove it damaged a lot of the surrounding area. I can only speak very quietly now, like a whisper, and it hurts when I do, so I usually text.

"What about sign language?"

I know it, but few others do, so it isn't all that useful. Mostly, I prefer to listen and watch.

A silence drifted between us, but I understood him better now.

The silence wasn't uncomfortable or heavy as it had. Now that I knew his quiet wasn't just because he hated me — he might still hate me, of course — I could handle it better.

You look happier.

I smiled at the words, then spoke without looking up at him. "I don't like silence from other people. It's harder to read people when they're quiet, and in my experience, quiet usually means mad. It's impossible to try to keep someone happy, to make sure I don't piss them off if they don't say anything. I'm glad to know you're quiet because of a different reason than that I'd pissed you off."

The phone in my hand dinged. *You've found quiet means angry? Do you mean you often dealt with people's anger?*

The question took me back for a moment, to living with my father, with Kyler Williams. He'd barely been a father to me, but he was the only one I'd had.

"Yeah, I have," I admitted. As soon as I whispered it, though, I backtracked. "Don't mistake me—I'm not some victim. I wasn't abused by angry people. I was always well protected as a kid. No one ever even dared to spank me." I laughed softly as I thought back, sorting through so many memories of my childhood.

My father had been an absent piece of shit, but others in my life? They'd filled that place. My mother— even if I didn't remember her much—Nem, the Quad, even Jarrod later. They'd all watched out for me, best as they could.

"My father was a serious man who didn't abide by mistakes or rebellion. He expected a lot out of me, and I don't think I ever really lived up to any of it in his eyes."

Which is why he tried to kill me, I guess.

I touched my side, the scar from the bullet wound he'd left me with, the one I kept hidden. It always made me feel pathetic, as if nothing more than a sign that one of the few people who was supposed to love me unconditionally hadn't. He not only hadn't saved me, but had been the one to shoot me just to hurt Nem, just to cause pain to others. He hadn't even shot me because he was mad at *me*, but because I was that unimportant to him.

A burning in my eyes made me blink quickly to clear it away.

The phone chimed again. *You look up at the sky a lot. Why?*

I gave Tor a smile as a thank you for changing the subject, for trying to draw me out of the painful memory. Even if he didn't know what had caused it, he'd paid enough attention to know when my mood had shifted.

So I answered him honestly. "I was alone a lot when I was a kid. Everyone around me was always too busy for me. I'd had enough one night, when I was ten, and I called one of the men who did our security work. He was like family to me, but because my father sent me away to boarding schools, I hadn't seen him in a long time."

As I told the story, the desperation of that night came back to me. I'd called Dane, needing to hear his voice, to feel as if I hadn't lost everything that mattered to me. My mother had been gone, my sister gone, then I'd lost my home and my father and the Quad when he'd sent me away.

"I told him I was running away, that I didn't want to be in boarding school anymore and would take a train to them. Of course, I didn't realize that I was in another country and couldn't cross the ocean on a train, but it was the only threat I had. The bodyguard, he was like a brother to me, and he told me to stop, to look up at the sky. I did it, and he told me he was looking at that same sky, that no matter how far apart people are, they're still connected. They're still on the same Earth, under the same sky. He told me to look up whenever I felt lonely and know that the people I care about, the people who care about me, are looking at it, too. It made me feel like I wasn't abandoned, that I wasn't totally alone."

As soon as I poured out my story, I chuckled. "I guess that sounds pretty pathetic, huh? And, I know, the poor, lonely rich girl doesn't really have any room to complain."

Everyone has problems. No one has a perfect life. You don't have to pretend to be okay when you aren't.

The words on the screen blurred, and this time just blinking couldn't deal with the tears. Instead, I used the back of my hand to wipe them away, embarrassed to have Tor witness the little breakdown. "Sorry," I rushed out, sitting up and turning to face him.

With the lights in the backyard off, I struggled to see the details of the man before me. I'd seen him enough to know what he looked like normally, but he wasn't the type I could just stare at. It seemed he caught me each time I tried, as though he'd honed his senses so well that he felt when people looked at him.

His hair was dark and his eyes held a golden hue. He had a mustache and a goatee, both thin and well groomed. A septum ring hung from the center of his nose, small enough to fit snug against him. Despite that, he didn't look like some rebel.

His hair was buzzed to his scalp on the sides and back, with the top longer, wavy, and pushed to one side. He was lean, and usually wore business-casual clothing, all seemingly expensive enough to fit in anywhere but not so trendy as to draw attention.

In fact, everything about him screamed a person meant to blend into the background.

It made me wonder who he was.

Who *any* of them really were. I'd spent a week here and I knew little more than the basics.

I knew Hayden ran a security company, that Vance was a womanizing artist from a rich and famous family, that Tor couldn't speak and that Char was a dick.

That was it.

You shouldn't get close to us.

The message made me frown. "I don't have much of a choice, do I? I mean, you all brought me here. I get that I might be in a worse position if you hadn't, but that doesn't change that I'm your prisoner right now. I can't go anywhere, can't reach out to anyone, so you four are all I have." Just admitting that aloud tanked my mood further.

Worse…as the days passed, I couldn't stop myself from recognizing that the longer this took to resolve, the worse it could get.

I normally spoke to Nem, Jarrod or the Quad daily. Since moving, the longest I'd gone without contact had been three days, and that had been during finals.

Sure, Jarrod had bought me some time, but even if they hadn't worried about the lack of calls, I had no doubt they monitored the security of my apartment. They'd know I hadn't come or gone in a week.

It wasn't a question of if they would come looking, but rather when.

I glanced at Tor again, the same thing hitting me that had before. No matter these men's pretty faces, the civility they treated me with, they were men accustomed to violence.

That sort of thing left a stain on a person, and maybe because I'd grown up surrounded by it, I could always spot it on a person. It was in the way they walked, the way they held themselves, as if by spilling blood a person's very being changed.

Tor might have treated me with respect, might have not given me reason to fear him, but that didn't change that he was capable of horrible things. If Nem came here, if the Quad did, they'd risk themselves for me.

That was the last thing I'd ever wanted. My family meant far too much to me.

I glanced at the phone in my hand, wondering if I could call Nem.

The phone chimed, signaling another text. *This phone can only send or receive calls or texts from Hayden, Vance, Char and myself.*

"So no calls to family and friends, huh?"

Your history shows you don't have any family, and from what we saw of you at the college, you weren't close with anyone. Who would you call?

Telling him that I wanted to contact the head of a huge crime syndicate in California would probably not help me at all, so I sighed. "You're right—I don't have anyone to call. You can go back inside. I'm just going to watch the stars a little longer."

I expected him to get up, to head back inside and leave me there. He'd done his job, had checked on me, had made sure I wasn't going to run away or cause problems. Instead, the phone chimed.

I'll stay.

And just like that, I didn't have to look at the stars by myself for once.

* * * *

Vance

"This is a shitty idea." Char sat on the sofa, his phone in his hands as if he'd grown bored with this entire meeting.

Which I understood. Meetings were dull, and I hated anything dull. Life was too short and too full of amazing things that I wanted to experience. The thought of spending it in things like meetings felt like a horrible waste.

It was like going to Paris and eating American fast food.

"Lorien is being careful," Hayden said, his take-charge attitude chafing me as it always did. He was the golden boy, the good one, the one who liked creating rules and following them. "He wants to find out who has her, but he can't figure it out."

Boring.

"That doesn't mean dangling her out there like a worm on a hook is a good idea," Char snapped.

Our phones chimed, and I glanced down at the text from Tor. *Didn't think you'd care what happened to her.*

Char snorted, the sound as dismissive as any sound could have been. "I don't, but she's a card we can only play once. If we fuck this up, we don't get another shot. If he gets ahold of her, we're done."

"We'll be careful," Hayden pressed. "But waiting around isn't getting us anywhere. Lorien wants her, is still looking for her, but he's covering his tracks well. None of our contacts can follow the trial back to him. If one path isn't working, running down it will only get you farther away from your goal. We have to change tactics."

"So what are you suggesting?" I asked.

"We've kept her out of sight for her safety, but we need to let Lorien know where she is, now. If he sees her, if he realizes that she's around, he's more likely to make a move. Every time he does that, we get another clue, another attempt to nail him down."

"So you're telling us to, what? Just parade her around and hope he hears?"

"If he's paying attention, he'll notice the second she shows back up at school."

It's not enough to know she's back — we want to give him a view of how to get her, Tor texted.

"So we need to make it clear who has her so Lorien has to make a move?" Char says.

"But in a way that keeps her as safe as possible," Hayden added.

I frowned, the answer obvious to me. It was strange, since the others tended to be better at planning, better at such underhanded things, but here I was with the clear answer. "I've got an idea," I said.

The other three turned their gazes toward me with questioning looks. It was a surprisingly nice feeling, really.

"And what idea is that?" Char asked, his tone incredulous.

I smirked, unable to help it. "I think it's about time you finally let me have my way with her."

Chapter Seven

Tor

Kenz's apartment was both what I expected and what I hadn't. It amazed me how she challenged my preconceived notions while also living right up to them.

"Nice place." Hayden whistled low as he peered around the large penthouse apartment. It fit perfectly with the idea of her being some rich, spoiled brat who lived off her father's estate. The views were fantastic, even during the day. After sunset, I would bet it all lit up, sparkling as bright as the night sky.

It was the sort of place that cost millions, though from what we could find, she didn't own it. Instead, she rented it. The bank records Char had managed to get showed five thousand dollars rent paid on the first of every month to a rental agency, the payments made automatically.

It all seemed above board, even if the apartment itself was far more than a kid her age needed.

It had four bedrooms and five baths, according to the records online. The furniture was nice, but it all matched perfectly. Either she'd rented it furnished or she had a decorator to pick out pieces like that.

I pulled at the coat I wore, disliking the uniform. I'd worked jobs that didn't require uniforms like that, which meant it chafed. Still, I knew exactly how useful a good costume was when it came to getting into places I wasn't supposed to be.

Such as Kenz's apartment without her. A tan jacket with the name of a repair company worked wonderfully to make people look the other way.

Hayden walked into the space with more comfort than I had. Then again, he had more experience dealing with others, with spending time in close proximity to them. As a bodyguard, Hayden had to often spend time in the homes of others.

Me, though? I rarely interacted with others beyond the absolute minimum necessary. I didn't enter a home unless I intended to kill the person in it, for the most part.

Which left me with a strange sense of unease in Kenz's living room.

It felt like signing Kenz's death, as though by my presence in her home, I'd marked her in some way.

I shook off the sensation, needing to focus on our task.

With Kenz at the school, all eyes should be there. It gave us a great chance to check out her place, to see if there was anything we needed here, any clues as to why Lorien wanted her.

Hayden started in the living room, immediately opening drawers and cabinets without the least bit of hesitation. Since he had this area worked out, I headed for the hallway.

As far as I understood, Kenz lived alone. The penthouse took up half of the top floor, which meant only her one neighbor shared the hallway. It limited the number of people who would notice guests.

From what we had found out, she didn't have friends come over. The people she knew at school, from her job, had never come to her place. However, the lobby security notes did show visitors from time to time. Those visitors did not sign in with names as everyone else did, telling me they held some amount of sway to convince security to let that pass.

It made me uneasy, wondering why they had come, how she knew them and just who they were.

I opened the first door, frowning when I found an empty room.

No bed, no dresser, no desk. It appeared by all accounts that no one used this room. The closet had no belongings and the bathroom showed no signs of use.

If the place had been furnished, they would have put things in the extra rooms, right?

When I couldn't figure it out, I went to the next room. The same store repeated in three of the bedrooms — empty.

It wasn't until I went to the first door on the other side of the hallway that I found anything. Inside was a bedroom that brought me up short.

It looked like the room of a teenager…

Never had Kenz seemed quite so young as she did when I looked in here. A large bed sat in the middle of the room with a pink comforter, the bed unmade and messy, as though she'd gotten up in the middle of the night and never made it back.

Then again, that's exactly what happened, isn't it?

The bed had a white lace canopy over it, with strings of lights that ran along the fabric.

A fluffy white rug sat on the floor, though it showed signs of use. This room didn't fit the rest of the apartment in the least.

A reluctance kept me at the threshold, some knowledge that I didn't belong in a space like this at all.

I certainly wouldn't have pegged Kenz as the sort of woman to have a room so comfortable.

Or *pink*.

If Char had been here, he no doubt would have said it looked like a unicorn had thrown up in here.

I forced myself to step into the room. I had a job to do, and my personal feelings would only get in the way. I first checked the bathroom, finding similar décor there.

A smile tugged at my lips when I spotted a unicorn toothbrush holder and matching rainbow soap dish beside it. Any eight-year-old girl would have been proud of a room like this.

For a moment, I tried to picture her here, brushing her teeth, smiling, going through life without a care.

That wasn't her anymore, though. It couldn't be. I shouldn't feel bad about it. I hadn't targeted her, hadn't torn her old life away. Lorien had done that.

We might have stepped in, but she was better off than she would have been in his care. Lorien did not have the reputation as a kind man, after all.

Still, no matter how much I tried to justify it all, that kernel of guilt ate away at me.

I checked the cabinets in the bathroom, finding the normal things a woman her age would need. On the counter, a single orange pill bottle sat. I picked it up and read a name I didn't recognize on it. She had no roommate, and I didn't recognize the name as an acquaintance of hers. I slid it into my pocket before moving on.

After the bathroom, I went to her closet. Clothes packed it full, despite how large the walk-in closet was. In fact, it was a closet so huge, it had a bench at the center, as though someone might tire themselves out from changing.

Talk about a world I know nothing about.

Shoes lined one area, the shelves lit up as soon as I'd opened the door. I knew nothing about clothing, but even I could tell that every item in this room had cost a small fortune.

A locked case sat along one of the walls, and inside? Jewelry shone, bright and tempting. It all appeared real, with silver, gold, diamonds, rubies, emeralds and gems I couldn't even hope to name.

I wasn't a thief, though, so I'd never cared much about things like jewelry. Beside the lit-up case, however, was an actual safe.

If she kept such nice items in the locked showcase, I could only imagine the worth of whatever remained in the safe.

This girl is so far outside of my league.

Which was fine by me. This was a temporary alliance—nothing more. What did I care if just one of her necklaces could buy every home that I'd lived in growing up? None of that would matter once we finished this.

"You find anything?" Hayden walked into the room, a notebook in his hands.

I reached into my pocket, fished out the pill bottle, then tossed it to him.

Hayden caught it, lifting it so he could read the small, printed words. "Anti-anxiety meds."

I pressed my lips together. She hadn't struck me as overly anxious, but who knew if that was true? Maybe she just hid it well.

"They say to use during panic attacks, flashbacks or when struggling to sleep." Hayden frowned, staring at the bottle for an answer. "Has she had trouble sleeping?"

I thought back to the first night, the only night I'd watched her sleep. After that, we'd gotten another room for her set up and properly secured.

I pulled out my phone and quickly typed a response. *She slept the first night she was with us.*

Hayden nodded. "Maybe she doesn't really need these. A lot of people get prescriptions and abuse them. She doesn't strike me as an addict, but that doesn't mean she isn't one. Lots of kids her age, especially rich ones, end up depressed or looking for an escape from the pressure. We'll bring these back, but I don't think I'm going to give them to her. We'll see how it goes." He tucked them into his pocket, then held up the journal he'd found. "This was on the kitchen counter. Looks like she uses it as a planner."

Which was likely a lot more useful than whatever was in her bedroom.

I held my hand out, then opened the book when Hayden gave it to me. Her writing was amazingly neat, and it seemed she drew all the pages herself. Perfectly done squares and doodles of vines and flowers dotted most pages, along with her daily plans and to do lists.

It was far more organized than I would have expected. Most people her age—especially rich art majors—weren't known for being on top of things. I pictured flighty kids, those who missed classes and assignments and never knew what day it was. Instead, this journal showed each day of her life mapped out, each thing that needed to get done.

I skimmed through the pages, surprised by just how good her art was. Even though these were hastily done, the attention to detail on the petals and leaves proved her skill.

She seemed to have little social life. Her daily schedule had things in it like school, work, grocery shopping, cleaning and going to the gym in her apartment building. Her days were scheduled full, yet none of it seemed like free time. She didn't include dates or meeting with friends or anything of that sort.

Worse? None of it gave me any idea as to how she might know Lorien or why he might want her.

"I still don't have a clue," Hayden admitted. "She seems like a normal college student. I didn't find any evidence of her knowing Lorien, of her knowing anything about his world, any reason he'd find an interest in her. It just doesn't make sense."

I peered around the room, wondering what we might have missed.

The safe.

I'd assumed more jewelry sat in it, given its location, but what if that wasn't the case?

I gestured toward the closet before heading back into it, Hayden's heavy steps telling me he followed.

How he could walk so loudly, I would never understand. Then again, his point was to be present, and others knowing he was there only helped him. He *could* walk softly, but he never did unless he had a reason.

I tapped the top of the safe, then raised my eyebrow.

"It could just be jewelry," Hayden said, a hesitation in his tone that implied he didn't fully believe that. "But, given how expensive the stuff in the glass case is, it's hard to believe she'd have anything nicer to put in a safe." He peered at me. "Can you open the safe?"

I nodded, a quick jerk of my head. While I wasn't a thief, I did have to track my targets, find out information about their whereabouts, and at times bring back proof my clients wanted. That required accessing sensitive information, which was the sort of things people liked to keep inside locked safes.

That made it a useful skill to be able to get into said safes.

The process took longer than it should have, all things considered. It went to show just how nice this particular safe was, how serious the person who installed it was about keeping their secrets private. The better the lock, the better the prize, after all.

When the lights on the front flashed green — the sign that I'd managed to bypass the programming and reset it — I twisted the front handle, the lock clicking open, before I pulled open the door.

A light inside flickered to life, illuminating the contents.

And just like that, I knew there was more to this girl than we had realized.

* * * *

Kenz

I am in so much trouble.

I knew the feeling well, had experienced it plenty of times to identify it the moment I walked into the house with Char by my side.

As if the day wasn't bad enough already.

I had a massive headache from the constant switching of Char's personality. I couldn't keep up with him going from sweet and charming and funny to downright hostile. The only time he seemed happy in the least was when we were surrounded by others. The second he got me alone — he reverted right back to his bad mood.

Is it me?

Probably not, but I couldn't help taking it personally. Even still, something inside me wanted to figure it out, to work out why he acted that way and how to get closer to him, no matter how foolish the desire was.

And now, after that, I felt the crushing tension that came just before a lecture.

How many times had the Quad done that over the years? Sat me down because they'd known something and wanted me to come clean?

Then again, if I'd never broken beneath the Quad's interrogations, I doubted these four stood a chance.

At least, I told myself that. In reality, my knees trembled, and my heart raced. What if I messed up? What if I said something wrong and ended up outing myself?

What if I put Nem in danger because I was weak?

I swallowed hard and faked a smile just as I entered the living room to find Tor, Vance and Hayden already there like parents whose kid had come home two hours past curfew.

Steady, girl. You've been through worse.

Hayden and Tor wore nearly identical expressions, ones I recognized even if I'd never seen them on these specific faces.

Annoyance.

I let out a hesitant laugh, one that doubtlessly came across more unhinged than I'd meant it to. It didn't sound like the chuckle of someone amused but rather a nervous attempt to cover discomfort.

"Do you have something worth laughing about right now?" Hayden asked, his tone *exactly* like Dane's when he wanted to trap me, when he knew everything but wanted me to spill about it anyway.

I swallowed down the laugh, though that didn't help the pounding of my heart or the sweat on my palms. "I was just thinking about how my old bodyguards would sit me down like this when I got into trouble."

"Oh really?" Hayden crossed his arms over his chest, staring at me with a heaviness that made it difficult to breathe. "And what did you do to annoy *them?*"

The implication that I'd done something to annoy these four didn't go over my head.

I gulped as I took a seat on the couch, the empty spot clearly meant for me. "What didn't I do? I mean, they were my bodyguards for a long time, so I had plenty of chances to really make them mad." I tried again for that laugh, rewarded with the others not moving a bit.

Guess I won't get out of this that easily.

"I remember one time my father said I couldn't go to a friend's house. He didn't think the friend was a good fit for me. They were poor, someone who only got into my private school because they were brought in for a quota. The girl was nice, though, so I didn't care. My school had security, so I didn't have bodyguards during school hours. They dropped me off and picked me up. Well, I ended up forging my mom's signature and using that to let me go to my friend's house after school one day."

The memory of that day ran through my brain, warming me. Her name had been Portia and she'd lived in this little house in the area of town my father had told me never to go into.

Which was hilarious, considering I later discovered my father controlled that area, that all those thugs and delinquents that made that area bad reported to him. The worst parts of that area were all owned by my father.

Portia had lived with only her mother, something I'd understood since my father had always been working. Her mother had made crackers with peanut butter and I'd gotten to watch TV and play with toys, acting normal in a way I rarely got to.

"I had a great time feeling like a normal kid, at least until two of my bodyguards showed up to take me home. They sat me down just like this to lecture me."

"Your bodyguards did, not your father?"

"My father was always busy, so I rarely saw him. My bodyguards, they also worked for my mother and sister."

Hayden broke in. "Sister? I thought you were an only child?"

Shit.

It reminded me why I hated having to lie, because it was too easy to end up saying something that couldn't be taken back. I'd watched Dane lie enough times to give it a shot, though. "She wasn't my real sister. She was a cousin who just lived with us sometimes, so I always thought of her as my sister."

Char snorted, the sound implying he didn't believe me in the least.

When no one actually called me out, I went on. "So my bodyguards lectured me about the dangers of going off without protection, that their job was to keep me safe, and that to do that, they needed to know where I was at all times."

"Did that work? Did you behave after that?"

I rubbed my palm against the top of my thigh, trying to figure out how to voice the chaos in my head. "I didn't like worrying them. None of my problems were their fault, after all, and they really did care about me. I agreed I wouldn't run off anymore."

I recalled Colton's frown when I'd agreed, as if my bending to their will didn't please him. I hadn't understood the meaning behind his look at the time, but later? Later I figured out how much they fought between wanting to give in to me, wanting to make me happy, and what they owed to my parents.

I didn't envy them for having to walk that line.

"Well, maybe you can learn to be a good girl for us, too," Vance said, his tone thick with meaning and promise.

And I did not care one bit for the way it made my stomach flutter. How could a man get that sort of reaction with just a few words? It seemed entirely unfair.

"So, do you want to stop lying to us?" Hayden asked, steel in his voice. It was the tone of a man who was sure of himself, who already knew everything, like the bait in a trap.

"I don't know what you're talking about," I said.

Tor grabbed a bag from behind the couch, one I hadn't seen, and dumped the contents out onto the table.

The stuff from my safe…

Piles of cash, all unmarked bills in differing denominations, spilled across the table. In addition, a number of identifications and passports in all different fake names, along with bank information for each. The last item struck the table with a loud thump, sitting there like a scorpion.

A pistol, the 9mm Colton had taught me to shoot, the one he'd bought for me before I'd moved here.

I hated the thing, but the only way the Quad had agreed to me moving so far away on my own was if they felt I could defend myself. That had involved self-defense with Rune and shooting lessons with Colton.

I stared at the items on the table, my brain refusing to offer any explanation. *Useless thing!* While Dane could have come up with a lie in a heartbeat, then would have sold it like his life depended on it, I lacked that skill.

"These aren't the sorts of things some rich college student would need," Hayden said. "These identifications are meticulously made. If I didn't know better, I might have even thought them real at first. They wouldn't come easily or cheaply. All the banking information is untraceable, and it gives you access to no less than ten million, from what we were able to track down."

"Then there's the issue of the gun," Vance said, a smirk on his perfect lips. "You seem like a nice girl, so why do you have something like that?"

Always bury your lie in the truth. Dane had taught me the best way to sell a story was to give them something real along with it.

"My bodyguards gave that to me in case I needed it. Even though, after my dad died, I'm not in a lot of danger, there are still people who could target me. They wanted to make sure I was safe."

"From what I can tell, you haven't had bodyguards for a while. That gun is new. Not only is it new, but it lacks the identifying marks a legal gun would have. You didn't buy that at a store, and the only people who need untraceable weapons are criminals," Hayden said.

Why did they have to be this smart?

I took a deep breath, then met Hayden's gaze head-on. "I wanted to live a normal life. I wanted to be just like any other college student, to move away after my father's death, to live my life on my own terms. I didn't want bodyguards, to draw attention to myself, any of it. That didn't change that people worried about me. When I moved, my old bodyguards got me those things just in case."

"So you're still in contact with them?" Char asked.

"Sometimes," I hedged. "They check in on me, but that's it."

"What else do they do?" Hayden asked. "If Lorien is interested in you, maybe it isn't about you at all. Maybe they're involved in things that you're now caught up in?"

You're closer than you think, but not quite on the mark yet.

I had little doubt that Lorien was after me due to my connection to Nem, to my family line. It wasn't the Quad—most likely—but rather my parents that had Lorien after me. Him knowing who I really was was the only thing that made any sense.

I couldn't say that, though, so I shook my head. "I'm sure they aren't caught up with Lorien. They don't leave the West Coast." True, at least for the most part. Nem kept them too busy to leave California let alone the West Coast. They only came out this far when visiting me.

None of the men appeared convinced. Then again, when someone couldn't find an answer, they tended to latch onto any little hint or clue because they had nothing else. It meant they weren't likely going to let go of this so easily.

"What are their names?" Char asked.

"What?"

"Your bodyguards. You want us to believe you, to trust your story no matter how little sense it makes or how obvious your lies are, so tell us the names of your bodyguards. Give us the contact information to them or their company so we can verify it."

Which was the one thing I absolutely could not do. Not only would it blow my cover and put me in more danger, but it might just endanger the Quad and Nem, too.

I'd never claim I was anything other than a coward, but that was too far. I refused to cross that line.

And no lie would satisfy them, not about this.

So I pressed my lips together into a thin line and shook my head.

"Not going to tell us?" Char asked.

"No."

"You realize that we're willing to do whatever it takes to achieve our goals, right?" Char crowded me, bending forward and setting a hand on the back of the couch.

I leaned as far away as I could, but it didn't help, didn't change that he'd caged me in with his body, that his dark eyes were right in front of me, the green flecks in them bright.

"I know," I whispered.

"And you'll still remain silent? You'll risk whatever we do to you for what? For a couple of bodyguards?"

I nodded.

"Why?"

"Because they'd do the same for me. If you want to hurt someone, I won't make them your target."

"So you'll take their place? You'll make yourself the target?"

"Yes." Finally, an answer with some conviction. My voice still trembled, but I had no doubt of my answer. I was terrified, but I would never give up the Quad, no matter what happened to me. "I know that I'm weak, that I'm not as brave as the people around me, not as strong, not as capable. I might be a coward who everyone else has to pick up the slack for, but I won't let you hurt people I care about. It doesn't matter what you do to me, I won't betray them."

Char blinked slowly, his expression different than the two I recognized. It wasn't the friendly one he showed others or the malice he offered to me. Instead, it was something like confusion, as if his brain had to make sense of the words I'd said.

After a long moment, he pulled away with a huff, then stormed out.

I glanced at the other three, wondering if that was the end.

Tor gathered the items off the table — including the gun — packed them away, then left.

Hayden nailed me with a hard look, one that said he wasn't done with the conversation even if he'd lost this time. "I'm going to tell you something it sounds like you already know but don't understand. I am a bodyguard. I deal with keeping clients alive. Just like how your bodyguards told you that keeping secrets from them would only endanger you, I'll tell you the same. Whether you like it or not, right now my job is to keep you safe. Keeping secrets is only going to make that job harder." He didn't wait for me to respond before leaving as well.

Only Vance and I remained in the room, and he stared at me with the same easy, amused smile as usual.

"Get dressed," he said. At my expression — which probably showed my confusion — he laughed. "We're going out. Wear something nice. I believe Hayden brought some of your clothing, so pick out a pretty cocktail dress."

He didn't ask me, didn't wait to see if I'd agree, before rising and walking out.

It left me alone in the living room, the tension from before still there, still crushing me. That anxiety that swamped me at night so often remained, bounding around inside me, not allowing me to breathe deeply or settle.

And now, after all that, I was going somewhere with Vance?

All I knew for sure was that that man was not good for my heart.

Chapter Eight

Kenz

When was the last time I'd dressed up like this? I pulled at the hem of my cocktail dress as I sat in the passenger seat of Vance's fancy sports car.

It was far from the first time I'd been in a car like this, though it was probably the time I was the least comfortable with it. Vance had yet to tell me anything other than he was taking me out on a date.

"You can't be *that* nervous." The way Vance could look so comfortable while driving around in a half-a-million-dollar car annoyed me. He should be the nervous one, darting through traffic while headed for some fancy restaurant.

Instead, he looked one hundred percent at ease.

He probably does this all the time.

Get a girl in a car like this, shower them with affection and compliments and fancy food and the odds of ending up alone at the end of the night were pretty slim, after all.

He'd dressed up in a suit, and it sure suited him well. The black gloves were still in place, but I hardly noticed them anymore. They were just a part of him.

"I'm not used to dates," I said.

"No? A pretty young girl like you? I figured you'd have at least ten guys on the hook, all of them simps willing to do anything you want."

I snorted at the wholly inaccurate guess. "I'm not into having men 'on the hook.' Besides, I'm busy with school."

"Why work that hard? Art is easy."

"Maybe for you, it is. For the famous, talented Vance Moore, it's all so simple. For the rest of us, though? We have to practice and learn and give it our all or we'll never make it."

He furrowed his eyebrows, the action making him appear older. I knew from the stories that he was in his late twenties, but that was about it. Magazines constantly covered him, but it was more about his exploits with women than anything else. In fact, I'd rarely seen an article discuss his art in years, and even those had been focused on older work. "You've got money. You could buy your way into the right gallery. An education is about making your art better, but succeeding in the art world is about who you know and how much you're willing to sell yourself — that's it."

His words were so cold that I shivered, the temperature in the car having plummeted to match his mood.

He'd never been sweet or caring, but these words rang hostile.

It wasn't a flip, not like Char, but instead like I'd peeled back a scab and exposed a deep wound to air. He reacted the way an animal protecting itself would.

Which showed it would be best to avoid that conversation.

"You look nice," he muttered, his tone sullen.

Was he trying to apologize for snapping at me?

No, he isn't the type to say sorry.

"Thanks," I offered, afraid to do anything to make us slip back into the tension from before. "It's been a while since I dressed up."

"Not a lot of chances at college?"

"Nope. They have dances or mixers sometimes, but those are casual. I also don't go."

"Why not? Isn't that part of the whole student life? Don't you want to make the best of your years here?" His voice almost came out like an ad for the college.

"I like my life to stay quiet."

"You also didn't have anyone over to your place that we could tell. Makes me wonder why you're working so hard to keep other people away. Some people like Char or Tor are just private people who value their solitude. You, though? You're more like me, like Hayden. You like to talk, to be around others, to listen to them. Why deny yourself that?"

I stared out the window at the lights that streamed by instead of at him. It made the rest of the world feel fake, like a movie screen playing outside the car, just a figment of my imagination. Instead, it was only Vance and me in the whole world. Maybe that feeling got me taking. "I've moved around a lot in my life because of my father. I never got to set down roots or become part of a community. The only people I cared about either left me or risked themselves for me and got hurt. I learned that letting people get close to me never did them any good, and it hurt too much when I was left all alone again. It's better to keep things casual."

Vance didn't answer, taking so long that I turned toward him. We sat at a red light, the engine idling loudly, and he stared right at me as though I'd said something that made no sense.

I kept my mouth shut, not sure how to make the moment better, how to laugh off the truth I hadn't meant to utter aloud.

I had no idea how long we remained locked in that moment together, lost in the words I'd said and the many I hadn't. Why was it that Vance always looked at me as if he understood? As if he got even the things I hadn't said? It made me feel far too exposed?

A honking behind us broke the spell, and I looked forward to realize the light had changed to green, long enough ago that the other lane had already gone.

Whatever Vance might have said died in his throat, because he turned his attention back to the road and sped the car along so quickly, the momentum pinned me to my seat.

And, as it had done so many times, that glimpse of Vance made me wonder just how much of himself he hid.

* * * *

"Why are you looking at me like that?" Vance didn't ask the question with the same attitude Char would have. Instead, every word out of his mouth felt like an invitation.

"You're unfair."

"Oh yeah? How so." He smirked and set his arm on the table between us, leaning in.

The restaurant we ate at was incredibly nice, the sort of place I hadn't gone in a long time, not since before my father's death. In the year since then, I'd eaten, best I could, as a college student. I'd enjoyed ramen places and diners and fast food.

The freshman twenty is a real thing.

"You're rich, famous, handsome and talented. It's unfair that you're charming, too. No one person should have so much in his arsenal."

Vance said nothing at first, the words sinking in slowly. Finally, he laughed. "You really know how to disarm a man, huh? I have to say, you look a lot better dressed up than I thought you would. I should have expected it, given your upbringing, but for some reason, I struggled to picture it."

His gaze moved over me, and it felt like a caress each place he looked. My shoulder, the curve to my neck, the exposed area above the neckline of my dress.

I dropped my gaze when I couldn't hold it any longer. "I've gone to a lot of places like this, dressed up for business get-togethers with my father. I'm just glad the dress still fits okay."

"Oh, it fits better than okay."

"Do you ever knock it off with the lines?" I wanted to say they didn't affect me, that I ignored them and felt nothing.

What a lie.

Even if I knew he was just toying with me — probably out of boredom — that didn't stop the way my pulse sped when he uttered such charming lies. In my old life, men had been far too afraid of my father to speak to me like that. No one flirted with me because they feared what might happen to them.

And since moving out here? Well, I hadn't exactly welcomed such entanglements, hadn't put myself in places where men might try it, so I hadn't built up a defense against it.

Which made me want to laugh. The idea that I could tolerate getting abducted and threatened without too much reaction, but a few smooth pick-up lines lobbied my way had my palms sweating was laughable.

"They aren't lines," Vance said. When I lifted my eyebrow, he snickered. "Well, maybe they are, but that doesn't make them untrue."

"Right," I muttered, taking a drink of my water to cool my burning cheeks.

"I'm serious." Vance waited until I lifted my gaze to his bright blue eyes before he continued to speak. "Believe it or not, I don't lie to women. I won't pretend I'm not a womanizer, that I haven't enjoyed more than my fair share of them, but I don't like or trick them into my bed. Every woman who spends time with me knows the deal, that I'm not planning to settle down."

"What woman would be okay with someone telling them they only want sex?"

"I don't *only* want sex." He held his hand up to silence me when I opened my mouth. "Don't get me wrong, I want sex, but that's not it. I enjoy women in general. I like to talk to women, to spend time with them. And what sort of women want that? Smart ones, usually, and confident ones. Some of them might hope they can get more out of me, and who knows? It's possible one could catch my attention and change my mind. Most, though? They like the way I make them feel. They like the time together, to feel like they are beautiful and important and special even if it's only for one night."

"One night?" I asked in a whisper, the meaning behind that enough to have my mind supplying all sorts of scenarios. While I hadn't actually had sex before, I wasn't such a prude to not know what it entailed, to have watched porn and seen enough movies for my imagination to take over.

"Yeah. Sometimes one night is all you really need, and I promise, I can make one night feel like a whole lot longer." He leaned in and set his hand on mine, the touch warm and gentle and reassuring. "I can make one night worth it for you, Kenz."

"Is that why you brought me here? You probably just haven't gotten to go out and find a booty-call because you have to watch me."

"There are enough of us to handle that. If I wanted to go out, I could."

"So why haven't you?"

He shrugged as he dragged his thumb over mine, the touch soft despite the way it felt connected to every erogenous spot on my body. "Because I find you entertaining. I love spending time with women, but sometimes it becomes monotonous. You've interested me enough that I haven't felt the need to go find anyone else."

I swallowed hard, unsure how to react. Each word he spoke made me fall deeper into some haze, making me feel as though I'd drank something stronger than water, as if I were drunk on the atmosphere alone.

Which reminded me just how dangerous Vance was. He wasn't the others, but he had a threat all his own. Vance could make me fall for him.

I had no doubt about that—he was too smooth, too smart, too damned handsome. If he really wanted something, I doubted I could resist.

Maybe I was pathetic and too needy. It felt like so long since someone had honestly complimented me. I'd been respected, given false words of praise all because people hoped to get something from my father, because they wanted something from me.

Those words had always felt like poisoned candy— sweet at first but that would eventually kill me.

Somehow, Vance's words landed different. They shouldn't have, since I couldn't believe he didn't whisper these same words to countless other women, but the idea of believing him, of accepting them, was too much.

So much had changed, so long I'd tried so hard to be something more, and here Vance was telling me I was good.

Not my name, not my money, not anything but *me.*

As the waiter passed by, I called out to him. "I changed my mind. Can I have a Long Island Iced Tea?"

When the waiter left, Vance chuckled and drew back, the loss of his hand chilling me. "Needing a little liquid courage?"

"When in Rome," I muttered.

Twenty minutes later, a nice buzz had taken me over as I ate the food from my plate. We'd ordered a few different things to share, giving me the chance to try an assortment of items, all of them amazing. I'd kept an eye on my blood sugar, since I rarely drank, but my before-dinner insulin seemed to be doing its job.

And the alcohol had smoothed over my nerves. It quieted down that voice in my head that screamed to be careful, the reminded me Vance teased all women, that I was nothing special. The cocktails had put that voice to sleep so Vance's compliments slid through me, beckoning me, letting me believe them for a while.

"You don't drink much, do you?"

"Not really," I admitted.

"Why not?"

The drinks allowed the words to slip from me so easily, as if I couldn't hold them all myself. "Alcohol makes people out of control, and I don't like to be out of control. It's not safe."

"Not safe? That's why you shouldn't drink alone, not unless you're home. I'll take you drinking whenever you want, love."

Love? The word glided from his lips like the best promise, like he whispered it into my ear when we were naked and pressed against each other.

I like that. It was dangerous, sure, but I couldn't help enjoying the way it sounded.

The thought of drinking again with Vance, of letting my guard down, it tempted me. My head spun, my heart racing, and I couldn't tell if that was because of Vance or the alcohol at this point.

All I knew for sure was that I needed some air, to cool down my heated cheeks. I got to my feet, stumbling slightly when it seemed I'd thrown off my alcohol-to-heel height ratio.

Yet, I didn't topple. Instead, a strong arm wrapped around my waist and pinned me to a solid body.

"Easy," Vance said. "There's a patio space. Let's take you out to sober you up a bit, hmm?"

I nodded, letting him take my weight, walking far easier as I leaned against him.

The patio was lovely. Strings of lights looked like fireflies and were strung up above a stone floor. In the corner, a water feature bubbled, the sound relaxing.

A cool breeze stroked across my heated cheeks, and when I went to pull away, Vance tightened his arm around me.

"You're not steady yet, so just stay here a little longer." His fingers pressed into my side, his arm wrapped around me, the touch like a safety net that I'd wanted so badly.

It felt like when the Quad used to tuck me in as a child, when I'd thought someone could keep the whole big bad world away, when I'd trusted others to do that.

Vance caught my chin and tipped my face up toward him. It let me stare into his eyes, drawn in by the bright blue. How could a man have eyes that pretty? The blue wasn't silver like Nem or Jarrod's. Instead, it was vibrant, standing out due to his blond hair.

He rubbed his thumb along my jawline, a smile tugging at one side of his lips. "Don't drink with other men."

"Why not?"

"I don't want anyone else to see this face. Turns out I'm a pretty selfish man, huh?" He laughed softly as if to mock himself and his own foolishness.

Yet it had me set a hand on his chest, the thumping of his heart heavy against my palm. He was an artist, yet his physique showed he worked out. He wore a sweater so soft I fought the urge to rub my cheek against it.

He really was handsome, wasn't he? It was easy to forget, but right now? Between the lights strung above us and the bubbling fountain and the alcohol, I forgot all the reasons this was a horrible idea.

I wanted to be a normal girl, just for a little while. I wanted to have dinner with a cute boy who liked me, to behave foolishly, to do things for no reason other than I wanted to.

A flash to the left made me frown.

"Showtime," he whispered, the words making no sense right away.

"What's that?" I asked, pushing back slightly, a history of watching out for danger screaming in my head.

"We've come to a busy, romantic, famous restaurant. A tip to some tabloids let them know. Now Lorien will know who bought you and why."

It took a long time for my brain to work through his statement, but the moment it did, it sobered me right up.

I was an idiot. I'd let myself believe that tonight meant anything, that Vance had meant any of it. How could I have been that stupid?

My eyes burned but I couldn't tear my gaze from his, from that damned half-smirk he wore, from the bright blue of his eyes. I blinked rapidly to clear away the sting, not wanting to let a single tear escape.

He leaned in closer.

I flattened my hands against his chest, pushing, but Vance had a hold of me too well. Before I could really resist, his warm lips pressed against mine.

It wasn't a gentle kiss, a sweet one. He tilted his head and used his grip on my chin to angle my own the opposite way. Quickly, he deepened the kiss, his seeking tongue teasing the seam of my lips. I gasped in surprise, giving him access to delve deep, to stroke against my tongue.

The kiss told me a few things.

He knew exactly what he was doing.

I was entirely outmatched by him.

And lastly? I'd never forgive myself for falling for his tricks.

* * * *

Vance

"The news is everywhere." Hayden clicked off the television as I walked into the living room.

"That's what happens when there's a juicy story," I said. I'd grown so used to the stresses of living in the spotlight that I'd learned to use it to my advantage.

After getting followed around as a kid, I'd figured out trying to avoid the tabloids was pointless. They'd make up stories if they had nothing, which meant giving them something worked to my advantage.

By the time I'd reached my teenage years, I'd learned to play the game. I'd figured out that seeding stories worked out far better for me.

There were times I hated it, of course, but hating something didn't change reality.

I glanced down at my gloved hand, then shook my head.

Can't change reality, no matter how much I want to.

"Is Kenz okay?" Hayden asked, the sentimental bastard.

"She's pissed, I'm sure, but she'll get over it."

The truth was, she hadn't spoken a single word to me after the kiss. Sure, I'd laid a good on one her, but it shouldn't have been *that* big a deal. She was probably angrier that I hadn't told her the plan, that I'd sprung it on her.

But if I had told her, I doubted she could play the game for the cameras. She was too honest, and if she'd known the plan, she'd have acted anxious and awkward, assuming she agreed to play along at all.

"So how long until Lorien knows?" Char asked.

"He'll know by morning at the latest," I answered. "I expect that by the end of tomorrow, we'll hear something from him."

"Like what? You think he'll just call you up and ask if he can buy the woman you bought from an auction? He's way too careful for that," Char said.

"Oh, sure, it won't be that obvious, but he'll reach out one way or another. He went to far too much effort for Kenz to throw it away now, especially at the idea that some rich playboy bought her out from underneath him."

I could picture him raging right now, as he saw the news. From what I knew of Lorien, his ego ran his life. The mere thought that someone, in his eyes, so far beneath him taking something from him wouldn't sit well.

And that would drive him to make choices he otherwise wouldn't.

The padding of bare feet against hardwood floors made me look behind me a moment before a clearly angry and still rather liquored-up Kenz stormed into the living room. Her cheeks still held that red tint and her eyes had a glassy quality that showed she hadn't sobered up despite the drive home and all the pacing she'd probably done in her room.

And this side of her made me grin wider. Why was it that I liked it? Sure, she'd been cute in her dress and heels, fitting in perfectly with the atmosphere and environment of that restaurant, but I preferred her this way.

She still wore the dress, but she'd removed the shoes. That alone had dressed her down, made her look more casual even in the figure-hugging black dress.

"You asshole!" she snapped.

The curse word from her lovely pink lips took me by surprise, and it took everything I had not to break into a laugh at her.

Even I knew better than to piss a woman off too much.

Men would punch someone for it, but a woman? They tended to wait until the right moment, then take a man's balls for going too far.

I liked my balls in one piece and to stay exactly where they were.

"You should probably sleep off all that alcohol," I said. "I'd hate for you to say something you didn't mean."

"Oh, trust me, I mean *everything* I'm about to say." She pointed her finger at me, the action drawing attention to the silver rings on her fingers. She wore a bunch of them, and they caught the light as she moved.

"Kenz," Hayden said, his voice soft and coaxing.

"Stay out of this," Kenz snapped without looking his way. "This is between the playboy and me."

Hayden closed his mouth, and wasn't that amazing? Normally he meddled so much that nothing could get him to shut up. Leave it to this little fireball to sideline him so well.

Which meant she was all mine for the moment. Even if it was due to anger, I couldn't stop my glee at being her whole world right now.

"So go on. What's so important that you stormed all the way down here to confront me?" I crossed my arms and waited, giving her the floor.

"How *dare* you use me like that!"

"Like what?"

"You lied to me. You took me there to show me off, to plant a story in the tabloids, and you didn't even have the decency to tell me about it first."

"I didn't say anything because if I had, you wouldn't have relaxed and looked like you were enjoying yourself. We needed the pictures to look natural, like we were on a date, and I've seen you lie. You suck at it. No one would have believed it if you'd known ahead of time."

She pressed her lips together, and beneath the anger? Hurt?

It made no sense to me at all. She tore her gaze from mine, staring instead at the far wall as she blinked quickly then looked up at the ceiling.

Is she going to cry?

Sure, women crying wasn't anything new to me. Women liked to use tears like a weapon, like another way to manipulate those around them. They rarely swayed me because I knew the trick so well.

Yet, watching Kenz try so hard *not* to cry caused a strange tightening in my chest.

"Why are you so mad? It was a kiss, Kenz. I never lied to you. It was a date, and I had a good time. The fact that I did it knowing cameras would be there didn't make anything I said a lie."

"You really are heartless, aren't you?" She turned to leave.

But something inside me refused to let her go, especially when I still didn't understand what had triggered her so much. It was one kiss, and honestly? It was a really damn good kiss. I saw no good reason to be *this* angry over it.

I grabbed her wrist with my left hand, needing to make sense of this. "What are you so mad about? Are you pissed it ended at a kiss? Because I wasn't lying. You are beautiful, and I do find you interesting. You want me to prove it? Come to my bedroom, and I'll spend all damned night showing you."

A stinging in my cheek made me release her and step backward.

She'd slapped me? I touched the spot, my eyes wide, the reaction totally unexpected.

Worse? The tears that had finally escaped her eyes, the ones she hadn't managed to keep from falling. "That was my first kiss, you asshole. I won't ever forgive you for stealing it."

With that, she rushed out, leaving me and the others in the living room.

What was this feeling inside me? This gnawing ache that made me want to rub my hand against my chest, to ease that tightness?

Well fuck, I think this might just be guilt for the first time ever...

Chapter Nine

Hayden

"What's this, a bribe?" Kenz lifted her dark eyebrow as she stared at the bag I held out to her.

"It's egg bites." I shook the bag as though she were a cat, and I offered her a treat. "Do you not want them?"

She pressed her lips together, then snatched the bag from me. "Fine. Bribe accepted. So what do you want in exchange?"

"You should always ask that *before* you take a bribe," I reminded her. "However, I've already gotten it. I just wanted you to cheer up a bit."

She snorted softly before getting into the passenger side of the car as I held the door open for her. I closed it, then went to the driver's side and slid in.

Kenz had class today, and because we'd properly set up a good story, I was able to go with her as a bodyguard. At least that put me right in my comfortable lane.

Because she'd gotten splashed on all the covers of tabloids as Vance's new woman, Vance had been able to contact the school and explain the situation. Stalkers and other threats were common against people in those position, which meant the school had been only too happy to accommodate a bodyguard, especially if that meant Vance might participate more in the school.

Hell, I suspected the dean had visions of a new 'Moore Wing' if he kept Vance happy.

All that political maneuvering wasn't my strength, so at least I could feel useful and in my realm of expertise today by protecting Kenz.

I pulled the car out of the driveway and onto the road as Kenz nibbled bites of her breakfast, which I'd picked up earlier to have it ready. She had dark circles under her eyes, a sure sign she hadn't slept well.

Then again, she hadn't seemed to sleep well in general. Each day that passed had her appearing more and more run down. I recalled the pills I'd found in her bathroom, the ones I hadn't told her about.

Maybe she needed them?

"About last night," I started.

"No need."

I gave her a sidelong glance at her quick refusal.

"I'm sorry I lost my temper and made a fool of myself. I understand why that was the plan, but in the future, I don't want to be kept in the dark. You all may have your own plans, but this is *my* life, too. I deserve to know what's going on."

I wanted to agree, to promise to tell her everything. She was a client right now, and I hated the thought of her upset or harmed, even emotionally. However...I knew better.

The reality was that protecting a person often meant keeping things from them. Few clients I'd had would yank a bodyguard in front of them to take a bullet, but that didn't mean we wouldn't take the bullet.

People did a lot of things that weren't best for them, and it was my job to protect them from everything — even themselves.

"I promise that I'll tell you what I can," I said.

Her sigh told me she understood exactly what that meant. Still, she didn't press. Instead, she looked down at her food and laughed softly. "One of my old bodyguards would bring me candy when I was sad."

"Oh yeah?"

A softness in her expression showed how much she cared about her bodyguards.

I understood that, had seen it with a few longer-term clients. When spending so much time with a person, it was easy for lines to blur, for people to mistake proximity for family.

I didn't care for the way she clung to them, though. Given Vance had taken her first kiss, clearly they hadn't done anything inappropriate. Still, I found myself annoyed with them for a reason I couldn't pinpoint.

Or maybe I just don't want to pinpoint it.

"They had to tell me no a lot. It was before my mom died, so I still had a parent around, but she was busy, too. She also wasn't the warmest person. Maybe they weren't either, but they were all I really had. I remember one time they said I couldn't go to an ice cream party that a classmate was having. I couldn't go because they worried it wasn't safe. Also, my glucose levels weren't all that well controlled and telling a seven-year-old not to eat ice cream and cake at a birthday party was just about impossible." Her voice held such fondness, though sorrow tinged it.

I'd found that whenever she spoke about her past, she had that same mixture. She'd had a family of some sort — even if it consisted of people paid to protect her — but the sorrow exposed her loneliness.

"He brought you candy?" I pressed so she'd keep going.

"Yeah. I found out years later that he had a bunch of bags of sugar-free candy that he kept just to give to me, to cheer me up. Since I couldn't go to the party, they had a special party at the house, just us. He had a chef come and make a sugar-free version so I could have it, and we ate so much we felt sick."

"And your parents? Were they there?"

She shook her head, but it was with the resignation that came with time. She didn't seem to even blame her parents' absence. "They were busy. They both worked a lot, so I didn't see them all that much." She peered at me, then chuckled softly, the sound lovely after the tears the night before. "Don't look at me like that. I missed them, but I understood, and I was luckier than a lot of others. I didn't have to worry about much, and I had other people in my life."

I reached out to pat her leg, to tell her how strong she was, but froze halfway there.

What are you doing?

I pulled my hand back. Sure, I knew exactly how much of a difference a little physical contact could make. There were times when, after an attack, a client needed a hug, needed someone there to assure them they weren't alone.

That was all part of my job.

This was different though. I'd reached out not because I saw a client in pain, but because I saw a woman hurting.

She's young enough to be your daughter. Knock it off!

I scolded myself and placed my hands on the steering wheel to keep them occupied before I made that same mistake again.

"Are you happy to get back to class?" I asked.

The smile she offered said she knew I'd changed the subject, but she allowed it. "Yeah, I am. It feels like weeks since I've barely created anything."

"Why haven't you?"

"I don't have much of my stuff. I've got pencils and my sketchbook, but no paints or canvas."

I cursed at the fact I hadn't thought about that. It stung, a failure to think about the wellbeing of my client. "You should have mentioned it. We could have picked that up at the store."

"I didn't feel much like drawing when I first got here anyway. Stress isn't good for the artist, you know? Being in class means I'll have assignments, though, so that'll force me to work. When I don't draw, it feels like this creeping, crawling sensation inside me. Sometimes I think art is the only outlet I really have, the only way to get rid of that."

"Other than the anti-anxiety meds?"

She sucked in a sharp breath, then looked out the window as though to avoid my gaze. "So you found those, huh?"

"Yep. When we went to your place to pick up things and make sure no one had broken in, I found them in the bathroom. They had a different name on them. You don't look that upset," I pointed out when she didn't react.

"I'm used to not having any privacy. It's not like I ever had any growing up. If I got upset each time it happened, I'd spend all my time mad."

"So why are they in a different name?"

"Because I didn't want anyone knowing about them. My old bodyguards would ask about it and worry if they knew, so I used a fake ID I have that they don't know about to go to the doctor."

"And why do you have them?"

"Because I have nightmares," she said, her voice soft. "I sometimes struggle to sleep, because I can't calm down, because I close my eyes and I see..."

"See what?"

Kenz sighed and shook her head. "That's not something I want or need to share."

I opened my mouth to argue the point, but I couldn't come up with a reason. She wasn't wrong—I didn't have the right to dig too deeply into her head. Judging from the way she spoke, she had plenty of hang-ups in her life. Ripping open those wounds would do neither of us any good.

"If you find you can't sleep, just tell me."

"You won't give me my pills?"

"Not all of them, no."

"You think I'll do something with them?"

"You're in a hard place right now. People have done crazier things when up against a wall, and sometimes by the time you realize the risk, it's too late to do anything. So if you need one, I'll give you one."

"So I guess I'll go without."

"Why? You only need to tell me."

Kenz closed her eyes, leaning back in her seat as though the conversation had ended. I thought she wouldn't answer me until, after a long silence, she spoke once more. "If I'm bad enough to need one, I'd rather just lose sleep than let anyone see me like that."

And just like that, this terrible sense of foreboding hit me. I'd lost clients before, had suffered through the guilt of failure. No person was perfect, and if someone wanted to kill someone else, there was little anyone could do to prevent it.

When Kenz spoke, though, I couldn't shake the feeling that she would be my next failure.

* * * *

Kenz

I hadn't managed to draw a thing. After getting our assignment, other students had started to work. They'd sketched out rough outlines of what they might want to do, but me?

The blank page had stared at me like some albino snake that would strike if I got too close. I'd picked up my pencil, but I hadn't been able to touch the graphite against the paper.

So despite three hours in class, I hadn't gotten a thing done.

"That's it," Hayden said as he drove me, breaking me out of my own pity party.

"What?"

"You've been sighing non-stop since we left. If I take you back to the house now, you'll just go into your room and hide the rest of the day."

"So? Doesn't that make it easier for you to protect me?" I knew my words were snarky, but so what? If I wanted to play the part of angsty, rebellious teenager, I might as well.

He pulled the car into a parking spot outside of a small set of buildings. The brick path out front had people walking and the large glass window showed off the wares of the places.

A pizza place, a café, a tourist shop with shirts and knick-knacks and an art store.

Hayden said nothing before he got out, slid a couple of coins into the meter, then came over and opened my door for me.

"What are we doing here?" I got out of the car as I asked. Even if I didn't want to go anywhere except for a hot shower and mindless television, it seemed my manners had been instilled so deeply I couldn't resist when someone did something nice for me.

"We are going to pick up the supplies you need for your art, then we'll order pizza and bring it back for dinner."

"And what? Have a paint night?"

Hayden frowned for a moment, that already familiar way he tried to make sense of something I'd said that he hadn't expected. "Those get-togethers where women drink and paint? I think you had enough alcohol yesterday, didn't you?"

My cheeks burned at the memory. I hadn't been wrong about what I'd said or done to Vance, and I didn't regret my actions, but I wished I'd been sober for them. It would have been better to have faced it without the alcohol. The high ground was a lot more unsteady when it rested on top of a mountain of liquor.

"Fine, I won't help you paint. You'll be all on your own and when you fail? I'll make sure we hang up the atrocity in the living room."

"You are a cruel woman." His voice held fondness.

I laughed, the feeling nice. After yesterday, laughing had felt impossible. Wasn't it funny how quickly life could turn around? How no matter how horrible things felt, it only took one small push to find joy again?

I stared up and into Hayden's dark eyes, taken in by how kind they seemed. He was one of the few people in the house who didn't make me feel as though I had to hide myself, like he was trying to get one over on me.

Was that because he was a bodyguard? Because he was used to dealing with clients?

Was he just handling me?

Does it matter?

Accepting kindness, no matter who gave it or why, was sometimes the only way to survive.

I parted my lips to ask him why he was being so nice to me when he froze, the shift in his expression a sure sign of trouble. A crackle in the air signaled danger, a tension I'd recognized from a life of knowing someone might target me.

Before I could say anything, before I could move, Hayden spun away from me, keeping me behind him, allowing me only the briefest glimpse of a knife sailing toward him.

I froze, far from the first time I'd witnessed someone facing off against someone else for my good.

How many times had a bodyguard stood between me and harm? How many had suffered wounds that had been meant for me? How often had someone been harmed because of me?

As quickly as the world stopped, it sped again. Hayden lifted his arm to block the knife, using the momentum to knock the attacker's hand to the side.

The blade slipped from his grasp and hit the ground. Not that the attacker was finished.

I backed a few steps away, knowing I couldn't do much to help. Rune had hammered that fact into my brain young, that me getting involved would only increase the risk. A bodyguard couldn't properly focus on a fight if he had to keep protecting me because I wouldn't stay back.

So no matter how much I wanted to jump in, I held myself from doing so, giving Hayden the room to maneuver he needed.

And maneuver he did. He seemed so nice when he spoke to me, had made me feel safe around him. At times, I'd almost doubted he was actually a bodyguard, that he was capable of the violence that job took.

Hayden cleared up any confusion on that point with the way he moved. He easily dodged the attacker, despite the man being very large. I'd spent most of my life around large and dangerous men, and even I would have given this guy room.

If I'd just spotted the two outside, I would have bet my money on the attacker, yet Hayden easily kept up with him.

"Out of my way!" the attacker shouted and darted his gaze past Hayden to land on me.

The hatred in those eyes made me take another step backward. It always threw me when I saw that, when I came face-to-face with anger great enough to want to hurt me.

How could someone *want* to do harm? How could they so easily be okay with it?

Even with all I'd been through, I wasn't sure I'd ever truly wanted to hurt another person, to damage them.

The man lunged past Hayden, headed straight for me. I didn't get the chance to even move back again before Hayden grasped the man's arm and twisted, using the momentum to throw the man to the ground.

A gun slid from the man's pocket and hit the sidewalk. He reached for it, but Hayden moved faster. He placed a booted foot on the man's hand, trapping him, before grabbing the weapon. He released the clip so it hit the ground.

"Who sent you?" Hayden leaned forward, placing more weight on the man's hand.

"I suggest you stay where you are." The new voice struck fear into me, the way it sounded so sure. There, to the other side of Hayden, stood a man with a gun pointed at me.

Hayden's expression tightened, but he didn't release the man whose hand he still kept in place.

"Drop the gun," the new man said.

Hayden tossed the gun back, and it landed in the grass near me. Not close enough to reach without jumping toward it, but close enough for a chance, especially because it hadn't ended up too far from the clip.

"Now, let's keep this civil. There's no reason anyone needs to die, is there?"

"I'm not letting you take her," Hayden answered, his voice strong.

In fact, he was so certain that I believed him. No matter how hopeless things looked, he made me think he could still win.

"You don't have much of a choice, do you? And if you die here, what good does that do her?" The man shook his hand, drawing attention to his gun. *As if we'd forget about that.* "I have the upper hand, and a firefight here will certainly leave casualties. In fact, it wouldn't take much for one accidental bullet to hit your client.

I'm sure you would hate to see that, wouldn't you?" The man walked closer, then touched a finger to my shoulder, sliding it along the front to my heart. "It would be so easy for a stray bullet to go right here. What a needless tragedy that would be."

Hayden set his jaw in a hard line, and the flicker of his eyes screamed that his brain was working, that he was trying to find another path out of this.

Sometimes you're all you've got on your side.

I recalled Jarrod's words as I'd recovered from my last gunshot wound. He was so different from the Quad. The Quad taught me to listen, to keep my head down, to let them handle things.

Jarrod had instead told me that I couldn't merely rely on others, that sometimes *I* had to do what needed to be done. It was fine to let Hayden handle the heavy lifting, but when things crashed?

Sitting in a sinking car hoping someone would find me wasn't the best idea. Sometimes, a person had to step up.

The man slid his fingers into my hair, tightening his grasp into a fist.

It took me back to Rune's lessons. Most women pulled forward, away from the grasp, which did all of nothing for them.

Stay calm. I knew what to do, had practiced it so many times with Rune who could easily put this guy through a window if he wanted.

I reached up and back, wrapping my fingers around the man's wrist tightly, then twisted my body. I held tight to him, ensuring he couldn't rotate that hand, twisting it so I was ducked down in front of him, his arm straight, his hand still wrapped in my hair. It pulled at my scalp, but that was the least of my issue.

I twisted more, forcing his arm to bend in a way it normally didn't. Panic bled into his movements at the threat, which made it easy to yank hard enough for him to release my hair. I didn't let go of his wrist, instead pulling him forward and moving that arm behind him, pulling it high up on his back.

I didn't dislocate it, but I doubted the ligaments were too happy right now.

He jerked, the motion causing me to loosen my grip enough for him to escape. Even so, he didn't move that arm too well. Instead of trying to take him on again — without surprise on my side, I knew I was well outmatched — I dove for the gun still on the ground.

I wrapped my fingers around the pistol, my other hand reaching blindly for the clip. Once I had both, instinct and muscle memory took over. I slammed the clip in and rolled, pointing the gun directly at the man who'd held me.

He huffed, then shook his head. "You don't have the backbone to shoot me."

I flipped off the safety, my hands steady.

It made him stop and study me.

He was right, of course. I could handle the gun, but the idea of actually shooting anyone? Of taking a life? I couldn't come to terms with that, couldn't even imagine it.

Still, the man stared until he let out a laugh, telling me he'd called me on my bluff. It seemed my lie didn't last all that long.

He took one step toward me when a figure appeared behind him. The figure moved so smoothly that I couldn't identify them at first, the way he shifted as if made of nothing but water and shadow. Silver flashed from the sunlight just before a blade sank into the man's side, between his ribs, angled up on the left side.

He didn't have time to make a noise before his body slumped down, leaving the man behind him standing there alone.

Tor.

He held the blade in his hand, snapping it shut with an ease and comfort that showed he was well acquainted with the weapon. He slid the closed knife into his pocket, then met my gaze.

That look froze me in place, especially with the blood coating his hand. The same blood that pooled around that man's body.

Tor pulled his gaze from mine then shifted backward, gone as quietly as he'd arrived. In fact, it was so smooth I might have wondered if I'd seen him at all, like he could have just been some apparition.

Except the blood proved he'd been here.

Someone touched my hand gently, and I jerked backward before realizing it was Hayden. He extracted the gun from my hands—I hadn't noticed I still held it.

"We need to get out of here before the police arrive," he said and pulled me to the car. He didn't wait for me to sit as he did usually, but instead almost shoved me in then rushed to the driver's side.

It made me look to the side, to see the man Hayden had pinned getting up, unsteady on his feet, rushing to check on his friend. When he didn't get a response, he looked toward us once, then took off.

Hayden sped the car off just as the sirens blared in the background, the sound like a reminder that this had been real.

Sure, I'd understood I was in danger, but it hadn't hit home before. It had felt like some distant worry, with this Lorien person not even seeming real. I knew differently, now.

Worse, it wasn't just my life on the line. I thought about the man who died, the bystanders who could have been hurt, the two men who had protected me.

So many lives in the balance and for what? I took a deep breath, wishing it shocked me more, that this was the first time I'd been in this position.

Instead, it just felt like the suffocating cage that I'd always existed in. It seemed like it didn't matter what happened, how far I went, I was always going to find myself locked in here.

* * * *

Hayden

Kenz had said nothing on the way back to the house. I would have preferred to check her for injuries there, to reassure her, but all my attention went to ensuring we didn't have a tail. While taking care of her emotions was important, it wouldn't matter if she was killed.

Now inside the house, safe from prying eyes, I had Kenz wait in her room as I checked in with Tor.

A text back and forth let me know the police had arrived, but they knew nothing. Tor had snuck into the local shops and erased their camera footage to ensure we weren't caught there. People ran away when it came to violence, which meant the odds of anyone getting a clear look at us was slim.

Even if anyone had, they'd know we weren't the aggressors.

My old life would have had me reaching out to the police, to explain the situation, but now?

That wasn't the life I had, not right anymore, not for this. It was far too personal and much too dangerous.

Vance was still out—who knew where—and Char was meeting with contacts. Tor would remain out of sight, at the place of the attack, to see if anyone showed back up there.

It left Kenz and I alone for the evening.

I carried a warm sugar-free chai latte in one hand and a package of graham crackers in the other. My knuckles struck the door, knocking softly so as not to startle her.

Most people, after living through something like that, crashed. I expected to walk in and find Kenz a mess.

Thus the warm drink and carbs.

"Come in." Her strong voice took me by surprise.

I entered the room, leaving the door open behind me. Kenz sat at the desk, her planner open, her pen sliding across the page smoothly.

She glanced over her shoulder, taking notice of what I'd brought. "I'm not hungry." She turned back to the journal.

"People tend to crash after things like that. Some food can help that not happen." I set the items on the desk beside her instead of giving her another chance to refuse. My job was doing what a client needed, no matter how they felt about it.

"I'm not about to *crash*. You don't need to worry so much."

I sat at the end of her bed, making it clear I wasn't going anywhere until we spoke. "I had a client, a singer, who was getting stalked by a crazy fan. The man jumped out of the shadows and grabbed her arm, trying to yank her into the bushes. I saved her and apprehended the stalker, who got arrested. She said she was fine, so I left her be."

I took a deep breath as the memories of that night came back to me, the way the girl had looked fine. "The next morning, she didn't get up on time. When I went in to wake her up, I found her unconscious with an empty bottle of pills beside her. That attack had been the last straw for her. Even though she survived it, it had made her feel hopeless, and I hadn't seen it. The ambulance got there in time, and she pulled through, but I learned my lesson. I'd trusted that she told me the truth, that she was okay. I won't make that mistake again."

Kenz sighed and set her pen down. "I appreciate that, but that girl isn't me. I really am fine."

"It's okay to be upset, to freak out. Anyone in your position would after going through something like that. You don't have to pretend to be okay, especially not in front of me."

"Do you really think that's the first time I've been attacked? That it's the first corpse I've seen?" She twisted, and her expression chilled me to my core.

I'd expected her upset, even frantic, especially since she took anti-anxiety meds. People who took those weren't usually the steadiest, after all. Instead, here she was, appearing entirely unbothered by what she'd just gone through. It took me so by surprise that no words came to me, nothing to help me make sense of this.

She didn't raise her voice, didn't yell. In fact, she spoke with such an even tone that it seemed what happened hadn't touched her at all. "You really don't know me at all, do you? You all laugh at me for being naïve and young, but you know *nothing* about me. This isn't the first time I've seen someone die, that I've walked away from something knowing it had been close, that I'd almost been the body on the floor. So if you're here to reassure me or because you think I'm going to break down..."

Her voice trailed off, the hardness in her expression slipping away.

She reached out and touched my forearm, her fingers gentle as she pulled my arm, the move so surprising I didn't react at first.

"You're hurt," she whispered.

I dropped my gaze to find blood soaked into my suit jacket. "It's not deep," I assured her. "It happened at the start, when the man swung the knife at us. I hardly noticed it."

She blinked slowly, her expression flat, her skin quickly losing its color. After a long silent moment, she rushed out of her chair and into the bathroom, then came back with a first-aid kit clutched in her hands.

Now she acts like she's panicked?

She'd dealt with the attackers without so much as a whimper or complaint, had used a hell of an impressive self-defense move, had even slid the clip of that pistol back into the gun with the certainty of a person used to guns, yet one little cut and she behaved as though the knife had hit a vital organ?

Who the hell is this girl?

"It's fine," I told her again as she kneeled on the floor in front of me. It made her appear even smaller, even younger, and my mind went straight into the gutter for one shameful moment.

Then again, with how busy I always was, I hadn't made time for anything like women in months. Who could blame my primitive brain when a girl this pretty got on her knees in front of me?

However, she was young enough to be my daughter and in no position for me to even think about such things, so I tried to wrench my brain from that.

She tugged at my jacket until I removed it, then tried to undo the buttons at the cuff of my shirt. Her fingers trembled, making it impossible to work free the tiny pearl buttons.

I wanted to tell her again I was fine, that she didn't have to worry, but I had a feeling it wouldn't help any more than it had before. Sometimes panic only eased when the person saw everything was okay with their own eyes.

I extracted my arm from her death grip and undid the cuff, then rolled the bloodied fabric to my elbow. The shirt was done for anyway, since getting blood out of white shirts was a losing battle.

Just a fact of the job.

Once the wound appeared from beneath the sleeve, her eyes widened at the deep slash. It still bled, oozing slowly now, and probably only because my movement had reopened it.

I thought she'd freeze, that the panic beating at her would win. Leave it to Kenz to be stronger than she appeared, yet again, because she took an alcohol swab from the first-aid kit in her trembling fingers.

She tore one open, leaving the trash in the lid of the kit, then went about cleaning around the wound. Her touch was amazingly gentle, careful.

Nothing like when I treated myself or, worse, when one of my colleagues did it. I hired bodyguards for my company, people who knew how to do first aid and could stitch a wound if needed, but they'd never learned good bedside manner.

I wouldn't mind getting hurt more if I had Kenz here patching me up afterward.

I shook away the unwelcome thought, both because it felt too dangerous and because the last thing I wanted was to panic her like this again.

"You don't need stitches," she said, her gaze pinned to her work.

"I told you it wasn't bad."

"You didn't even treat it."

"I knew it only needed to be cleaned and wrapped, and I had to contact the others then check in on you."

"Why would you ignore this just to make sure my little feelings weren't hurt?"

I caught her chin with my other hand, then lifted her dark eyes to mine.

She really is astoundingly lovely.

It was far from the first time I'd noticed it, but it might have been the first time I'd really accepted it, that I'd recognized it or allowed myself to think it.

Her hair was long and loose, tumbling down over her shoulders. Between her dark hair, her dark eyes, her dark eyebrows, her skin seemed to glow. Light freckles dotted her cheeks, but unless I was this close to her, I doubted I would have noticed them.

She didn't dress flashy, despite the fact I had no doubt the clothing cost a bundle. Instead, she still looked young and casual, like the most welcoming sight that was sure to get anyone to lower their guard around her. Or maybe that wasn't her clothing at all and just her personality.

"You are more important than some little scratch," I assured her.

My words had been meant to calm her, to even make her smile. How many times had I told clients that I would happily trade my life for theirs? That was why they hired me, after all, to keep them safe. The fact that I would pay that cost always reassured them.

I expected the words to do the same for her. I wanted her to take a deep breath and see that mark as proof that I would do whatever it took to keep her safe.

Except, that didn't happen. If anything, more color leeched from her cheeks.

She twisted, tearing her chin from my grasp. "Then you're a fool," she whispered as she finished cleaning the wound.

"A fool? I'm not going to argue that, but how is it you figure?"

Kenz took a large bandage from the first-aid kit, opened it, then covered the gash, pressing at the edges to ensure a good seal. "Make sure to keep this clean and change the bandage every other day. If you can't get the bandage on yourself, just ask." She gathered the trash in one hand, then closed the lid with the other and stood.

She was fleeing. I'd fought enough in my life to recognize when a person did that, when they retreated. What I *didn't* know was why.

Without thinking about it, I caught her wrist gently. "Why am I a fool?"

Kenz didn't look at me, and I got the sense she saw something else, something from her own past. "You're a fool for being so willing to throw your life away, for thinking that someone else's life matters more than yours. Life is precious — all life — and no one should be so quick to offer theirs up."

"That's my job, Kenz. It's my place to stand between people and the things that want to hurt them. That's why they hire me."

"And you think that makes me happy? You think that you treating your own life as expendable is going to make me feel all safe and sound?" That chilling edge to her voice had returned, the one that sounded as if pain and trauma had honed it. She shook her head and let out a long shaky sigh. "The last thing I want is someone trading their life for mine. I can tell you right now that if you do that, I won't ever forgive you."

When Kenz tugged her hand, it brought my gaze down to where I held her. I could so easily keep that grasp, and I wanted to. I wanted to keep her close, to explain it all to her. She was too naïve, too innocent to understand the world, the real danger there.

Only that reason explained how she could spout such optimistic nonsense. If she really understood what could have happened to her today, she'd have been happy to have me as a shield. People valued their own lives more than anything else in my experience.

Except, I couldn't force her to understand, and a part of me wanted her to keep that sweetness. I didn't want the world to harden her, to force her to see things she didn't want to see, to live with the harsh, ugly reality of what people really were.

So I released her, and when she left, when she went into the bathroom and shut the door, I knew our conversation was over.

Which was for the best, right? She didn't need to become more intertwined with our lives than she had to. If we kept going, we would finish what we had to and Kenz?

She could go back to her perfect little life, none-the-wiser of the monsters in the world.

Chapter Ten

Char

My cheeks ached from smiling, but I hardly noticed it. Sometimes, when I slid into one of my many personalities, I sank so deeply that my own thoughts turned fuzzy.

"You are adorable," I told the woman who leaned in closer and put her hand on my arm.

She traced a design on my bare skin, the most obvious come-on I'd seen in a while. "You're just being nice, I'm sure."

Kenz sighed beside me, the sound loud enough to cover up the fake-shy laugh of the woman.

I turned to see Kenz with her gaze down, on her notebook, even though she hadn't actually drawn anything. It had been that way for a few days, though. She would take out that sketchbook and a pencil, but never touch the graphite to the paper.

Why?

Some sort of weird artist's block?

"What are you doing after class?" the woman asked.

"Kenz and I are getting some lunch," I said.

"Oh yeah? I guess it is about time for that. I haven't eaten all day! There I go, forgetting to eat." The woman narrowed her eyes toward Kenz. "That's probably not something she deals with, is it?"

Ouch. Sometimes the viciousness of women astounded me. Men, we tended to use our fists to deal with things. When pissed, we either ignored it, settled it with a good fight, or threw a few vulgar insults then moved on. Women, though, they could identify the exact thing that would wound someone the worst. They spotted that weak point and attacked it with amazing precision.

Even if untrue—and it sure as fuck was untrue to imply Kenz had any issue with weight—those sorts of ugly words stuck.

And the other part? The incredibly obvious fishing for an invite from this woman might as well have been a huge flashing sign above her head—*notice me!*

However, I saw no way the woman might prove useful and no desire to waste time playing a part around useless people. "Well, maybe next time we'll all go together! I'd invite you, but we made reservations at a busy place and it's too soon to add another."

The woman stuck her lips out in a pout that made her look like a toddler puckering up for a kiss. "Here, at least take my contact information. Kenz there can survive on her own for a little while—she's used to it." She jotted down a string of numbers on a piece of paper she tore from her sketchbook and pushed it across the table to me.

"Sure." I tucked the scrap into my pocket.

"Well, that's it for today," the professor at the front of the room said. "Your end-of-year exhibits are coming up. I know it seems like it's a long time from now, but it sneaks up fast. Don't procrastinate, because rushing is the death of art. If you have any questions, *please* reach out to any of your professors. We're here to help, after all, and that exhibit will determine your placement next year — and whether you have a place or future at this school. Now, have a good weekend." He offered the last part with a smile, as though to erase the sting of the rest of it.

Then again, this was one of the workshop classes Kenz had, where each student worked on whatever they wanted to, giving them time to apply their skills rather than listen to a lecture.

And Kenz had spent the entire time staring at an empty piece of paper.

What was her problem? Just stress? Or maybe she was the spoiled rich girl I thought, and she knew she could buy her spot next year no matter if she worked hard or not.

Kenz packed her things, so I did the same, tucking my tablet into my messenger bag. It was easier to fake it on a tablet, which meant I could play the part of art student by having pre-made pieces already saved there. I didn't look much like a bodyguard, so being her friend was a far easier tactic.

On our way out, a number of students stopped me. They all offered me that same charming smile, the one I hated.

It was fake, just a mirror of my own false smile. They liked me because I knew how to play them, how to get the reaction I wanted. Life was easiest for charming people, so I'd learned easily how to play that part. It opened every door that I needed.

People talked when they liked someone, and I was an expert at getting people to both like me and to talk.

And each time someone stopped me, Kenz paused and stood by my side, silent but not rushing me, either.

It also reminded me that despite so many people knowing her, she rarely interacted much with them.

"You look good today, Char," a girl said as she got off the elevator just before we got on.

A quick glance gave me the rundown. *Holland Kissley, twenty-five, got in on a scholarship, hard worker but parties too much because she struggles to say no to her old friends.* Her facts rested on an index card in my head, the same as all the others, just bits of information filed away for future use when I needed them.

"Thanks," I said with a smile. "Is that a new skirt? You wear it well." I dragged my gaze over her, pretending to be smitten.

Yet I didn't feel a thing. I never did.

The doors slid shut, closing Kenz and me in alone. I let the smile fall away, noting the ache in my cheeks, the throbbing of my head from playing the part for so many hours.

"Are you going to eat at that disgusting place around the corner again?" I shuddered as I recalled the cheap hole-in-the-wall diner she adored, that she dragged me to most days.

Kenz turned to look at me, a line between her eyebrows. "Why do you hate me?"

Her words took me by surprise, the last things I expected her to say. "I don't hate you."

"Right." She turned her gaze from mine again, staring instead at the corner of the elevator.

I should let this go. I knew nothing good would come from this conversation. Let her think I hated her if she wanted – what did it matter to me? The last thing I needed was for her to know more about me, for me to admit to anything that might give her a weapon to use against me.

Despite warning myself, though, my stupid mouth opened and asked, "Why do you think I hate you?"

"You always smile when you talk to other girls – no, to anyone. You're nice and you're kind and you're sweet. Then, as soon as you're alone with me, you change."

"And?"

"And the only thing different is me. I'm the common variable. The only thing I can figure is that you really dislike me, but I can't figure out why, or what I've done."

I tilted my head as I watched her, even as she tried very hard *not* to look at me. "So you think that friendly side is really me, huh?"

"I think that most people are at their realest when they're happy."

I shook my head at her stupid idea. She'd gotten it *all* wrong, hadn't she?

But everyone got that wrong. Hadn't I learned my lesson enough times?

I turned toward her and closed the distance. Even if she hadn't wanted to look at me, the way she jerked backward said she'd still been paying attention to me. She retreated, but she had nowhere to go, not in the small elevator together. As soon as she pressed against the wall, I crowded in.

I wasn't that tall, which meant I only had to look down a few inches to stare right into her wide pretty eyes.

I offered her a false smile, even if it made me sick to my stomach to play this game. And why? Normally falling into these personalities made me feel safe, let me hide, but right now?

It made my head throb worse.

"You like this, huh?" I lifted one hand and brushed my fingers over her soft cheek, rewarded when red colored her flawless skin. "You want me to be nicer to you? To tell you just how lovely you look in your outfit? To tell you that the bronze eye shadow you have on brings out your eyes? That you make my heart race just by smiling?" I leaned in closer, making sure my breath tickled her ear, dropping my voice to a sensual whisper to her.

She sucked in a breath, and I knew if I pressed my hand to her chest, I'd find her heart racing.

Yep, this is what she likes.

I took a step backward, dropping the act, surprised by how heavy it had felt. "You're like everyone else, every short-sighted, shallow asshole who wants smiles and fake words, just as long as they're pretty. I don't hate you, Kenz, but I fucking hate having to play this game so people feel comfortable. Life sucks, and it isn't always pretty, and fuck you for wanting it to be."

I turned away, the anger inside of me almost frightening. I'd dealt with people like this all my life, had learned time and time again that only the outside counted, that nothing beyond the surface level mattered, so why did it make me this angry to find Kenz was no different?

She wanted the fake me, the one I showed to everyone else. She assumed I hated her because I didn't put on that show for her instead of realizing the truth.

I'd shown her the real me, something I rarely did, and her response?

To spit on me and ask for the fake me.

When will I finally learn that no one wants the real me?

* * * *

Kenz

I took a deep breath as the makeup artist applied blush to my cheeks. I never loved having my makeup done, but I'd sat through it enough times to tolerate it.

The woman seemed nice enough, but that didn't make me more comfortable.

"You look like you're getting ready to walk the plank," she said with a laugh as she tilted my face to see her work in better light.

"I'm not used to being on camera," I admitted. Being in public? Sure, I'd done that plenty, but it was a different matter being filmed. Everything I'd done had been quiet, the sort of people who didn't want anything about them recorded.

"Well, if you're on Vance Moore's arm, you're going to need to get used to it. That boy has a camera on him most of the time."

I'm not on his arm. At least, not really. This was just part of his plan to make sure Lorien knew exactly who had me.

They wanted to push as hard as they could, force him to take notice, to make another move. It made me feel like a piece of meat they dangled in front of a starving dog.

However, I had no reason to tell this woman any of that. The reality was that my only choices were to try to escape — and that was a big if — or put up with these men and their plans.

Even if I could escape, it would mean I had to either explain to Nem how I'd failed, how I needed her to swoop in and rescue me, or give up my entire life. Neither option appealed to me.

Which put my ass in this chair, following along with the plans of others — like always.

There was a risk to this stupid plan, of course. Nem, Quad or Jarrod might see it. If they did, I doubted they'd wait on the sidelines quietly. They wouldn't know what was really happening, but having a boyfriend would draw attention.

However, they were an entire country away. Vance had assured me that this interview would be released locally, which should reduce that risk. We only needed Lorien to see it, after all. Plus, we wouldn't use my full name, which hopefully would prevent it from getting picked up by a search engine keyword watch.

"You look beautiful." Vance's voice warmed me, and just as quickly I stamped out that fondness.

His pretty words were all lies, after all. Maybe not the words themselves, but the underlying feeling, the promises they held, those didn't exist.

The makeup artist turned, smiling widely. "She's easy to work on because she's already very pretty. Just a little polishing is all it takes."

Vance came into the room just as the girl gathered her things and left, seeming to feel we wanted a minute alone. Once she shut the door, Vance let his gaze move over me. "You really do look lovely."

"Keep it to yourself." I got out of the chair and ran my fingers through my hair. It had more curls than usual, making me appear fancier than I preferred. I loosened a few with my fingers.

"You're still mad?"

"No."

"You are such a woman, saying you're not mad when you're all but snarling."

I turned toward him, unwilling to appear weak. "There's a difference between being mad and being smart. I've always thought that when someone shows you who they are, you should believe it. You've shown me who you are. I get it. We're good."

"Well, this little attitude of yours won't play well for the camera. We need to look the part of a happy couple to sell this."

"Lorien knows you bought me. Why would he think we were happy? Not a lot of women dream about becoming someone's property."

Vance sighed, then picked up a napkin from the counter. He grasped my chin, holding my face still as he rubbed off the lipstick the makeup artist had put on. "You really are a lot of work, you know that?"

"You're just used to women who fall at your feet."

He smiled as though recalling fond memories before grabbing a lipstick from behind him. He set it down, then grabbed another, holding them up beside me. "It's more fun when they do that, I'll admit. I mean, who doesn't enjoy a well-behaved woman who's more than willing to please?"

I scoffed at his statement, but froze when the meaning really hit me. How often had I wanted to be that person? How often had I shoved down how I really felt to fit a mold? Even if I complained, I always ended up bending to my mother's whims.

I'd been ready to walk down the aisle to marry a man twice my age just because my father told me to...

Vance opened one lipstick, a soft pink as opposed to the bright red the makeup artist had chosen. He applied it to my lips, his expression focused.

It was strange to see him serious. He finished, then set the lipstick down on the counter. "There. That color fits you much better. Bright red is for women who need the extra pop, but you don't."

His words threatened to soften my feelings, but I refused to let them. I knew better, didn't I?

When he set the lipstick down, I found myself watching his actions, the way he used his left hand, the awkward way he'd done everything with that hand.

"Why do you wear the gloves?" I asked.

The air in the room disappeared, as though that question had sucked it all out. Vance didn't answer, didn't even look at me, but his muscles went rigid beneath his black turtleneck shirt.

It reminded me of how he'd acted when I'd looked at them before, the way it immediately shut down any warmth inside him.

He turned away from me and took a few steps toward the door as if he hadn't heard me. He paused just before he left. "Make sure you play your part. Your life depends on it."

He left me with those threatening words.

But was he really threatening me or just trying to throw me off the trail? I had the sense that Vance was the sort of man to snarl when people neared his wounds.

And suddenly I wanted to know about those wounds, even if I knew it would only hurt us both all the more.

* * * *

I thought I'd be ready for this. I'd stood in front of huge groups before, when my father had paraded me around like a game piece.

I'd shaken hands with people powerful enough to determine the course of the country, with people who could have snuffed out anyone without a second thought, and it had never scared me. I'd grown up used to that sort of thing.

Many of those people felt safer than the rest of the world because I understood them.

So when Vance had told me about this little interview, I'd thought it was nothing new.

How wrong I was.

Hayden stood to the side, off screen, watching over us. No doubt Tor was somewhere, Char too, but neither were the type to actually show themselves. I'd bet they were in the shadows, hidden away. It made me feel almost safe, as foolish as that was.

I should know better than to let my guard down around these men.

"So, tell me how you met," Pam, the interviewer, asked. She had blonde hair that had obviously cost a bundle to get and maintain, and she used the perfect non-geographical accent. Clearly, the woman was a pro.

We'd already agreed to let Vance do most of the talking, since he'd do a better job than I did.

Vance sat to my left on the small couch — the size no doubt intended to make us sit close, to give the viewers better optics. He answered with such ease, not showing an ounce of discomfort at the idea of being on television in front of potentially millions of people. "I met her at her college, actually. I was doing a meet and greet there, and she spilled coffee on herself. What can I say? I'm a sucker for a damsel in distress."

"You mean you just like it when you can get a girl naked right away?" Pam said with a chuckle.

"Well, there's that, too, I guess. However, she turned me down that day. I'm surprised I recovered, honestly."

Pam looked my way. "You turned him down? Did you not know who he was?" The look of pure shock on her face nearly made me laugh.

"I wasn't really looking for romance," I admitted. Char had told me to stick with the truth — best I could — because I sold that better than an outright lie.

"So, if you turned him down, when did you two get together?"

Vance jumped back in, rescuing me. "It was the next evening. I saw her at an event, and I knew I had to have her. Everyone was looking at her, but she didn't seem to care what anyone thought. I guess I liked that about her."

"The women you're usually out with are models or actresses, and from what I've heard, they're the ones who do the chasing. What was different this time? I mean, it is the first time you've come out publicly like this to announce anything."

Vance's smile could have charmed the surliest of people, and I wondered for a moment if he'd learned that. Had someone taught him just how to do it? Was he like Char, in that way? "I'm used to being chased, I'll admit, and there's something nice about that, about being wanted. I think everyone craves that, deep down, even if they don't like to admit it. The thing is, that gets boring. Things that come too easily don't keep people's attention for long. Kenz, here, she was different. It was like, the moment I saw her, everything else faded out around her. I saw her and I knew that no matter what it took, what it cost, I had to have her." His words could have melted the most frozen of hearts, and it took me reminding myself that he didn't mean them for me not to fall.

Pam appeared smitten, however, so at least he had her on the hook.

She turned her gaze to me, but there was no doubt she didn't look at me the way she did him. "And you? What made you finally give in? What made you realize you wanted him, too?"

No way to avoid this question, is there? Vance squeezed my hand tighter, as if to remind me to mind my manners and remember the plan.

"I thought he was a playboy," I said. "I thought he was just kidding around with me, that he didn't mean anything, and I'm not the sort of girl who's interested in becoming another trophy for some man whore." The insult slipped from me before I thought better of it, and a tighter squeeze said Vance didn't appreciate it. "The thing is there's more to him than that. He's driven when there's something important to him. It's almost impossible to say no when he's willing to do anything to get what he wants."

"That sounds less like love and more like Stockholm syndrome," Pam said with a laugh.

I shook my head, trying to fix that before I risked our plan. "I don't mean it like that. I meant that...I saw a different side of him. He seems like he doesn't care about anything, like nothing matters to him. That's all I knew about him. However, after spending some time with him, I glimpsed another side of him, one he doesn't show many people. He has this serious side of him, a part that wants what he wants, that works hard to get whatever it is. It's the side he uses when he creates his art, and it's the one I saw when he talked to me. I don't like the public side, the carefree playboy, but when I saw that other side of him..."

A smile tugged at my lips, one I didn't even plan as I remembered when he looked at my drawing, when he'd given me advice in that room after I'd changed. "I like that side of him."

Silence made me look up again to find Pam staring at me.

No, not just Pam but everyone. Even Vance looked over at me, his expression unreadable and nothing like the face he showed most people.

I hadn't said anything that weird, had I?

"That is amazingly sweet," Pam said, her voice dreamy. "I don't think I expected something like that."

Vance recovered quickly, replacing that wide smile. "You see what I fell for her? It's not easy, trying to date a normal girl, but you can see why I need to. I mean, she's a once-in-a-lifetime girl."

"Do safety concerns worry either of you? It's not unheard of for you to have problems with obsessive fans, after all."

Vance slid his arm around me, pulling me closer, the action so casual that it made my heart speed. "Her security is a priority for me, of course. I've hired an amazing security company to stay with her, to make sure she doesn't suffer just because I love her. I could never forgive myself if I let anything happen to her."

Pam nodded, then a glint in her eyes made me sit up straighter. It reminded me of when someone stopped playing a game. Her gaze sharpened, and she leaned forward. "Do you think this will get you back to work?"

Vance went still, his fingers digging into my arm. "Excuse me?"

"It's been five years since you released a new piece of art. People have been clamoring for more, but we've seen nothing from you. Some people have speculated that you had a mental breakdown, since you disappeared from the public eye around the same time. Others said it's a drugs issue. Now that you've found yourself a muse, can we expect new work from you?"

My arm hurt from where he held me tightly, but a glance to the side, to that false smile and his gaze locked on Pam, told me he probably didn't realize he was doing it.

"Who knows?" His voice came across friendly, but a chill rested beneath it. No one else seemed to notice it. Was that because I'd gotten closer to him? Because I knew him well enough to read him better now? "Maybe."

"Any comment on why you took the hiatus?"

I flinched when he held tighter again.

Looks like it's my turn to save him. "You know the strangest thing I've learned being with Vance?"

Pam shifted her attention to me, annoyance clouding her expression. She couldn't tell me to shut up, but she sure wanted me to. "What's that?"

"I always thought living in the spotlight would be fun. To be admired and celebrated by hordes of fans? I mean, that sounds like a dream come true, right? I've learned that isn't the case, though. I've seen what it can do to a person. It's a heavy burden to bear. Beyond that, I'm an artist as well, and I know the toll that takes on a person. Vance doesn't owe anyone answers for why he's taken a break or when he'll come back. If people truly support him, they'll wait until he's ready." My words came out soft, but from my heart.

Vance was a shitty person in a lot of ways, but I remembered seeing his work, and I knew how much it had mattered to him. If he hadn't worked in five years, he had a damn good reason.

The pain in my arm eased, and a glance to my side showed Vance staring at me with a questioning look, as if trying to figure me out.

It made me wonder just who the real man was. When he stopped pretending, when he wasn't the famous artist or the playboy or the celebrity, who was he?

Chapter Eleven

Vance

I couldn't stop my brain. The whole way home from the interview, I'd stared out the window without speaking, ignoring any attempt to draw me into conversation.

The idea of working through my own thoughts while also holding a conversation struck me as impossible.

Not that many people gave a damn whether I spoke or not. Even Kenz had only tried once before falling silent and leaving me to my own misery.

And didn't that say something about how badly I'd screwed up? Kenz, who was nice to a fault, had given up on me. Then again, what had I ever done to give people reason to support me?

I stared at the large white canvas in my room, the one that mocked me. No, not the one — there had been so many. Each time I tried and failed to turn it into something beautiful, I'd get a new one to hang, like some reminder of what I'd lost, what I couldn't have.

Why did I do this? Why did I insist on having that blank canvas right where I saw no matter what? It was the first thing I saw in the morning and the last thing before I shut my eyes at night.

I took a pencil in my left hand, hating the way it shook, both from anxiety and from a lack of use.

That damn interviewer's words echoed in my head, her questions. How could they still bother me so much? It had been five years of people asking when I'd release new work, so when would I hold a new exhibit? My managers, patrons and various people in the art world contacted me weekly to ask, and I always responded the same way.

When I find a new muse.

What a bullshit answer... I didn't need a muse, I needed...

I shook my head, unwilling to let the idea go further. What was the point? Where would it get me? Sometimes we lost things and those things ended up gone forever. No one could go back in time, could change what had already happened. All we could do was try to live with it.

I brought the pencil up toward the virgin canvas. The first stroke against a new piece always set the tone. It was like a first kiss—special and memorable and important.

My mind went back to Kenz in the living room, to how she'd told me she'd never forgive me for taking her first kiss.

I really am an asshole, aren't I?

The graphite came closer to the canvas, but the shaking in my hand worsened. Still, I forced myself.

Maybe this time it would be different. Maybe this time, I could do it, I could create *something*, I could find my old self.

In my brain, I saw Kenz, her sweet smile, her dark eyes, the shy way she'd glance to the side and avoid my glance, especially when that cute pink flush colored her cheeks. I moved the pencil against the bumpy surface of the canvas as I drew the line of her eye, trying to stay light, the image so strong in my head that it already felt alive.

I pulled the pencil away and stepped backward to survey my work.

A messy almond shape sat there, in the middle of all that white, the line jagged and dark. It looked like a toddler had drawn it.

I pressed my lips together, anger and loss mixing together until they overwhelmed me and I yanked the canvas off the easel. The wood frame broke when it hit the floor, the corner coming apart, but that wasn't enough for me. I set one foot on the bottom, grasped the top edge and pulled.

The canvas tore, and I didn't stop until nothing but strips of white littered the floor.

Even with the voodoo doll of my anger in pieces, the fire in my chest didn't diminish.

My gaze found a bottle of scotch on the dresser, one my manager had sent me a year ago in celebration of an exhibit that had gotten me in a spot in a prestigious art magazine. I'd never opened the bottle, feeling like it was one big joke.

But right now? The idea of numbing this anger sounded like a fantastic use of the alcohol.

I tucked the bottle beneath one arm and used my left hand to rip off the foil cover, then pulled the cork from the top.

Fuck glasses.

Glasses were for people who planned to only have a little, and I needed the whole damned bottle to drown the feelings inside me. I grasped the bottle by the neck, tipped it up and savored the burn as I gulped.

Fuck it all.

* * * *

Kenz

The seat at the table where Vance usually sat remained empty. Everyone else had eaten, but Vance never showed.

I took the empty dishes into the kitchen, stacking them beside the sink despite Hayden's complaints. He didn't care for me chipping in with the housework, always telling me not to worry about it.

His footsteps echoed into the kitchen behind me. "I can handle that."

"I don't mind it."

"We didn't bring you here to turn you into our housekeeper." His tone came out clipped, as though me helping actually offended him.

"I'm living here, aren't I? I might as well help. I'm not as useless as you seem to think."

"I never said you were useless," Hayden said on a sigh. "I just know you're in a hard place right now. You had a lot of things happen—none of them your fault—so the last thing I want is for you to feel like you need to be taking care of us. I mean, if anything, we put you in this position. I'd rather you focus on your schoolwork or something for you."

I laughed at the way he spoke, his tone sulky. "You're a lot nicer than I would have thought." I rinsed the dishes before I loaded them into the dishwasher, the motions automatic. I'd gotten pretty good at this, at least, over my time living alone.

"You'd be the only person to say that."

I glanced over my shoulder to find Hayden with his arms crossed, staring at me. He wore a basic black long-sleeve shirt, the front a V with buttons that showed a bit of his chest. He was rather handsome.

The thought hit me so fast that I wondered how I hadn't noticed before.

Because finding your abductors good-looking is a stupid cliché that signals serious mental issues.

I laughed at my own thought and shook my head, bringing my focus back to my work. "You are, though. You always look after me and worry about me."

"That's my job," he reminded me.

Ouch. It was true, of course, but having him tell me that so coldly made me have to force my smile. I didn't want him to see how much it stung. It took me back to the Quad, who had also protected me because it was their job, their duty, a debt they'd had to my mother.

It's never about who I am as a person, is it?

"I know," I said, hoping my voice was strong, that he wouldn't catch the way it wavered. "I know I'm just a client. That doesn't mean I'm not grateful. If a doctor saves my life, I'm still happy they did it, even if it was because it's their job. So, even though it's just because you have to, I'm still glad."

"Kenz..." Regret colored my name. Had he just realized how mean his comment had been?

Except, I didn't need an apology from him. I didn't need people to say sorry for the truth. We were all stuck in this world, all at the whims of the way things were.

Besides, it would only make me seem all the more pathetic as he tried to explain it away.

No thanks.

I closed the half-full dishwasher. "It's fine. I'm going to make a plate and take it to Vance."

"Why?"

"Because he didn't come to dinner. He needs to eat, after all."

Hayden said nothing while I piled food onto the dish, then set silverware on the edge. I grabbed a water bottle and tucked it beneath my arm.

I recalled the look on Vance's face, the silent way he'd stared out of the window in the car after the interview. Then he hadn't come to dinner? I couldn't shake the worry about it.

Hayden spoke softly as I passed him. "You shouldn't get too close to us."

I paused, but kept my gaze forward. What was I supposed to say back to that?

He went on. "We aren't the sort of people you should interact with more than needed. Remember how you got here, Kenz, and the world we live in. Your best bet is to do as your told, keep your distance, and go back to your own life when this is all over."

"I'll go back to my life when this is over, but that doesn't change anything for now. I can't ignore someone in pain."

He didn't stop me when I walked out, headed up the stairs, then down the hallway that led to Vance's room, Hayden's warning echoing in my head.

I hadn't gone into Vance's room yet. I'd seen Tor's room, since I'd spent the first night there, until they set up my own room and felt sure I wouldn't run. That was it, though.

And why did I feel nervous about it?

Vance and I had a certain comfort between us by this point. It wasn't a happy comfort, of course, but more of an understanding. It was like a pap smear — I hated it, but I knew what would happen so it wasn't that stressful.

Yet somehow, after the way he'd looked at that interview, it made me anxious about intruding on his personal space.

The man's words could come out vicious when he wanted them to.

I knocked on his door, the plate balanced on my other hand. No answer came.

Had he gone out? Maybe I just hadn't heard it?

A crash inside made me frown. *Guess not.*

Standing outside wouldn't do a thing, so I gathered my courage, twisted the handle and pushed open the door.

I'd expected his room to be spotless. He seemed as though he didn't care what people though, but at the same time, he always appeared flawless. I assumed that would continue with his room.

Boy was I wrong…

Except, as I peered around the room, I realized it wasn't just general messiness. Clothes weren't strewn across the floor or trash piled high on surfaces. Instead, white scraps of fabric were all over.

No, not fabric. I recognized it after a moment. The only thing out of place in the room were the scraps of canvas.

Well, other than shattered glass on the floor, and Vance on his hands and knees in front of it, a small wastebasket beside him. He picked up the shards of glass and dropped them into the trash.

"Fuck," he muttered when one of the pieces slid across his fingers, a drop of red welling up at the tip. The word came out strange, without the defined way of speaking I'd grown used to from him. He normally spoke carefully, each word perfectly enunciated. Basically? He spoke like a man who came from a superb private education.

This time, he said the word drawn-out, slow and unclear.

A strong acidic scent hit my nose, and I identified it as alcohol.

That explained the way Vance spoke, at least.

He reached for another shard, even with the blood dripping from his gloved finger to the ground.

Before I could think about it, I rushed forward and dropped to my knees in front of him. "It'll hurt if you get alcohol in that cut," I told him.

I set his food on the ground beside him, then went about picking up the glass, dropping it into the basket beside him. It was easy, at least. The bottle had been an expensive brand — no surprise there — so the pieces had all been large.

"Why're you here?" Those words slurred more than just the one word had, but even if he complained, he sat back and watched me work.

"You didn't eat dinner, so I brought it to you."

He glanced at the plate, then laughed. "Not hungry."

"But the food will soak up some of that alcohol."

"Exactly the problem." He leaned his back against the dresser beside him, then lifted one knee and rested his forearm on it. "I don't need to be clear-headed. That bullshit's not for me, not today."

I continued to clean the glass up, his words heavy. Normally, everything he said came out like some joke, like he didn't give a damn about anything. He flirted and he laughed and he seemed untouched by the world around him.

Was that just a façade? Because it wasn't this man in the least. This man watched me as if he were thinking, and I had to wonder, what did he think?

He probably wished I'd leave. Vance wasn't the kind of man who would want to show his weakness to anyone, so me intruding and forcing my help on him wouldn't sit well.

Too bad. If people screwed up too much, they got help whether or not they wanted it.

"Why did you destroy that canvas?" I kept my voice soft and quiet, as though the question would be less invasive if I whispered it.

Vance looked toward the shreds of canvas. Sadness rested in his blue eyes, dimming them, glossy from the alcohol.

Just how much did he drink?

"I didn't like it," he said.

"Why not?"

"That interviewer said, didn't she? Five years is a long time. People lose skills." His words sounded like bullshit to me, like an easy lie in place of the hard truth.

"Eat, please." I finished with the last shard. A touch to the floor showed that very little alcohol spilled, which meant Vance must have drunk nearly the whole bottle before he dropped it, right?

He was actually doing pretty well, then. If I'd drank even a fraction of that, I'd have been on my ass.

"No. Nights like this aren't meant for food."

"What are they meant for?"

"Liquor and beautiful, easy women."

"Well, you've drank more than enough, and I'm the closest you have to a beautiful, easy woman. So why not add food to the list, then sleep?"

He huffed a sound that could have almost passed as a laugh. Hell, it was *almost* charming, making him look younger and more carefree than even his normal mask did.

He was angry, now. Angry and lost and fearful. These were things I'd never expected to see from Vance.

He twisted, grasped the edge of the dresser to haul himself up. Any questions I had about if he'd polished off the entire bottle tonight went away when his hand slipped and he came crashing back down.

I crossed the short distance between us, trying to help, but as it turned out, catching a man that large was a stupid idea.

I wasn't all that large and I sure didn't work out enough to even hope to keep him upright. None of that stopped me from trying, though.

And as a reward for the effort, he took me down along with him. The breath knocked out of my lungs when I hit the floor beneath his weight.

He really was more solidly built than I'd realized. He wasn't the type to show it off, usually wore clothing that covered his body, but being up against him like this made it so much more obvious.

I groaned as I stared up to find his face above me, our positions so close that if I didn't know better, it would feel like lovers.

Is this how it would feel? I didn't have any experience, had no idea how that would really feel, but with his liquor-tinged breath spilling over my lips, I felt drunk on him.

A red mark on his cheek told me he'd struck the dresser on his way down — it would probably darken into a bruise come tomorrow.

"You hurt yourself," I whispered as I lifted my fingers to brush over the spot. "You should be more careful."

"What does it matter? Sometimes I wonder if I destroyed this face, this name, would I be free?"

I frowned at the hopelessness in his words. I hadn't ever seen him like this. "You're too hard on yourself."

He sighed and leaned in. My eyes slid closed on their own and I expected the press of his lips to mine, just like before. All that anger I'd felt, when I'd raged at him over stealing my first kiss, it all disappeared.

Why?

Out of pity? Because he seemed so damned sad that I couldn't even imagine rejecting him? Or maybe it was just plain old hormones that made me think a kiss might just be worth it.

Except, something warm pressed to my forehead instead of my lips. When I cracked my lids, I saw he'd rested his head against mine.

"You don't know me," he said in a voice so breathy, I nearly couldn't make out the words. "No one does, not really. They see who I am on camera, who I am when I'm doing interviews, but they don't know me. Hell, do I even know anymore? What was the point of any of it? The public, they just want the pretty version of me that they've seen on cover magazines and my art, but no one sees *me*."

I reached my other hand up, to cup his cheeks on both sides, forcing his face far enough away for me to see him clearly. He didn't open his eyes, though. It was for the best, since I'd bet if he had, it would have broken this rare, honest moment between us.

"I know you," I assured him. "I know you're arrogant, and you think you're God's gift to women, and that you enjoy people talking about you and making a scene. I also know that you're kinder than you let on, that you're serious about your art, that you're sensitive even if you like to hide it. I don't know everything about you, but I know you're not nearly as bad as you think."

His weight grew heavier on me, as if some of the tension inside him had released and he sagged against me.

Had my words meant that much to him?

That pulled me in even more.

"Come on, let's get you into bed," I said and pushed at his shoulder.

He grumbled, but rolled off me. The process was slow, a constant two steps forward, one backward. I'd get him up, then he'd stumble, even with me under his arm, and he'd catch himself on the wall.

Eventually, though, we made it. He collapsed on the bed, not trying to break his fall in the least.

"You shouldn't drink this much," I scolded him as I kneeled and unlaced his shoes. The leather was nice, the craftmanship undeniable. I didn't know much about men's fashion, but I had no doubt he'd paid a lot for them. I removed them, then pulled off the no-show socks he wore beneath.

When I rose, he tried to undo the buttons of his shirt, but was having little luck.

He was like a large toddler. Was this what it was like to have children?

If so, I understood child-free folks much better.

Part of me wanted to tell him to just get under the covers, to go to sleep fully dressed. Drunk people did it all the time. He'd drank enough to pass out, so what he wore didn't matter. Come tomorrow, he could shower off the sweat of liquor and wash his sheets.

Except, given the way he tried and failed to get his shirt off, I had a feeling he'd just keep at it until he got it or knocked himself out of the bed.

Stubborn drunk.

I kneeled on the bed and shooed his hands away. "Let me."

He jerked back, as if afraid to touch me, then glared.

"You shouldn't look at me like that," I muttered as I worked free the buttons, trying hard to ignore each inch of skin revealed. I pretended I was undressing a toddler, like I'd said before, rather than a very attractive man who I had no doubts would give me *everything* if I just asked him to. "I'm helping you, after all. You should be nicer to me."

"I'm always nice." His pout was downright adorable.

"No, you're not. You may say things that sound nice — sometimes — but they're not real."

"I always tell you how pretty you are."

I laughed at that, at the way it brought back all the times he'd done just that. "You would tell a ninety-seven-year-old she was pretty if you thought you could get something out of it. Either you lie when you say it to everyone, or you have such low standards that you think everyone is pretty."

He pressed his lips together, then tore his gaze away, staring at the ceiling instead of me. "Well, I really do think you're pretty."

"Oh yeah? And when did you start thinking that?" I tugged the hem of his shirt from his pants so I could undo the last buttons, the fabric now resting open and loose, revealing his entire chest and stomach.

And *boy* did he look amazing.

"Not at first." Vance's words made me frown for a moment as I thought back to what we'd been talking about. Before I could get offended, though, he kept speaking. "When I saw you at your college, I thought you were just another hanger-on. I was there to see what you were like, to see if there was anything special about you, and I didn't see it."

"You see? Not nice."

He went on as though I hadn't spoken. In fact, I had no idea exactly how much of what I said made it through the liquor and into his cloudy brain. "I thought you were pretty when I saw your sketchbook."

"What?" The question escaped me when it was the last thing I'd expected.

"Hair and makeup and cleavage and clothing don't mean a thing to me. Those are easy to get, especially in my world. Anyone can buy a pretty face or a better body. So whether you were pretty or not physically never mattered to me. When I saw your sketchbook, though? I liked that."

"You looked at a few rough sketches. Those were hardly worth you noticing."

He shook his head and slung his arm over his face. Was he hiding his eyes? His expression? "I could see your passion. When some people draw, they draw what they think the world wants. They give them pretty skylines and bright colors and whatever will sell. What I saw in your sketchbook was deeper than that. It was like you'd peeled away your skin and bled on the page. Each line *meant* something, and when I saw that, I couldn't stop thinking about you." He laughed softly, the sound full of pain. "That's when I thought you were pretty, because I couldn't stop seeing that sort of thing when I looked at you. I'm jealous of that sort of openness. Not a lot of artists can put their entire soul out on the paper like that."

His praise hit differently than it usually did. Normally, he treated me like a piece of meat he wanted to chew on. This, though? It made a smile tug at my lips, the compliment the sort of thing I actually wanted to hear from him.

Still, he was so drunk, he had no idea what he was talking about. Come tomorrow, he'd end up forgetting all about it. I didn't push him about eating anymore, because he'd drank so much that he'd probably end up choking on the food anyway. I didn't want to have to clean his vomit up, either.

Sleeping it off would do him the best.

"Aren't you going to finish stripping me?" Vance peeked at me from beneath his arm, the look beyond adorable. This playful side of him made my heart speed.

"You're impossible, you know that?"

"You don't let me get close any other time. Gotta strike while the iron's hot, right?" He offered me a lopsided grin that made him look downright boyish.

I wanted to tell him no, but at the same time, he needed sleep. "Fine," I muttered. "But don't get any bright ideas, okay?"

"No worries," he assured me. "After how much I drank, I don't think I could even get it up."

"Imagine the newspaper headlines from that— notorious playboy impotent?" I unhooked his belt, then undid the button at his waist, all the while telling myself this was just taking care of him. This was no different than a nurse undressing a patient.

Professional. *Yep.* That was what this was. Totally freaking professional.

"Don't make jokes like that, or I'll get hard *just* to prove you wrong."

"You're contrary enough to do just that," I admitted before unzipping his pants, then grasping the waist of his pants. I pulled them down, getting them off only because Vance cooperated by lifting his hips slightly.

He wore a pair of black boxer briefs, and, even without touching, I was sure they were incredibly soft.

He also filled them out *very* well. The fabric was snug against his thighs, showing the muscle he'd cultivated there. A white elastic band ran low on his waist, the V of his abs disappearing beneath the edge.

I'd never found men in underwear all that appealing, but I suddenly understood the attraction. He was flawless, and if he wasn't drunk—and an asshole—I might have made a move.

"Don't stare so much."

I jerked my gaze up to his at the tone he used, one unlike his previous. It was full of lust, deep and coaxing. A similar heat rested in his blue eyes, as if alcohol be damned, he'd have me either way.

And seeing him undone like this did it for me. He still had his shirt and gloves on, though the shirt was open to show off his body. His skin was unbelievably pale, his nipples pink and flat and so tempting I nearly reached out to stroke one.

What the hell are you thinking? I sucked in a breath to try to calm myself. I wasn't some animal who couldn't control myself or my wants. I was *not* going to molest a drunken man just because he looked good.

"If you look at me like that," Vance whispered, "I'm going to get the wrong idea. I already took your first kiss—keep looking at me like that and I'll take a lot more."

That woke me up.

The fantasy of sleeping with Vance was a far cry from the reality. He'd proven willing to do anything it took to get what he wanted. He'd proven he wasn't really interested in me, that he was just playing. I couldn't lose myself to desire, because I'd only end up hurt later.

So instead, I tried to keep my voice steady, to not let him know how much he affected me. "Take the shirt off, then get under the blankets."

He pulled in a deep breath, the action making his chest rise, reminding me of how good he looked, then shrugged out of the shirt. It wasn't easy, but he managed it.

Never thought a man in underwear and gloves would look this...erotic.

Maybe it was just Vance—he could make a rainbow clown wig and red nose sexy.

I gathered the discarded items and tossed them into the laundry hamper in the closet. Lastly, I grabbed the water bottle from the floor, the one I'd brought, and the food. I set both on the nightstand beside him, then helped cover him with the blanket when it seemed he couldn't manage it on his own. "Drink water. Dehydration will make you feel so much worse tomorrow if you don't. I'll leave the food, too, in case you wake up and want to eat something."

I peered around the room, seeing his phone on the ground. When I picked it up, I had a moment of hesitation.

Vance was in no position to notice, was he? I could call Nem from this…

The phone they'd given me could contact no one but them. With this, though, I could reach out. One call and it would be over.

Nem would come with the Quad, with Jarrod. They'd slaughter these four men who had dared to trap me, would take me back to my real home. If Lorien wanted me, if he was stupid enough to come after me, they'd deal with him, too.

Just one call and I'd be safe.

Except, when I looked at Vance, his eyes closed, his position so vulnerable, I couldn't.

These men had bought me from an auction, had imprisoned me, had endangered me, planned to continue doing that, yet I was worried about *them*?

I really was an idiot.

I set the phone on the bed beside him. "If you need anything, call me. For now? Just sleep it off."

He didn't move, his face relaxed and vulnerable there right. It drew me in, and before I could think twice, I leaned in toward him. My brain returned to me a split second before I touched my lips to his, before I made that mistake, and I aborted.

Instead, I kissed his forehead.

When I went to pull away, something wrapped around my wrist. I looked down to find his hand clinging to me. "Stay," he asked, his voice small.

I couldn't help it—I couldn't walk out, not when he spoke to me like that. "Okay, for a little while." I sat on the side of the bed, then brushed my hand over his head, running my fingers through the curly strands of his hair.

His breathing evened out as he fell back asleep, as if just my presence relaxed and soothed him.

He slept fitfully at first, small sounds leaving him. After the first fifteen minutes or so, my back started to ache, but each time I shifted, when I thought about leaving, he'd reach for me again.

Looks like I'm going nowhere.

He huffed, kicking his legs like a kid who couldn't get comfortable. He tossed his blanket down, showing off his chest again, sweat beading on his forehead.

It was warm and humid, and alcohol tended to make people feel even hotter. "Stupid clothes," he muttered beneath his breath, then reached down for his underwear.

Before I could even come up with a way to stop him from stripping, he removed the boxer briefs and flung them to the ground. Thankfully, the blanket kept me from seeing anything.

I guess he sleeps naked.

Not all that shocking for a man like Vance.

He brought his left hand to his mouth and took one of the fingers of his glove between his teeth, then pulled it off. It was the first time I'd seen him without those gloves on.

People often said he wore them due to his art, that they were to protect his hands. I still recalled when he'd told me to protect my own, that for artists, they were so important.

His left hand was just as pale as his chest, his fingers long and lovely. It was funny since the rest of his body was so large, so manly, that his hands could seem so graceful.

He hooked the thumb of his left hand under the wrist of his right glove, then yanked the black fabric off, tossing it to the floor with the same annoyance he'd used for everything else, as though he really hated wearing anything.

When my gaze went to his right hand, I froze. It looked *nothing* like his left.

And just like that, I knew I'd seen something I was never meant to.

* * * *

Vance

My head pounded as I came to, and I wondered if it might just explode. Had I hit it on something? Was this an aneurysm?

Whatever it was, the idea of fully waking up seemed like a horrible idea. I could only imagine this would get worse.

Something moved beside me, making me laugh.

A woman by my side would make even a headache like this not seem so bad, after all.

I swallowed, my throat dry, and the taste of stale alcohol explained the pounding in my head.

It'd been a long time since I'd overindulged like that. A few drinks? Sure. I enjoyed dulling my senses just a bit, the nice relaxation that happened when I could let things go and not worry so much. Blackout drunk, though, was something I'd put behind me a long time ago.

I opened my eyes, curious to see whatever girl I'd brought him with me.

And boy did I not expect to see a certain brown-haired girl beside me.

Kenz slept, her eyes closed, her lips pulled into a half-smile even in her sleep. Just seeing her like that made my chest tighten.

Had I slept with her?

While I couldn't deny I sure wanted to, the idea that I actually had struck me as weird. She wasn't the type to give in like that. I never figured I'd have a shot, yet somehow, she was in the bed beside me.

Then I noted that she was dressed fully.

Weird.

If I did get her into bed with me, I knew I wouldn't be satisfied with some quickie where we kept most of our clothes on. No, I'd want to strip her down fully, to see every inch of her pretty body, to make sure I remembered it all.

So had we not slept together?

The night before remained fuzzy, but little bits flashed through my head. The interview, the liquor, dropping the bottle.

Right, she'd come to check on me, to bring me food. *Sweet girl.*

Most of the night remained a mystery, and the idea of waking her up right now to continue hit me hard. If she was half asleep, could I convince her? Maybe she was a morning person, because my cock certainly was.

I shifted, ready to press my lips to her throat, to tease her until she woke panting and desperate, when I froze.

On the nightstand sat my gloves, the familiar black fabric resting there as if they were important.

They were.

I jerked my hand up, my right one, and to my horror, it was bare.

Exposed and mangled and ugly.

A soft groan came from the sleeping girl just before those dark eyes of hers opened. She looked at my face, then at my hand which still was there.

No shock registered in her expression, and that made my heart plummet.

It meant she'd already seen it the night before. Any chance I had to lie, to hide it, they were gone.

After how hard I'd worked to keep it to myself, I'd gone and gotten drunk and shown her the part of myself I'd wanted no one to see.

Just great...

Chapter Twelve

Kenz

I rubbed my lower back, the muscles sore and tight. As it turned out, trying to sleep in someone else's bed wasn't great for a good night's rest. Worse, Vance was a horrible bedmate.

He might be talented when it came to pleasing women, but he tossed and turned and hogged the blankets like a selfish jerk.

And this morning hadn't gone any better.

"You hurting?" Hayden asked from beside me, his sharp gaze locked on my back.

"Just a bad night of sleep." No need for him to know what had happened. Vance had woken early enough that when he'd rushed into his bathroom, I'd snuck back to my own room with no one being the wiser.

"Well, you wouldn't be the first person to lose some sleep in Vance's bed."

Or, maybe I hadn't been as sneaky as I'd like to think.

"It wasn't like that," I rushed out.

Hayden shook his head, though his expression remained tight. "I'm not judging you. You're an adult, you can do as you please." Even as he said that, he sighed. "Though, I don't want to see you get hurt. Vance isn't the type to settle down, and you don't strike me as a one-night-stand girl, either."

I wrapped my arms around myself, trying so hard to look totally unaffected. Blushing would just prove I was a kid. "He drank too much, so I was just taking care of him."

"All night?"

How to explain that? The truth was better than anything else. "He just looked so sad and lonely, I guess. Nothing happened, though. I'm not dumb enough to mistake what he's like. I just couldn't leave him there alone."

"So you just slept there?" Hayden lifted his eyebrow as though my words didn't make any sense. After a moment, he chuckled softly. "You're probably the only girl who has ever spent the night in Vance's bed without anything happening."

No doubt he meant to make me laugh, but I wasn't in a laughing mood.

"Have you ever seen Vance without his gloves?" I asked before I could think better of it. He probably didn't want others to know, but I couldn't stop thinking about it.

Especially because I got the sense he wouldn't say anything to me. So far, he'd avoided me. After his shower, he'd snuck out of the house so fast I hadn't caught a glimpse of him.

Hell, I wasn't even entirely sure he'd come back at all. It was in the shock on his face, the way he'd pulled away and tucked that hand behind his back.

I had no idea exactly how much damage had been done or how it had happened, but the fact he hadn't done any art in five years suddenly made sense.

He had gnarled skin over the back of his hand, and from what I could tell, he only had two fingers — his thumb and pinky finger. What appeared to be slid over the back of his and around the side was some sort of prosthetic that replaced his middle three fingers. They hadn't moved, and the way I'd seen him grasp things or use that hand fit.

He wore the gloves to hide that, and he'd removed them because he'd been hot and drunk out of his mind. His expression showed he hadn't intended for me to see.

Hayden remained silent for a long moment, and the quiet there told me the truth.

He knew.

If he didn't, he'd have asked me what I meant or laughed off my question. Instead, the tension suggested he knew exactly what I was talking about.

"He showed you?"

I shook my head. "Not exactly. He was drunk and took them off, but he didn't realize it — not until he woke up."

Hayden rubbed his hand against the back of his neck. "That explains why he ran out this morning, I guess."

"I didn't react badly," I rushed out. "I would never."

Hayden set his hand on my shoulder, the touch heavy and calming. "I know. I'm not saying you did anything wrong. Vance is very careful not to let anyone see, and I'd bet you were the last person he'd want to know about it."

"Will he come back?"

"Yeah, he will. He's stubborn and difficult, but he's as invested in this as anyone. He'll finish this, no matter what."

"How did it happen?" I asked.

Hayden shook his head. "Sorry, but I'm not one to gossip. I wouldn't have told you anything if you hadn't seen it yourself. If you want to know what happened, you'll need to ask him."

"That's why he hasn't come out with any new work in so long, isn't it?" The memory of the shredded canvas came back to me, how it had been spread across the floor of his room. The anger needed to do that made a lot more sense.

I stared down at my hands and wondered how I'd feel.

Art mattered to me. It made me feel complete, and I didn't even have a career yet. How would I react to having it taken away? To have my hands damaged in a way that made it impossible to do what I most loved?

I couldn't blame him for his 'I don't give a damn' attitude when I thought about it like that.

Hayden squeezed my shoulder, freeing me from the horrible thought. Still, I understood Vance in a way I hadn't before.

"Come on." Hayden moved his hand to my back and pressed me forward to get me moving.

"Where are we going?" We'd already gone to turn in my work to the professor, since I couldn't attend classes regularly.

"Somewhere fun."

"That didn't go so well last time," I pointed out, thinking about our failed field trip to the art store.

"Yes, well, this time I'm watching much more closely for tails. Trust me, Kenz, I won't let anything happen to you."

And why was it that all it took were those few words and I immediately did trust him. The world didn't feel nearly so scary with Hayden beside me.

And that felt more dangerous than any threat against me.

* * * *

Tor

The tension in the house was obvious. The least observant person would have felt it, but I was especially untuned.

Because I rarely spoke, I noticed more than most. Subtle changes in others were clear to me when normal people might have missed them.

This tension had started this morning, when Vance had snuck out of the house, carefully avoiding Kenz.

Of course, Kenz had left his room early in the morning, so it didn't take much to guess what had happened.

Or, perhaps not... She hadn't appeared embarrassed, as though sneaking out of a room after a one-night stand. Instead, her expression held worries and questions.

Likewise, I hadn't known Vance to ever avoid people after casual sex. If anything, he acted proud of his indiscretions, more likely to flaunt such things like a victory lap. Certainly not to hide them.

So what actually happened in that room?

My gaze landed on Vance, who stared at his right hand.

Ah, that's it?

I knew about his hand — we all did. It had brought us together, after all. We all wore our wounds from that fateful night, from the event that had altered the course of all our lives.

Still, he'd never spoken about it. He'd never admitted anything, never removed his gloves, never said a word about it.

I knew he'd gone to physical therapy, because I preferred to know what the others were up to. No matter how much pain he must have been in, or how difficult tasks were to complete, he had never allowed anyone to see his struggle.

I would be a useless hitman if I couldn't spot a near useless limb, though. Over the past five years, he'd gotten better at using his left hand for most things. He'd also gotten different.

He'd grown colder, with the smile he wore less honest as time went on. He would buy those canvases, but I had year to see him finish or bring any artwork out.

However, we weren't the sort of people to pry into each other's lives beyond what bound us to one another. We all walked our own paths, interacting simply because those paths ran parallel to each other.

And my silence gave me the chance to observe the others, to gather information, to understand them.

The leader, Hayden, who took on the weight of the world all himself. He was controlling and worried far too much, even if he would never admit it. Char, with his false face he showed to the world, too afraid to allow anyone close enough to reject the real him. Vance, who had lost a piece of himself and now walked through life hollow and in complete and broken.

And me, the hitman with so much blood on my hands that I knew better than to get close to others.

Then there's Kenz... My mind went back to the little spit of a girl who lived with us, who had created ripples on the pond that had been our settled lives. The way she perked up the moment anyone said a kind word went to show she craved attention, affection, but she wanted it too much.

The way she deflated when people didn't give her that praise, the fear in her eyes when she tried to care for others, it proved that she'd gone without that reassurance before in her life.

It made me want to know more about her, which was a strange desire from me.

While I watched others, while I saw everything, I cared little about the information outside my job. With Kenz, however, I wanted to interact, not just watch. I wanted to go nearer to her, to discover the secrets she hid, to...

I wasn't sure, honestly.

I'd never felt this way, so I didn't know how to define or explain it.

"They're late," Char muttered, seated on the couch with his feet up on the table. His mood was even fouler than usual.

Jealousy?

"Hayden said they'd be back in about half an hour." Vance jerked his gaze from his hand, as though he'd realized someone might notice.

"He spoils her," Char went on. "He acts like she's on vacation here, like she's on Spring Break or something. He should be tougher on her."

"You want to know a secret?" Vance set his bad hand on his stomach and covered it with his other. "Women are a pain in the ass, but they're worse if they're bored or upset. It's a lot easier to deal with them if you spoil them every once in a while."

Char snorted. "So you're as useless as he is, huh? We should have locked her up in her room and gone about our business without dealing with her much. Just brought her out when needed."

I lifted my eyebrow at that.

It was funny how differently the same idea could come from different people, how it changed the meaning.

Char meant *exactly* what he said, that he would have locked her into her room to keep her out of his hair. Hayden would have locked her up to ensure her safety. Vance would have made a joke about chaining her to a bed.

Me?

The thought of seeing her fearful or upset bothered me in a way I didn't fully understand. Would I have done it? Perhaps, but it wouldn't have sat well.

The front door opened, causing all three of us to swing our gazes that way.

We look like fathers waiting up for our daughter after she went out on a date.

It was downright embarrassing how far we had fallen, wasn't it?

Kenz walked in first, a smile on her lips. It eased me, seeing her happy. That smile had become less and less common recently, as though the crushing reality and threats had worn on her.

It was good to see it, now.

She had her arms wrapped tightly around a large stuffed animal, the creature distorted by her grip enough that it took a moment for me to figure it out. Was it a bunny?

Somehow, that seemed fitting. I could almost picture her like a rabbit, quick footed and far too easy to break.

Hayden came in on her heels, his gaze on her, his expression unusually soft. He needed to work on his poker face, because anyone who saw that would recognize that he did *not* merely see her as a client.

"You're late," Char snapped, his mood even worse now that they'd returned.

"I wasn't aware I had a curfew," Hayden answered.

"Dinner is usually at six."

Vance remained silent during their little back and forth. Did he not want to draw attention to himself? Whatever had happened between him and Kenz, he seemed unwilling to address it head-on.

Hayden set down the large bag he had on the table. "Well, lucky for you, Kenz is nice. She had us stop on the way home and pick up sandwiches from a shop."

"And the rabbit?" Char asked.

Kenz flashed an impossibly bright smile as she tightened her arms around the stuffed animal, as if that were the most precious item she owned. "We stopped by that new place that has all the really soft stuffed animals."

"I thought it would help you sleep," Hayden said, pink on his cheeks. "You had a few on your bed at your place, so I thought maybe you weren't sleeping well without one."

You could have just gotten one of hers.

The things people did said so much more about them than they realized. People's actions told a story, betrayed secrets, and this was no different.

Hayden had taken her to get something for her, a gift, and something rather personal since it was an item to sleep with.

What an interesting development.

The four of us had worked together for five years without much friction. Kenz was a bolt thrown into that machine, and now it ground as it tried to turn as it always had.

Kenz smiled at Hayden, and her expression held affection as well. Romantic? That I wasn't sure about. "Thank you — I love him."

Hayden nodded once, his lips softening, a smile pulling at the corners though he didn't allow it to spread. "Of course. It's pretty late, though, and you have a class you can't miss tomorrow. You should get to sleep. I hope he helps."

Kenz said her goodnights to the rest of us before, pausing for one long moment before talking to Vance. Clearly that discomfort would take a while longer to settle. She headed down the hallway, toward her room.

I pulled my gaze from where she'd gone to find the others staring that same direction.

A pull existed between each of us and her. If I were trying to destroy our group, she was the perfect weapon. She could have taken us all down without problem, sowing distrust and chaos in an otherwise peaceful setting.

However, what I'd learned long ago was that change wasn't always bad. Change signaled opportunity. It heralded a need to alter things, to adjust, and sometimes that adjustment led to successes that had been otherwise impossible.

So would Kenz lead to our salvation or our destruction?

And did I even care?

Chapter Thirteen

Kenz

I yawned as I reviewed the requirements for the end-of-year exhibit. I had a while to get in my pieces, but I didn't have nearly enough done.

I could pull from my old work, but that wasn't the point. This exhibit would determine my placement next year, and it mattered. I wanted to show my abilities, to prove how much I'd grown, to earn my place.

Yet I hadn't managed a single thing good enough for what I needed to do.

"You frown too much." Char had his legs out as we sat at the large park, beneath a tree.

It had surprised me that he'd brought me here, but I'd learned to never question kindness, at least not in the moment. If I complained or asked him why he'd done it, he'd probably take away the little outing, and I really needed it.

The breeze was lovely, even if the heat made me sweat.

"I was surprised Hayden said it was okay to come."

Char pointed at the large building just across the street. "That's the courthouse. Police are constantly coming and going here, so only an idiot would try to attack. Besides, I'm keeping an eye out." He paused, his lips tipping down. "Unless you don't feel safe having me as your bodyguard."

"I never said that."

"You looked pretty chummy with Hayden last night. Thought maybe you'd decided you only liked him watching out for you."

His tone was strange. He was always unpleasant around me, but the more I interacted with him, the more I could tell what sort of unpleasantness he felt at any given time.

There was normal unhappy for him, which was his baseline. Then there was annoyed — often when he had to interact with people he didn't want to. He had his hangry mood, when he missed a meal and started to snap at others for making noise. That was surprisingly similar to his mood when he had to wake up early as well.

This one felt slightly different. If I didn't know better, I'd have labeled it as jealousy.

I shook my head, telling myself that was crazy. Char barely tolerated me because he needed me right now. He'd done nothing to imply he felt anything positive about me that might lead to jealousy.

It meant I must not fully understand his moods yet.

"I'm fine with you," I told him honestly. "I just was making conversation." I allowed my voice to trail off after that, then flipped through the journal I had, staying quiet so as not to bother him anymore.

The paper inside was worn and yellowed, with scraps shoved in, pictures glued to different pages. I'd had this thing for years, like a collection of everything that mattered.

"You're being too quiet," Char muttered, his voice quiet as though he hadn't wanted to say it but couldn't help himself. "What's that thing?"

Instead of calling him on his bipolar attitude, I opened the journal wide and angled it toward him. "This is my idea book."

"What's an idea book?"

"I've been working on it for years now. It has lots of things — some small sketches, ideas for future work. I have quotes that matter to me, and images of artwork I love, or pictures of things that inspire me. I use it when I feel stuck on my art, when I don't know where to go. It reminds me that I've got this, that there are beautiful and horrible things in the world that I want to create."

He took the journal from me, but he didn't yank it like I expected. Instead, he held it with care.

He always confused me, somehow swinging between being an insufferable asshole and showing me a surprisingly sweet side, even if he hid it behind a layer of sarcasm.

He turned the pages gently, taking his time on each one. I didn't stop him because I had no reason to.

It wasn't some private sketchbook like a journal. Instead, I'd filled it mostly with pictures of landscapes or plants or animals I saw and liked. The artwork inside wasn't mine — printouts of paintings or sculptures that inspired me — or they were rough sketches that I didn't care if anyone saw.

"You have strange tastes," he said.

"Do I? What sort of art do you like?"

"I'm not an art person. People are complicated enough without having to deal with things as undefined as art or culture. I know enough to fit into a group and talk about art, but I don't really enjoy any of it."

His statement didn't surprise me. Most people saw art as unapproachable, like something only for the rich or snobby. It had always broken my heart that people felt that way.

"I always wanted my art to be accessible," I explained. "I honestly don't like art museums — too stuffy. I prefer going to the children's museums. They have to entice kids, and I think the art there is always so much more powerful. What I want isn't to get my work in some fancy gallery somewhere. I want kids to see prints of my work and beg their parents to hang it on their wall. I want people to see my work and smile or cry or feel something, but I want it universal. I don't want it restricted to just people who have art degrees."

Char lifted his gaze to mine but said nothing for a long, tense moment. He narrowed his eyes, then looked back down at the journal as though he hadn't figured out what to say back.

The way he often went silent made me uneasy, but I'd learned it was just him. I had a feeling he thought of something but didn't want to say it out loud, to risk anything by admitting it, so he hid those words away deep inside him.

"What's this?" He turned the journal toward me to show a large sketch I'd done over two pages.

My chest hurt the moment I laid eyes on it. I'd forgotten I'd even drawn that in there.

The picture showed Nem, the only color in the entire thing her red hair, done in colored pencil. Beside her were the Quad, each of them roughly sketched in but so easy for me to identify.

Bray, with his nose ring and sharp eyes. Rune with his long hair. Dane with that half-smirk and Colton, standing back slightly as if to watch over them all.

My eyes burned as I stared at it. Since Nem had come back into my life, I hadn't gone more than a day or two without speaking to at least one of them, but now?

It had been weeks. It was easier to ignore how lonely that made me when I focused on what had to happen, on living with these men, on what I had to do. Now, however, seeing that picture, it brought it all back.

I miss them so much.

"Who are they?" he asked.

I swallowed and forced a smile. "They're family."

"I thought you only had your father."

"That's the girl I said was like my sister, and those are the bodyguards who helped raise me."

He peered hard at the picture, and a part of me worried. I'd refused to tell them anything about the Quad, but now Char had an idea of how they all looked.

California was a long way from Florida, though, and while people knew the Quad, it was far less likely for anyone to know their faces.

Same with Nem.

I could have lied, but with the way my eyes watered and I fought back tears, I was pretty sure it wouldn't have worked. Char would have seen right through that sort of ploy.

"I miss them," I admitted softly. "I moved out here to be on my own, but I really miss having them around me."

A frown touched his expression, but it was yet again different from the others I knew. This one read like confusion. "If it makes you this sad, why move away from them?"

"Because I was used to them doing everything for me. I wanted to stand on my own, to make my own choices. I couldn't do that if I stayed under their wings." I laughed softly and shook my head. "And look how well I did on my own, huh? Targeted by some criminal, sold at an auction and abducted by you all."

"When this is over, are you going to go back to them?" He tapped his finger on the bottom of the page, careful not to smudge the drawing.

"Maybe I should. I mean, I'm causing so many problems for everyone. Maybe it's better to go back to the cage, huh? I'm just being selfish and making everyone else suffer for me." I peered around the grassy area in the park, the reality hitting home. "I mean, even right now, you're wasting your time here because you all are worried about me, because you want to make sure I get to go out and do things. Hayden was hurt because he wanted to take me to an art store to cheer me up. It seems like all my life, I've been a burden to everyone around me."

"Burden is a pretty strong word. Do you think they'd use it?"

I thought back to all the times others had had to take care of me, when they'd had to step up and risk themselves or take their time all for me. From schools where my father shipped me off to, to bodyguards and drivers and tutors and housekeepers and butlers. So many people who had watched out for me.

Those weren't even counting Nem, who had risked her life after nearly dying just to come back and rescue me, or Jarrod who helped to teach me to take care of myself and treated me like a daughter, or the Quad who had countless times shielded me from danger with their own bodies.

"Whether they'd say it or not, it's true. No matter what I do, I'm just a silly little girl who others have to protect and look out for. The fact that they're too nice to tell me doesn't mean it isn't a fact."

Char said nothing back at first, his gaze locked on the picture. When he did speak, he didn't look up. "I can tell they matter to you by the way you draw them. I'd bet they don't see you the same way at all. No one would make you smile the way you do when you think about them if they didn't care about you, too. That sort of connection is rare in the world."

"You see me as a burden," I pointed out.

"Well, sure, *I* do, but I'm an asshole." Char smiled at me, the expression odd. It wasn't the forced smile I so often saw, the one he gave to strangers when he played his part.

Was this a real smile? It held an edge, a sorrow, but that seemed just like him.

Why did it make my stomach flutter?

"You should smile like that more often," I said.

Immediately, he wiped the expression from his face. It was like the door I'd peeked through slammed shut in my face, stealing the glimpse I'd gotten beneath his defenses.

"Don't get this confused." His voice no longer held that slight fondness, having turned icy. "I'm doing a job — nothing more. I'm here because I need you to get what I want. Don't think for a moment you're anything special to me."

I thought I'd grown used to Char's attitude, to his cutting words, but it seemed he could still surprise me. I hadn't thought he'd fallen in love with me or anything, but the fact he could so clearly cut me down hurt. Maybe it was the hurt, but I found myself responding. "You don't need to be so afraid."

"Excuse me?" His question came out like a snarl, like a dog warning someone to stay back.

But I knew him, and I'd grown up around terrifying people. He couldn't scare me, not with his little attitude. "Trusting people, letting them in, it isn't nearly as scary as you think. You don't have to snap just to keep others away. Living like you are, too scared to let your guard down, it'll mean you're always alone. That's no way to live life."

He blinked slowly, his gaze hard. I had clearly gone *way* too far, but I couldn't help it. "You don't know a damn thing about me." His voice held no anger anymore, but the cold in each word was worse. It sounded like every bit of warmth or feeling inside him had leeched away. "I don't let people close because it's stupid to do so. People put on masks, they pretend to be whatever they think someone else wants, and they use that to get what they want. You act like I'm the only one, but I'm not. I'm just more aware of it than others, better at it."

"I don't pretend to be anyone but who I am."

"That's not true. I saw you with your little friends at school. You act differently. You act differently with your professors than you do with friends, and you act differently with me than you do Hayden or Vance or

Tor. You are just like everyone else – giving people whatever version of yourself you think works in your favor."

I wanted to tell him he was wrong, but he wasn't entirely. Sure, I acted differently based on the environment, but that was normal, wasn't it? "That's no excuse for retreating into yourself. How do you expect to find special people in your life? Love?"

"Love?" He laughed, a sound filled with venom. "Love is a fantasy, Kenz, just something we pretend exists because it makes us feel a little better."

"You just say that because you don't know any better. Love is real."

"You've fallen in love?"

"Well, not yet..." I thought about the few boys I'd liked and the way the Quad or my father had run them off.

"Then how *dare* you try to tell me off about it. You, who apparently hadn't even had your first kiss, want to lecture me about what love is?"

The condescending way he spoke pushed me to fight back. "And what about you? You don't know anything about it either!"

"I was married."

And just like that, the ground seemed to disappear beneath me.

Char

Fuck. The moment the words left my mouth, I regretted them. I wished I could gather them and swallow them down so they never escaped.

Especially when Kenz's eyes widened, and she went speechless.

I dropped my gaze, unwilling to look at her. Why did I say that?

Because she was challenging me.

It turned out I hadn't grown past the stage where people could goad me into whatever they wanted. At least, I hadn't when it came to this frustrating girl.

"You were married?" She asked me as though she couldn't quite wrap her head around it.

Ending it now would have been pointless, so I nodded. "It's not that hard to believe, is it? Yes. I was married for two years."

"How did you meet?"

"Does that matter?" When she said nothing, I sighed and answered. "She worked at a coffee shop I went to. She was always nice to me, always smiled at me and remembered my order. That seemed as close to love as I understood." I thought back to Isla, to how she'd worn that ugly brown apron but how it had fit her so well. She always looked so happy when she worked, sliding through the space as she made coffee like some dance.

Later, after we had gotten together, she always smelled of coffee. No matter how much she showered, that scent had clung to her hair, and it made me smile. At least it used to—now it made me a little sad.

"So if you know that, how can you say love isn't real?"

"Because it wasn't. She fell for the mask I wore, and I fell for the mask she wore. She saw the bits of myself I showed her, the ones I cultivated to make sure she liked them. I gave her the gifts I knew she'd want, said the words that would make her heart beat faster. Getting her to fall for me was nothing more than a game, than manipulating her feelings to get her to want me."

"That's not true." Kenz spoke with the same stubborn streak a kid certain that Santa was real used, as though she couldn't let go of the fantasy. "Love is complicated, but you can't spend two years with someone and have them not ever see the real you."

"Of course you can. I wore that mask so tightly, never letting it slip, never risking her seeing the real me. If she had, she would have run."

"What happened?"

I closed her journal, then handed it back. A part of me wanted to burn the book, as though it was responsible for my frustrations, for the way it angered me that she could hold onto so much optimism. "She died. Five years ago, she died without ever having seen the real me. Maybe I should thank my stars for that, that she died before she had to suffer through finding out I wasn't the man she thought I was. So before you lecture me about what I should do and how great love is, you should shut your mouth. You don't know a damn thing about love, life or me." I twisted, turning my back to her, unwilling to see her face.

She'd probably cry. She'd tell me how I was mean and heartless.

It's all true.

Something about those tears would bother me, though, and I refused to turn into Hayden. I wouldn't coddle or spoil her just because it made shit easier.

She sniffled. *Yep, here come the 'poor me' tears.*

Warmth surrounded me. I flinched before looking down to find Kenz's arm wrapped tight around me, her forehead against my back.

"What the fuck?" I asked when nothing else to say came to mind.

"I'm sorry," she whispered, her breath hot against my back, even through my shirt.

"Get off me." I shrugged my shoulders, but it didn't dissuade her. If anything, she clung to me tighter and shook her head. Wetness soaked into my shirt, telling me she no longer held her tears.

When she'd thought about her family, about her loneliness, she hadn't let her tears fall, but she did now?

"Fine, I'm sorry I was mean," I snapped when I had no idea how else to get her off me and end this.

"I don't care about that," she said. "I'm sorry about your wife."

"I already told you that love isn't real, so why are you sorry? I don't need your pity."

"It's not pity. Losing people is hard—I know, I've been through it. And I don't care what you say, I can tell you loved her very much. I can hear it in your voice, so just…let me hold you for a minute." Her words were broken by her own tears, as though she cried the tears I should have.

Then again, Kenz had proven herself empathetic to a fault.

"I didn't even cry when she died," I admitted. "Even when she was buried, when people spoke at her funeral, and everyone else was crying around me, I didn't shed a single tear. Can you really say I loved her if I didn't even cry?"

She held me tighter, plastering her body against my back. "Then I'll cry for you."

And I knew she would. Even if it hurt her, even if she didn't know Isla, even though I treated her horribly, the tears that escaped her now were all for me.

The pain in my chest that I hadn't been able to explain suddenly sharpened, and I finally understood it. It was Kenz burrowing her way into my heart, and I had a feeling no matter how much I resisted, she'd still win.

Chapter Fourteen

Hayden

Being around Kenz had gotten far more comfortable than it should have. It was strange, given I'd worked with plenty of clients for years at a time. In all those instances, however, I'd always maintained a professional distance.

I cared for them, of course, but I knew our places — they were a client, and I was a bodyguard. I worried about them, watched over them, and that created a false sense of closeness no matter what. However, it had always been easy for me to add in the correct distance for both of our sakes.

I couldn't seem to do that with Kenz, though.

Why not?

"What do you want?" Her voice brought me back to the moment, forcing me to scold myself for getting distracted.

I glanced around to realize she spoke with a woman who worked at a small coffee cart on the sidewalk at the school.

"Nothing, please."

Kenz pressed her lips together, giving me a look like she'd grown tired of my nonsense. "Well, you're getting something, so either tell me what you want or you'll drink whatever I get you." When I went to answer, she pointed a finger at me to silence me. "And let me assure you, I'll pick something pink with whipped cream just to punish you."

I couldn't stop my laugh at her fierce expression. "You have a mean streak, sweetheart. Fine, I'll have a café latte."

Kenz nodded, appearing pleased before she turned back to the barista and ordered both of our drinks. I scanned the surroundings, careful not to let my guard down.

It had been a few days without anything from Lorien, and that made me uneasy. All too often things went quiet just before they went very bad.

Given everything he'd done to obtain Kenz, I couldn't imagine he'd just given up. So why?

What was he planning?

"It's so nice to see a father visiting his daughter," the barista said as she handed over the drinks to Kenz.

Father? Ouch. It wasn't that I didn't know how we looked, or that I was unaware of the age difference, but I hadn't quite accepted I looked old enough to be her father.

I did some math in my head. I would have been around twenty when she was born.

Yeah, I guess I could be her father…

Kenz smiled, the comment not seeming to bother her. Then again, why would it? "He's not my dad," she corrected the woman.

But why tell the barista that? What did it matter what she thought?

"Oh he isn't? I'm so sorry! How rude of me." The woman rushed out an apology, her cheeks red.

Then again, that was like asking a woman when she was due only to discover she wasn't pregnant. It was a social misstep that was hard to come back from now.

"It's fine," I assured her. It wasn't the woman's fault that I was old as fuck, now was it?

Of course, it reminded me of what it looked like when Kenz and I walked side by side. Did that embarrass Kenz?

She didn't seem like it, but who knew?

Kenz handed me my drink and thanked the barista before we strolled off. She'd already taken care of her morning class and had a two-hour break before she had a meeting with her advisor about her exhibit.

"So what's that?" I gestured at the large bag slung over her shoulder. I'd assumed they were art supplies, but at her class, she'd only taken out a small sketchbook from the front pocket. What was the rest?

Kenz flashed me a wide smile before gesturing at the large grass lawn. "I thought we'd have a picnic for lunch!"

"Picnic?"

Her smile fell. "I swear, the food's good. I got up early to make it..."

"I'm sure it's good," I reassured her, unable to handle that beaten-puppy look she gave me. "I was just surprised."

"So you want to eat it?"

As if I could have said no to her when she looked at me with those pleading eyes. Hell, I was pretty sure she could have gotten about anything she wanted if she just gave me that crestfallen look.

"Of course."

It turned out that big bag wasn't just food. It also had a blanket folded up inside. She opened the blanket and spread it out on the grass, then kneeled and started to remove the food. She placed out multiple dishes, and it made me wonder just how early she'd woken to get it all done.

I'd left in order to work out, so I hadn't seen any of it. By the time I'd gotten back, about thirty minutes before we'd needed to leave, she was already dressed, ready and with this bag.

And a smile that I now understood. How could she be this sweet? To be excited about making me food?

I glanced around the grass, checking for potential threats. Instead of any dangers, however, what I spotted were other people having their own lunches.

Some were students in groups, but a good number were obvious couples. They sat close together and shared their food, laughing and having a great time. A few were stretched out, resting. One woman leaned against her boyfriend's arm. Another couple had a man with his head in his boyfriend's lap.

"Sit." Kenz patted a spot for me.

Without a way to say no, I did as she said, leaving plenty of space between us. Instead of asking me why I was acting weird, she went about making a plate of food for me.

Everything looked delicious, and I chuckled when she forwent adding any oranges to my plate. It amazed me how much she noticed, that she'd recalled I didn't like oranges just from seeing what I ate at the house.

Someday, she'll make a husband very happy.

Why did that bother me so much?

She handed me my plate, and I offered her a thanks before I set it in my lap.

Kenz made her own plate, then moved off her knees to sit cross legged, though the action meant she sat closer to me.

I scooted just a bit away, to put a more appropriate distance between us.

"Do I smell or something?" Kenz asked.

"What?"

"You keep moving away. It's hot, so I'm sure I've been sweating, but I'm clean."

I popped a piece of the food into my mouth, having to admit that she really did cook well. Still, her question rested between us, forcing me to address it. "I didn't want people to get the wrong idea."

"What idea?"

"That we're a couple."

"Why would that bother you? Because of the news reports about Vance and me?"

I hadn't even considered that fact, to be honest. "No. If any tabloids got pictures, it would be easy to explain that I'm providing security for you."

"So why do you care?"

I shifted in my spot, wondering why I had to explain this to her. "That barista saw it. I'm old enough to be your father, Kenz. If we sit close together, it might make you look bad."

She tilted her head, her look making me feel foolish. "You really think I care about that?"

"You should. When this is over, you'll still be here. This'll still be your school. You've got a future to consider, and you don't need to have people spreading rumors about you."

"You should take a page from Vance's book and not worry so much about what other people think."

"I don't care about it for myself. I care about *you*."

"Then you should know I don't care. They can think what they want. We know the truth, so what does it matter?"

She'd intended her words to reassure me, no doubt, so why did they bother me so much?

"Of course. I mean, it would be crazy to think we were romantic, wouldn't it?" I tried to keep my voice even, to not let her hear the bitterness as I said that.

Kenz reached out and set her hand over mine, the touch surprising me so much, I nearly yanked away. "That's not what I meant. I didn't say I don't care because we know it isn't true, but because I wouldn't care if anyone thought that."

"I'm double your age, Kenz. You should be smarter when it comes to men." Why was it that everything I said sounded like the advice an old man would give to a kid suddenly?

"That doesn't matter to me. I care about who a person is and how they make me feel. Their age or background or job or anything like that? None of that matters to me." She squeezed my hand, and if I'd been eighteen still, I wouldn't have been able to resist kissing her.

She was too damned lovely in the sun like this, her dark hair glossy, her pink lips tempting. I would have lost myself in the romantic moment and crossed that distance, onlookers be damned.

But I wasn't a kid anymore, and I had to think clearly even if she didn't.

I gently extracted my hand from hers. "Well, I care, even if you don't."

The way she dropped her gaze had me almost ready to apologize, but one of us had to be tough. It would be far less painful for her in the long run to let go of any strange notions she had now rather than letting them linger in her head.

After that, the conversation all but died. We both ate in silence, but the food had lost some of its deliciousness. The tension soured the flavor, made it tougher to chew.

When we'd finished, Kenz closed the containers and packed everything back up, working hard to avoid my gaze.

And boy did I hate that.

Sure, I'd needed to say what I had, to make sure she understood each of our places, but I didn't care for the dejected way she moved, now.

When she got up, I helped to fold the blanket, then handed it to her. She made sure our fingers didn't so much as brush.

That's for the best.

A strange feeling behind me alerted me. It was an old, honed skill, one that had kept me alive more times than I could count.

I twisted, tucking Kenz behind me as I did so. She stiffened but didn't pull away as though she'd figured out the reason I'd do such a thing so suddenly.

Sure enough, a familiar face appeared across the grass lawn, headed our way.

Bradley Chains, the man who ran the auction where I bought Kenz. I'd met him a time or two, of course, but we'd had little interaction beyond that. He ran the auction whereas I simply attended from time to time. We were in entirely different worlds.

However, his gaze locked on Kenz and me said he'd come to speak to us.

I didn't move, keeping Kenz safely behind me, until he reached where we stood.

"A college campus isn't the sort of place I expected to see you at," I said.

"It isn't. The days of co-eds and frat parties are long behind me. However, I felt this was a far more comfortable and neutral place in which to meet. People tend to get worried when I show up at their homes." Bradley dressed nicely enough to draw attention, yet he didn't appear bothered by it.

"Can you blame people? You're not the type to show up for coffee and chitchat."

He laughed softly as though conceding the point. "You have caused me problems, and I dislike when people cause me trouble."

"I have no idea what you're talking about."

"I prefer things running smoothly, and I have set up my businesses to do so. You and Lorien have managed to throw that off course, however, and I dislike it. I had ignored it at first, hoping you would work it out amongst yourself, but that has not happened. Instead, you have caused me a headache by having fights in the street and going on television for interviews."

When he put it like *that*, it didn't sound good, I had to admit.

"We won, so aren't you supposed to protect our purchase?"

"I would, if everything had been done properly. I don't think you truly want us to go into that, do you?"

The way he stared made it perfectly clear that he knew about the less-than-honest way in which we'd won.

I pulled my shoulders back, standing tall, ready to face him if he wanted to touch Kenz over this. Bradley wasn't known for being forgiving or lenient, so the fact we'd gamed his system wouldn't sit well with him.

"Attacking you here, in such a public place, would be foolish and I am no fool. You can relax. I came to talk — not to turn to violence. There has been enough of a public spectacle already, don't you think?"

"Then what do you want?"

"You need to sit down with Lorien and work through this. The petty issues between you are of no concern to me, but it is now risking *my* business, and that I will not allow. We will call a meeting for you and Lorien to discuss the matter and come to some sort of agreement."

"And if we don't?"

"It would be unadvisable. I am being exceedingly understanding at the moment given what you have done, and I wouldn't suggest you push my patience any further. My understanding is that Lorien will call into the meeting to retain his anonymity, which means you can pick the time and location. I will contact you next week." He paused, then shifted his gaze as if to try to see Kenz.

I set a hand out, keeping her behind me and out of sight.

"So much trouble for such a little girl," Bradley muttered and shook his head. "Then again, I recall when I had a flat tire one time. It halted my entire day, caused us to remain on the side of the road for hours as we waited for a replacement tire, forced me to cancel numerous meetings. When we finally had it resolved, I discovered the culprit—one tiny nail that had driven through the tire wall. It was funny that something so small could derail an organization as large as mine. It reminded me to never ignore even the smallest of problems, because they can cause a great deal of trouble."

With that, he nodded and turned his back, strolling away. He met up with bodyguards a ways off, having clearly left them so as not to worry us.

I waited until he disappeared from view, then went to turn. Something stopped me, however, and I realized Kenz had her fingers clutching my suit jacket, her face pressed against my back.

And now that I could focus on her rather than the threat, I realized she trembled.

Poor girl. I reached behind me to untangle her fingers from my jacket, entwining my fingers with hers in exchange. I twisted to face her, but she stared down. It made her hair hang forward, casting her face in shadows.

"You'll be okay," I promised her.

"How can you say that?"

"Because I'll keep you safe. I may not be good at shopping or dealing with women or picnics in the park," I laughed softly at the long list of my own ineptitude, "But I am *very* good at protecting people." I used the hand not holding hers to cup her cheek and bring her gaze up to mine.

Fear played across her delicate features, and I wished I could wipe that away. I wanted her to not know just how dangerous this really was, how much she could lose. I wanted to carry it all for her.

But I knew better than to think that was possible.

I couldn't take her fear away, but I could promise that I'd do everything I could, that I'd give every drop of blood in my body to keep her safe.

And if it came down to my revenge or her life?

For the first time, I wasn't sure what I'd pick...

* * * *

Nem

"Tell me to calm down one more time and I'll shoot you." I paired the threat with a good glare, the sort that normally sent people running.

"You shouldn't threaten to shoot people," Dane said.

"Why not? Do you think I won't?"

"That's not it. You just shoot people so often the threat has lost its sting." His smirk infuriated me, testing my already frayed nerves. The last thing any person wanted when as wound up as I felt was to have someone tell them to calm down.

That was the verbal equivalent of a nuclear launch button.

That's probably why the asshole said it.

Leave it to Dane to push me as a way to get my mind off whatever worried me. If it had been any other problem, it might have worked. This wasn't just any problem, though.

We weren't talking about a missing informant or someone who owed me money.

We were talking about my flesh and blood, here.

Instead of entertaining Dane any longer, I hit the button on my phone that connected to Kenz's number. I had it saved under *Fox* since I couldn't risk having her real name in my phone. Given that we had faked her death, I couldn't do anything that might cause others to catch wind of the truth.

I had too many enemies, too many people who would use her to hurt me if they only knew about her.

Even without me being an issue, how many would gladly try to turn her into a pawn? To marry her or otherwise sell her off because of her name, because of her bloodline?

Far too many, and no matter how much faith I had in myself, I knew it only took one lucky moment for a person to succeed.

The phone went straight to a voicemail, with just the number repeating since I'd told Kenz not to set a message.

"If Kenz went to the police, she could get you arrested for stalking," Bray muttered. "You've called her at least twenty times a day for two weeks."

I turned toward him, but his eyes were glued to the screen of his laptop instead of looking at me. Somehow that felt normal for him. In fact, I felt like I recognized him the most when the screen of a monitor bathed his face in a blue tint. "Like you aren't worried, too."

He sighed, then turned toward me. "We agreed to give her space, just like Jarrod said. You don't want her feeling trapped. Besides, she's an adult."

"Barely. She's nineteen!"

"Nineteen is an adult," Bray pointed out, his voice flat as mocking me for having to point out something so obvious. "You should have more faith in her."

"It isn't about faith. I just... I worry. She doesn't have as much life experience as we do."

"And how do you expect her to get any if you're always on her ass?" Dane asked.

I went to argue with them when it occurred to me just how stupid this was. "This is rich coming from you all! I don't know a more overprotective group than you all. Do I need to remind you that you, Bray, have trackers all over her phone. Dane, you like to call her school and apartment pretending to be other people just to spy on her and get information."

I turned to find Colton and Rune both sitting on the large sofa at the far end of my office, neither looking all that worried about becoming part of my targets. "Colton, when you heard that there was a teacher known for using his position to blackmail *favors* out of his students, you convinced him to quit before Kenz started at that school. And Rune?"

Rune lifted his eyebrow as if to tell me to bring it.

Fine. "You're the one who has a weekly subscription for pepper spray delivered to her apartment. I don't think any of you get to pretend you're innocent here, that I'm the overprotective jerk."

Rune let out a low chuckle, but it came out strained. The truth was, they might be trying to act fine, but I could read each of them.

They were worried.

"It's only been three weeks," Colton said. "She said she wanted more freedom, right? She said she wanted us to give her some space."

"Space is one thing. Falling off the face of the Earth is another. How do we know she isn't in trouble? That something didn't happen?"

"When I called the school, they said she's been attending classes," Dane said. "If she was in serious trouble, she wouldn't be going to class."

"But she hasn't gone to her apartment. The sensors only went off one time over these weeks. If she isn't sleeping at her place, where is she?"

"She *is* nineteen..." Bray pointed out, the only one brave enough to utter such a suggestion.

The thought of my precious little sister sleeping at some man's apartment made me want to reach for a knife and gut the idiot who even thought about touching her.

"I'll kill any fucker who touches her," Rune said without missing a beat.

And just like that, he soothed some of my anger. He reminded me why I loved these men, why we worked so well together. We were all twisted, all broken and dangerous and violent.

"Agreed," Colton said. "A few bullets would do well."

"A few? And here I thought you were good enough to put them down with one," Dane said.

Colton stared back, not even a smile to soften his words. "If any man screws around with her, I have no plans to end things quickly."

And what did it say about me that his threat made my body heat?

"So what? I'm supposed to just wait here and hope she'll turn back up?"

"Give her a little time," Bray said. "If you keep pushing her, she might run for real. You saved her so she could make her own choices, so she could lead the life she wanted. If we keep forcing her into this safe little box, are we any different than Kyler?"

The name of the man I had thought was my father for so long, Kenz's real father, Kyler, made my stomach clench. It took me back to when he'd shot at Kenz, when he'd been willing to kill her just to hurt me.

I hope that bastard is burning in hell right now.

If there was any justice in the world, my mother was getting to spend her eternity torturing him.

Still, I couldn't fully deny Bray's words.

I *knew* Kenz wanted more freedom. She wanted to stand on her own, to make her own way in life. I'd been there, too, knew how that felt. "She's just so young," I whispered.

A hand wrapped around my wrist, and after a tug, I found myself in Dane's lap, my knees pressed into the couch on either side of him. He was in an office chair that had no arms, and I could already imagine him explaining that *this* was the reason he preferred chairs like this.

"She's young, but she's smart and tough. She'll be okay."

"But how do we know she's okay? How can I trust that she can handle everything on her own? I don't want to control her—I just want to help."

Dane brushed his thumb against my cheek, fondness in his expression. "I know it, Nem, but it's like any kid. You have to let them go eventually, let them leave the nest. It's not easy, but if anyone understands that, it's you."

And I did. I remembered how much I hated it when Jarrod had hovered over me at first, when he'd trained me and always looked over my shoulder. I'd wanted to prove myself on my own, and I'd resented his safety net.

My phone rang, making me jump. Without leaving his lap, I leaned back to take the phone from the desk. Jarrod's name on the screen dashed my hopes.

"Any word?" I asked when I answered, not bothering to ease into the conversation. People like us didn't need those niceties.

"Nothing yet. I'm getting on a plane, and I'll be in Florida by the morning."

"Maybe I should go, too." The idea of letting Jarrod deal with it didn't sit right. I wanted to go there myself, to find her myself, to not rely on others.

It was *my* job, after all. Kenz was my sister.

"You're busy," Jarrod reminded me, the garbled announcements of an airport behind him.

"All this stuff can go to hell. I don't give a fuck about this bullshit, about running anything here. You know I'll drop it all for her."

"You can't do that. Part of the reason she's safe is because you keep things in order there. I'm sure everything is fine—she's just hitting her rebellious stage a little later than most teenagers. I'll find her, ensure she's okay, and report back in."

Dane plucked the phone from my hand. "Thanks, Daddy."

Jarrod's voice was muffled, since Dane had the phone, but I could still hear the annoyance in his voice when he answered. "I should have killed you."

"Probably. Since you didn't, though, you go find our wayward teenager and I'll make sure Nem here is *well* taken care of." Dane had a hell of a promise in his voice when he said that, and the look he gave me reminded me that my stress over Kenz had meant we hadn't spent nearly as much time together as I would have liked.

Jarrod muttered a response, but I didn't catch anything other than *asshole* before Dane ended the call and tossed the phone back to the desk.

"He really will kill you," I warned Dane.

"Oh, I know he'll *try*. Still, you're well worth the risk."

Dane slid his hand behind my neck and pulled me in, taking my lips in a kiss that was almost good enough to erase every worry in my head.

Almost.

He chuckled when he pulled back, then ran his thumb along my bottom lip. "Oh, it's that bad, huh? Not even I can distract you? Well, I guess that's the reason you aren't a one-dick kind of girl, isn't it? I have a feeling that between the four of us, we can get you entirely mindless. I mean, I *did* promise your father that I'd take care of you."

"I don't think he meant like this," I pointed out. Even as I spoke, I could *feel* the other men give up whatever they'd been working on. They came closer as if drawn by something, by the threads that bound all of us together, the ones that nothing could break.

"Well, then I guess if nothing else, I might as well give him something worth shooting me over." Dane kissed me again, silencing any objection, just as Bray, Rune and Colton closed in.

I reminded myself that Jarrod was handling the Kenz issue, that I had done everything I could, so I gave myself over to the moment, to these men, to the pleasure that I knew I could have.

I'd sacrificed so much, had suffered so much, to get this life. Now I had power, security, men I loved and family I protected.

And if it turned out someone had threatened that, that someone had targeted Kenz?

I didn't mind one bit showing anyone the monster who watched out for her.

Chapter Fifteen

Kenz

The weight on my shoulders disappeared the moment I saw Grisham. How did he do that?

Maybe it was because he was one of the first people I'd met when I'd arrived at college, because he'd guided me through my first year here, because it felt like he always had my back.

Whatever the reason, seeing his face let me plop in the seat across the desk from him and let out a long sigh.

"You look exhausted." He laughed as he shut the book in front of him the way he always did, giving me his full attention.

It was one of the things that made me feel better around him. He never multitasked, never behaved like I was a burden to him. After spending so much of my life feeling like one, it was a nice change.

Especially as I thought about Tor, standing outside the door, who followed me around today out of obligation.

"I'm having trouble sleeping." The fact everyone kept pointing that out made me suspect I looked even worse than I realized.

He nodded, then leaned forward and rested his elbow on the desk. "You've only got about two months left. How's your end-of-year exhibit pieces coming along?"

"Not good." My shoulders drooped. I hated having to admit to failure, especially in art, which was the one thing I was supposed to be able to do.

"Why not?"

"I don't know. I just can't seem to get my head in the game. I've tried a few things, but nothing feels right." I pulled out my phone and brought up the pictures I'd taken of the pieces I'd worked on. None were finished — just rough sketches, mostly — but they gave a general idea. I handed it over to Grisham. "I keep trying, but they all feel flat."

Grisham swiped his finger across the screen, scrolling through the images. Since this was the phone the men had given me, I knew nothing weird was on the camera roll, so I didn't mind him searching all he wanted. A line appeared between his eyebrows, the expression far from happy.

Guess I was right. These suck.

"I don't know what's wrong with me," I whispered, ashamed to bring him such substandard work.

"Everyone goes through this sometimes." Grisham handed the phone back to me, leaning across the large oak desk. "It's hard to find our voices as artists. There's an entire world out there trying to shape us, to tell us what we should do, how we should act, and too often, we fall prey to it."

Boy, he found the heart of the matter there. I thought about Nem, about the Quad, about Jarrod, about the men in my life now. They all wanted something from me, all pushed me toward whatever they thought was best, and me?

I went along with it all. I might have bitched about some of it, but in the end, I did as they wanted.

Was that the problem? Was I trying to please others with my art?

"Do you know why I took you on as a mentee?"

I frowned as I thought back to when I'd first arrived, when after one of my first classes, he'd approached me about becoming my student advisor. The college usually assigned those automatically, and my first had been an old man who had scowled and hardly said a word to me. I'd jumped at the chance to have someone like Grisham help me, instead. "No," I admitted. "It seemed like such a great chance that I didn't want to risk asking why."

He chuckled, then took a hard butterscotch candy from the jar on his desk and handed it to me, as he often did when I looked stressed or upset. "I'm tenured here, and I don't teach many classes anymore, so I don't serve as a student advisor unless I volunteer. I saw the painting you did for your entry piece, the one of that woman with dark hair."

My mother. I remembered painting that, how many nights I had stayed up late, each brushstroke as freeing as it had been painful. I'd almost not turned it in, fearful that putting my mother's image out there could be dangerous, but in the end?

I couldn't ignore that the piece mattered to me.

"Often people forget the purpose of art. It's to make the audience feel something. It's manipulative in a way, but so much more honest than most of our lives are. We create things to force others to experience what we want them to. Unfortunately, artists forget this. They think it's about widespread acclaim or sales or fame. They get stuck because they stop trying to make people feel something first and foremost."

"But Professor Callos always talks about audience, about trends, about how to create something that people want." I recalled the long, boring lectures where I'd jotted down notes as Callos had turned art into a marketing class, sucking the life out of my passion.

"Professor Callos isn't an artist. He's no different than someone who pours concrete driveways for a living. Creating something doesn't make a person an artist. When I saw that painting you did, I *knew* you had what it took to be an artist, a real one. You had the passion and ability to create things that made people feel. I always go to the opening exhibit to see the work from the incoming students, but in the past, I just walked by before leaving, never even pausing to look at something more than a second or two. When I saw your painting, though? I stood there until they told me I had to leave, that they wanted to lock up." He chuckled, the sound warm, as though the memory were a cherished one.

"Why, though? I mean, I worked hard on it, but it's hardly my best work. I've learned so much since then, have made things more realistic, more detailed, more impressive. What was different about that one?"

"You *felt* as you painted that. When creating something, if you feel nothing, the audience won't, either. I could feel your pain from the brush strokes, the shorter ones used around the eyes to show your hesitation there, the spots near the bottom that are discolored — probably from when you cried and your tears landed on the canvas. You let yourself experience pain when you made that, and that pain translated through the image to me. I wanted to know you better, to understand what you'd suffered so you could portray such pain."

I swallowed hard, dropping my gaze. He was usually friendly, but this was the first time it felt like he was getting personal. Worse, he picked at a scab I knew I couldn't allow to bleed.

"Who was she?" he asked.

I couldn't tell him the truth, but denying my own mother entirely felt wrong. Instead, I offered something close enough. "She was important to me. She was murdered over a decade ago, and I miss her."

Grisham nodded, his expression soft. "I figured as much. I've seen paintings done of those who have hurt the artist, and they're done differently. Likewise, I've seen pieces done for a loved one who died that are all nostalgic nonsense. That piece drew me because of its honesty. You showed your own pain and sorrow, but you didn't make her an angel. The slight twist of her lips showed a cutting tongue and her shrewd eyes implied a very calculating woman. The darker colors showed you missed her, but also held a certain level of anger, of resentment. Those things are fascinating, and the mixture is what creates truly great artwork. Nothing in life is simple. Things are never all happy or all sad. Life is an amalgam of beauty and ugliness."

He gestured at my phone. "What you've worked on for the exhibit isn't bad. It will secure you a spot next year, but nothing more. It isn't what you're capable of, what I know you can do. It's like a world-famous chef cooking boxed mac and cheese. You can do it, and it will be fine, but it is a far, pathetic cry from what you're capable of."

His words stung, worse because I couldn't deny the truth of them.

Had I really put my heart into anything recently? Had I let myself feel anything?

I'd painted that piece of my mother after my father had died, after I'd found out that he'd killed her. It had been one of the few times I'd given myself fully over to the pain of those events, to how conflicted I felt.

My mother had loved me, but I didn't remember much about her. Between my young age when she died and how busy she had been when still alive, we hadn't spent that much time together. Sometimes I thought rather than missing her, I missed what I'd wanted out of a mother.

"Putting our wounds on display isn't easy, is it?" I whispered.

"No, it isn't. Do you know why there are few great artists? Because it is terrifying to peel our skin off and bleed on a canvas, to open that window and allow strangers in to witness the darkest parts of ourselves. Hatred, jealousy, pain, every negative emotion that we're taught to pretend we don't have? Those are the things that connect us all and make great art. If you can't tap into that, you'll be forever falling short of your potential."

I tucked my phone into my pocket, hating that I couldn't deny what he said. Sure, there were positive feelings, good things, but they weren't the full truth. The reality always was a mix of good and bad, and so much of my life had been bad that I wasn't sure if I really made the good things. I didn't know them well enough to paint them, to make people feel them.

"Well, thank you," I said and pushed myself to my feet. "I'll think about what you said and start over. Could we meet in another week to look over my progress?"

Grisham nodded, staring at me hard, his glasses making his eyes appear even larger than usual. "Of course. I'm looking forward to seeing what you come up with."

I headed for the door, but his voice made me pause just as I reached for the handle.

"I believe in you, Kenz. I wouldn't have done all I've done if I didn't know you could live up to my expectations. Stop wondering if you're good enough, if you've got it or not. Not many people have what it takes to be great, so don't doubt yourself. I don't make mistakes."

And just like that, I knew that no matter how hard it was, I couldn't let him down. I'd spent my life letting people down, falling short of those around me. My life was in chaos, my love life nonexistent, danger trailing me, missing my family, and I could do nothing about any of that.

However, I *could* do this. I understood art, and I'd damn well have this one part of my life go right.

* * * *

Tor

Kenz was unsettled. The way she avoided my gaze and fidgeted, twisting the silver rings, on her fingers made it clear.

I wasn't sure what had happened inside the office, between Kenz and her student advisor, but whatever it was, didn't seem to sit well with her.

Then again, she had a lot going on. Her entire life had changed over the course of a few weeks. She lived with four men she didn't know, virtual strangers to her, and had no freedom or privacy from us. She couldn't leave alone, couldn't go anywhere without a shadow. Danger plagued her, and she wasn't foolish enough to not know it. On top of all of that, she had an important event in school coming up.

That sort of stress would wear on a person, and the bags under her eyes said she struggled.

"Where are we going?" Kenz sat up straighter, peering around when I took a left instead of the normal right. Tension lined her features, fear bleeding into the expression.

Right. She might worry it's a threat.

I reached over and took her hand, squeezing gently to reassure her.

She let out a shaky breath, suggesting she'd understood the gesture for what it was.

I steered the car through the smaller streets. In my experience, stress was best dealt with through physical exertion. There was nothing better for sleep than a good workout, and from what I'd seen, Kenz had had little chance to work out the nervous energy inside her.

The small parking lot had many open spaces, and I pulled the car into one of them. Once I'd turned the ignition off and removed the key, I got out.

Kenz followed suit, not asking me again what we were doing. At least she didn't appear fearful. She walked beside me, trusting me as we went.

Jayce Carter

I didn't think I'd ever had a person trust me like that, someone willing to follow a man like me in the dark without knowing where we headed.

Her gaze lifted to the lit sign above the front door. "Steel Self-Defense?"

I nodded and tucked my hands into the pockets of my jacket. Through the large glass windows, a class of students worked out on the large mats inside.

I held the door open for Kenz, and when we stepped inside, the young man behind the counter smiled.

"Tor! I didn't know you'd be here today."

I nodded in acknowledgment, then scanned my card at the reader on the desk to check in.

"Who's this?" the man asked, grinning as he looked Kenz up and down.

It wasn't an appreciative look, one that made me want to warn him off. Instead, he seemed pleased that I had brought someone along with me, like an old woman thrilled her grandson *finally* brought a girl home.

I didn't think I appreciated that sort of reaction.

"My name is Kenz." Kenz put her hand out, that sweetness that was so much a part of her capable of winning over the hardest of hearts.

The man shook hands. "Tor never brings anyone. Usually, he just comes here to work out. Sometimes he'll run classes for us if we're short, but he never really spends any time around people. To be honest, I was starting to think he was antisocial."

Kenz laughed, and already some of the tension she had melted. "He's a little antisocial," she whispered as if it were a secret. "But honestly, I have no idea why I'm here."

"Sounds about like him." The man peered at the class, then back to us. "We've got back-to-back classes today, so the main floor is full. Are you wanting to join?"

I shook my head. The last thing I would allow was for Kenz to practice or spar with amateurs. She might end up hurt, and I was far from okay with that.

The man took one look at my expression and laughed. "A little protective, are we? Well, private room three is open. Why don't you use that?"

I nodded and let his comment go, because what was the point in arguing over that? Especially because he was right...

Anyone else and I would have seen sparring as a necessary risk. A stray punch or kick were part of the reality. Why then was it that imaging Kenz in such a situation made my hands clench into fists?

The man typed into his computer, the keyboard noisy as he clicked the keys. "Okay, you're all signed in. You've got the room until we close." He smirked, then added on, "and don't worry, no one will bother you."

I narrowed my eyes, then set a hand on Kenz's back to get her moving. The man was just being nosey and invasive — it was hardly reason enough to react even if I didn't care for his words.

They brought up feelings and wants that I was wholly uncomfortable with. Kenz was...

I didn't know how to finish that statement, and worse? I knew it didn't matter. How I might feel about her didn't change our reality. It didn't alter who and what I was or make any difference in the fact I had no place in her life after we finished our task.

We crossed the gym, with others nodding at me in acknowledgment as we headed toward the private rooms. I went to room three and scanned my card, the lock unlatching since the room was registered to me for the time being.

I knew these rooms quite well — often practiced in them to stay away from prying eyes.

Plus, when I worked out in the main gym, I always ended up with people trying to speak to me. It caused an awkward moment when I had to try to mime to them that I couldn't speak.

In fact, I often carried a stack of basic cards with that written on them. Still, I preferred to work out and practice without an audience unless I was actually sparing or teaching a class.

Kenz looked around the room, the mirrored walls, the padded floors, the punching bags lining the wall. She didn't appear freaked out by any of it.

Then again, I recalled how she'd dealt with that man who had grabbed her before. Clearly, she'd taken some self-defense in the past. Anymore, it was common for women to take a class or two for their own protection. I had to guess she'd done so.

Kenz gestured down at herself. "I don't think I'm really dressed for any of this."

I let my gaze skim along her body, pressing my lips together when I realized what she meant. She wore a long black skirt with a lace overlay, paired with a crop-top, long-sleeved shirt. I'd grown so used to how she dressed that it hadn't even occurred to me.

I also try hard not to notice how she looks in such things.

I held one finger up before heading out to the front.

When I came back, I handed her the workout clothing I'd bought from the man at the desk. They didn't have a lot to choose from, but they had enough to work for today.

Kenz took the clothing, a sigh as if she knew she couldn't get out of whatever I had planned now.

I turned my back, facing the door to give her privacy. I expected her to complain, to ask about the locker rooms, but to my surprise she didn't.

She must have gotten used to having a security detail enough to realize semi-public places like that were best to avoid when possible.

The rustle of clothing behind me made my pulse speed. I hadn't started to work out, but I suspected I'd already hit my heart rate goal.

Despite the way I told myself not to react, not to think about it, my brain had other ideas. It supplied a fantasy of Kenz standing there, naked, so close that I could turn around and be on her in a heartbeat.

Would she push me away?

Would she flinch? Would she show fear?

I stared down at my hands, which appeared clean, but I knew better than to believe that. I shouldn't touch a girl like her, not with hands that had done the things mine had.

"Okay, I'm decent." Kenz's voice came out shy, and why did I find even that charming?

I turned to find her bent forward, lacing the sneakers I'd grabbed for her. When she rose, I considered strangling the man behind the counter.

I hadn't looked closely at what he'd given me, just paying the cost without much thought. Since there weren't a lot of options, it wasn't as though I had many choices.

Clearly, I should have paid *far* more attention.

Kenz was in a pair of black workout shorts that left all of nothing to the imagination. They were snug around her, high waisted so they stopped right at her belly button, and went to her mid-thigh. On top, she had a black and pink sports bra-top that might have been a bit too tight, given the way it created enough cleavage to make a young boy drool. The bra didn't stop just below her bust, instead with another few inches of fabric, meaning it functioned as a crop top as well. It left a small strip of skin between the shorts and top exposed, which wasn't that different from her previous outfit. Perhaps the skin-tight fabric made this feel so much more...naked.

"There's a sweater here too, but I'll be too hot if I wear that." She showed no signs of being uncomfortable in so little, no embarrassment about it.

Was it because she often wore clothing that exposed quite a bit of her or was it that she didn't view me as a man? Perhaps she saw me as a friend, as someone she didn't need to consider such things around?

I pulled in a deep breath to center myself, to remind me that I had more than enough self-control to deal with this.

I took her sweater along with the clothes she took off and put them into the bag I'd also gotten from the front desk. I set it near the door, then put our phones on top, her purse beside it.

Having a phone when working out like this was foolish. I'd shattered more than my fair share of screens before realizing that conversing via text during sparing was foolish.

However, a whiteboard on the wall with a dry erase marker on a chain next to it placed just for me showed why I used this room.

"So we're going to work out?" she asked.

I went to the large whiteboard, taking the marker in my hand.

You seem stressed. I thought some basic self-defense would help you relax.

A smile played across her lips. "You really read me well, huh?"

I take it your meeting didn't go well?

"I wouldn't say that. He gave me the advice I needed, but knowing what I *need* to do is different than being sure I can." Her own doubts hung heavy on the words.

It was something I'd noticed with her. She had little faith in herself. She didn't trust herself or her decisions. Why?

From what I'd seen, she was responsible and reliable. What had happened in her past to make her so afraid of herself? How had she gained so little confidence?

I could have kept going with the writing, but if she wanted conversation, I wasn't the best for that. Instead, I moved away from the whiteboard for the main purpose.

* * * *

An hour later and I had *no* question about whether or not the girl had been trained. She astounded me over and over again, countering my moves with the ease of someone who had practiced it many times.

She wasn't up to my skill level, of course, but she proved she could hold her own against most people who would want to grab her.

Just who taught her this?

I had to guess it was those bodyguards she spoke about so fondly. She claimed they were like brothers, but I couldn't stop a certain level of distaste. Too often women thought men around them saw them that way only to later find out it wasn't the case at all.

Was that the truth here?

I grabbed her from behind, wrapping my arm around her and pulling her against my chest. Touching her felt strange, still, but at least doing it this way meant I had rules, guidelines.

Kenz reacted beautifully. She didn't panic, didn't struggle mindlessly the way most people did. She remained calm even with me that close, with my larger size and strength restraining her. Kenz grabbed my arm and shifted forward, dropping her center of gravity to throw off my balance. When I was forced to readjust, she used the moment to twist and rolled me forward.

I flipped, my back striking the padded floors, forcing the air from my lungs.

Impressive. I'd expected her to stomp my foot, to drive her elbow into my stomach, even to bite my arm. Instead, she'd managed to put me on my back.

Except, it seemed she wasn't finished, yet. She didn't release my arm, twisting it but not so far as to harm my joint. It forced me to roll to take the stress off my shoulder—her exact plan, since she took advantage of that by sitting on my back and pinning my wrist to my mid-back.

"It's been too long since I've gotten to do this," she admitted with a breathy laugh.

She couldn't see my face, so I allowed myself to grin at her tone. How often did I have fun with anyone?

Still, I wasn't about to let her win. A man had his pride, after all, and she'd proven she wasn't some fragile thing who needed to be treated carefully.

I dug my toes into the mats for leverage, then shifted my hips to the side opposite of where she had my arm pinned. The last thing I wanted to risk was getting my shoulder dislocated because she accidentally yanked it the wrong way.

Sure enough, she released my wrist to avoid harming me. *Sweet girl.* I turned enough to grab her arm, then maneuvered her light weight easily. It would have been far harder to do this sort of thing with a full-grown man, but Kenz couldn't weigh more than one-ten or so.

I flipped us, pinning her on her back below me. She lifted one leg, no doubt to wrap it around my waist and regain her upper hand. However, after an hour of doing this, I knew her strengths and weaknesses.

She was flexible and had amazing leg strength. She wasn't vicious, which meant her punches were all of useless, but she managed throws and take-downs with ease.

I avoided the leg, then moved my knees to outside her thighs, trapping her biggest weapons. Afterward, I grasped both her wrists and pinned them to the mats, rendering her helpless.

I smirked down at her, knowing I enjoyed this *far* too much. It had been for her, to cheer her up and ease her burdens, but somewhere along the way, I'd ended up having a great time myself.

Except, when I stared at her face, my breath caught.

She panted hard, sweat on her forehead, a few strands of her hair that had escaped from her braid sticking to her skin. We were *so* close. When we hadn't been face-to-face, it had felt more like sparing, but like this?

It felt like lovers.

I waited for her to snap at me, to tell me to get off her, to lecture me for taking things too far.

I deserved that. I'd do it, moving away, offering an awkward apology for losing focus.

Except...she didn't.

Her pupils grew wider and her pink tongue darted out, running across her bottom lip. She shifted her legs, her thighs rubbing against each other, the action impossible to see as anything other than what it was.

She's turned on...

Two sides of me warred in that moment.

The smart part of me, the civilized and thoughtful part wanted to shove away from Kenz. It screamed that I should put distance between us, that this was just a reaction to stress and the difficult place she was in. She'd been forced into relying on four men without fully understanding just how dangerous we were, how terrible.

Of course she'd cling to us, would see the best in us. She had no other choice. It was a basic survival skill, to grow close to those who control our fates.

Except, the other part of me wanted to push more. The sight of her tongue and her damp lips drew me in, made me crave a taste of her. I wanted to spread her thighs around my hips and grind against her, to hear her moan and gasp for me.

I wanted to see her experience pleasure, to have her fall apart beneath me, to witness her first time having a man take her to the depths and heights of what she could feel.

And I knew I could do just that. She was so honest that I had zero doubts I could get her there, that I could please her.

Don't you dare!

I was a monster, but even after all the terrible things I'd done, I didn't think I could bring myself to look in a mirror if I took advantage of her here.

Kenz leaned up, her lips nearing mine, her eyes drifting closed. All I had to do was not move and it wouldn't even be my fault, right?

Red covered my vision, as though the blood of all those people I'd killed rolled through my mind.

I flattened my hands against the mats and shoved myself upright, moving away before she made contact. I hopped to my feet, catching a glimpse of hurt on her face as she opened her eyes.

She should realize how lucky she was that I thought clearly enough for the both of us. I had to trust time would show that.

I went to turn, to wrap up for the day, when my gaze landed on her stomach.

The hem of her crop top had ridden up, but it wasn't lust that hit me. Instead, the sight of damaged skin struck me, a gnarled scar there that I easily recognized.

Live the life I had, kill as many people as I had, and certain wounds were impossible to forget. The biggest among them? The telltale mark from a bullet wound.

The scarring there on her side said Kenz had gotten shot, and that the bullet could have easily taken her life.

Just what the hell had she been up to?

Chapter Sixteen

Kenz

Talk about awkward...

I'd say that Tor didn't speak to me the whole way back to the house, but that was pretty much normal. It wasn't his silence, but the *way* he remained silent. He never spoke, but it normally had a level of comfort. I always had the feeling I could speak if I wanted, that he was ready to listen.

That wasn't the vibe after he'd spotted the scar on me. He'd stared, his gaze locked on the mark even as I'd rushed to pull down the fabric and hide it. The embarrassment I'd suffered when he'd soundly rejected me had dissipated at his expression, at the reminder of the wound I'd suffered.

He'd tossed me the sweater, then waited until I'd put it on. His mood had soured so badly that even the friendly man behind the counter didn't seem all the chummy as we'd walked out.

That same mood had continued in the dark car, a heaviness that made it clear conversation was *not* welcome. It also suggested this topic was far from over.

Once inside, Tor handed me the bag that had my clothing in it, then pointed toward the stairs. His expression made me want to take a step backward.

It was strange. I *knew* Tor was dangerous. He reminded me of Colton, of someone not only well acquainted with death but comfortable with it. Maybe my own twisted upbringing meant I found comfort in that.

When I'd met nice guys, I'd felt nothing. Even when people laughed with me, when they told me to go for it because some guy who hit on me seemed sweet and rich and funny and whatever else, I'd experienced no spark. If anything, they made me uncomfortable, always waiting for some dark truth beneath that nice façade.

Maybe that was why I got along with these men — they were honest, at least.

However, Tor's entire vibe had changed. Instead of some silent guardian, I was faced with the expression of a hardened killer. This didn't feel like the same man I'd sparred with, the one who listened quietly when I spoke, who sat beside me and made me feel less alone.

I didn't take the step back, though. This was just another face of the same man.

So instead, I nodded and headed for my room. No doubt they'd all chitchat together, gossiping about what Tor had seen and what it might mean. I'd bet I had a long damned time before I could hope to get to sleep.

Instead of letting myself stress about it, however, I figured I might as well get comfortable. Once I reached my room, I picked out my most comfortable pajamas and ran a hot shower.

I'd worked up quite the sweat from sparring with Tor. Washing it all off would make me feel slightly better — at least, I hoped so.

The scent of my fancy shampoo soothed my nerves as I fell into the familiar motions of washing my hair. I scrubbed the massaging bar of soap over my muscles, knowing that come tomorrow, I'd feel it.

Tor had been careful not to go too hard, not to injure me. If anything, he'd been far more cautious than Rune was. Rune hadn't minded leaving me with bruises if it taught me a lesson, if it got me to move faster and react better. Tor, however, didn't seem nearly so tolerant about marks on me.

Still, even with that, I'd feel it tomorrow. It had been far too long since I'd exerted myself so much, and getting thrown to the ground would shake a person up no matter how gentle their opponent tried to be.

Yet…as I rinsed the lather from me, I had to admit that Tor's plan had worked. The exhaustion that had hung on me was still there, but it seemed that I could close my eyes and sleep for once. Some of that nervous energy that had bounced around inside me had lessened, as though I'd worked them out during Tor and my practice.

In fact, I had a feeling that if we worked out whatever discomfort sat between us, I'd ask him to do it again. I'd always enjoyed practicing with Rune, had even liked the few times Jarrod had worked with me while I'd stayed with him. There was this power that came from feeling as if I could defend myself.

Of course, given Tor's reaction at the end, I had no idea if he'd be willing.

The memory of how he'd pulled back when I'd tried to kiss me made my cheeks burn in a way that had nothing to do with the hot water or steam.

Well, even if he didn't want to practice with me, there was no reason I couldn't work on my own. Rune had taught me how to keep my body fit, what exercises were most important, how to train myself. Maybe it was time to take some responsibility for myself and make my physical health a priority.

I shaved, taking my time to drag the razor over my legs, under my arms, even my public hair. The shaving cream helped the razor glide over my skin, though it reminded me I really needed to exfoliate sometime soon.

A soft laugh bubbled up from my chest as I thought about Hayden standing beside me at the store, trying to figure out what a sugar scrub was.

By the time I'd finished everything, I had a feeling my time limit had expired. If I remained in here any longer, there was a good chance someone would end up dragging me out.

Or not. So far, only Vance had shown any interest in me, and that had been more about me being convenient than because he wanted me at all. I had a feeling the others would do about anything to make sure they didn't see me naked.

Maybe that's the trick. I just need to walk around naked and they won't bother me anymore.

The idea had merit, but I knew damn well I wasn't confident enough to try that. Nem would pull it off, no doubt. I was pretty sure she could host a meeting with the heads of every large crime syndicate in the country and being naked wouldn't cause her to even blink.

She was tougher than I was, though, and setting myself against her only forced me to acknowledge it.

I slid on my pajamas after drying off. They were old, now, but they mattered to me. I'd rarely gotten to see the Quad during the years after my mother's death, but they'd visited occasionally, when they could swing it based on their other jobs.

Bray had come to the small village where one of my many boarding schools had been. My father had ended up putting me in ones in small towns, since he thought I could get into less trouble than in the bigger cities. Bray had shown up out of the blue and signed me out for a day.

I doubted my father had put him on the records, but Bray could hack any computer system, so he had probably just added himself. He'd taken me for ice cream and listened as I'd rambled.

Bray had never been much of a talker, not one who made a point of having deep conversations, but he'd never failed to listen. I'd said I hated it there, that I wanted to come home, to them all, that I was tired of being alone.

He'd said nothing as he'd listened, as he'd let me pour out all my worries. When I'd finished, he'd patted me on the head and told me to follow him. I trusted him enough that I didn't even care where we were going. I'd have followed him anywhere, knowing if he was with me, I was safe.

We went to a small store full of comfortable clothing, the sort of things girls liked to wear when they had nothing special planned. Looking back, it made me want to laugh. Bray was hopeless when it came to feelings, so it wasn't a shock that he had no idea how to respond with words.

Besides, he was in a hard place anyway. He couldn't do anything about my problems. He was bound to my father, to obey him, which meant he was as trapped as I was.

So instead of empty promises he couldn't keep, or telling me to suck it up, telling me it would get better, he'd taken me to a shop and bought me anything I looked at. When I'd gone back to my dorm room, I'd buried my face against the soft fabric of the pajamas as if those were a sense of home. From that point on, they always made me feel as though I had a home, that I had a family that cared about me no matter how alone I felt.

Suddenly, I knew I needed that feeling, and when I put on the pajamas, I had that same sense that I wasn't alone.

My last task was to braid my hair back after towel drying it. I secured the bottom with a tie, then looked into the mirror.

Yeah, no wonder everyone asks if I'm sleeping well.

The dark circles under my eyes were the kind that people working graveyard shifts had. Maybe I'd luck out and manage sleep tonight.

"Kenz?" Hayden's voice floated through the door, into my little haven that was the steam-filled bathroom, breaking the peace.

"Time to face the music," I muttered before twisting the handle and opening the door.

If I had any question if Tor had ratted me out, Hayden's severe expression told me. I plastered a forced smile on my lips, pretending I had no idea what was going on. "Did I take too long? Sorry, but this house has the hottest water and the best pressure I've felt since moving to Florida."

Hayden didn't even smile back. So much for a nice little conversation. "Come on, let's talk."

"Right." I followed him down the long hallway, surprised at how not-worried I was.

Yet again, I'd faced off against the Quad. I'd survived interrogations from them since I was old enough to talk. These four couldn't break me, especially as I got to know them more and more. They might act tough—and don't get me wrong, they *were* tough—but they'd proven they wouldn't hurt me.

When we reached the living room, I had a moment of déjà vu, recalled when they'd questioned me about the contents of my safe. They all sat in the room, waiting, nailing me with hard, loaded looks as soon as I stepped into the room.

And for a moment, I regretted my clothing choice. There I was still damp from a shower, in a thin tank top and a pair of baggy cotton pants while the four men were fully dressed. Even the fact they wore shoes while I was barefoot set up the dichotomy of our power.

Instead of letting them see that, though, I sat on the couch beside Char and folded my legs beneath me. No one spoke at first, but I endured the discomfort from that.

I will not break first.

As usual, Hayden spoke first. "Let me see."

"See what?"

He narrowed his eyes, a rare show of temper. I guessed that proved how serious he found this. His tone brooked no argument. He wouldn't accept me just saying no, so one way or another, he'd get a look at the scar.

Which meant showing was a better option than having them force me—which I was sure they'd do, next.

I sighed and leaned back, gripping the hem of my shirt and lifting it. I tore my gaze from his, hating exposing myself so much.

In fact, a part of me wondered if I wouldn't have been more comfortable flashing every part of me to them rather than letting them see that scar.

Hayden kneeled in front of me, and I jumped when his fingertips brushed my bare skin, to the edge of the mark.

"Easy," Hayden said, his voice carefully soft. It wasn't the same coaxing, sweet voice he used normally, the one when he smiled at me. Instead, this came across forced, as if he used it to smother something deeper. He didn't pull back, tracing the edges of the scar. He set a hand on my shoulder and pressed me forward, finding the exit wound on the back, following the same manner he'd used at the front.

I shivered at his touch, feeling as though he tore open the wound.

"This is about a year old, right?"

I nodded.

"I'm surprised it isn't better healed. With all the lotions and beauty products you use, I figured you would have used scar ointments to make it fade faster."

I swallowed hard, unsure how much to say, afraid to open my mouth and let the truth tumble out.

I hadn't realized just how hard it would be to show anyone this. Only Jarrod had seen the wound, in the weeks after my injury, when he'd taken care of me. He and Sasha, the nurse and the woman he was now with, had watched over me while I'd healed, keeping the wound clean and helping me with the many tasks I couldn't do on my own.

Not even Nem or the Quad had seen it. I had the feeling Nem had wanted to, but if anyone understood privacy, it was her, so she'd never asked.

And now I have these four getting a front-row seat to the most painful part of my life.

Hayden sighed softly. "If you didn't use any ointment, you must have wanted the scar to stay. Why?"

"It's a reminder."

"Of what?"

"That life is short, and people will betray you if you give them the chance."

Hayden didn't pull away, his fingers still touching me, but he shifted back enough to look into my face. "What happened?"

"You've seen it. You all wouldn't be sitting here like I broke curfew if you didn't already know exactly what it was."

"Are you really giving us attitude right now?" Char snapped. "This is the time when a smart person realizes they've fucked up and try to do damage control."

"Yeah, well, maybe I'm not that smart, then. Or maybe you're asking stupid questions. Clearly, I was shot. What more do you need to know?"

Vance spoke, his voice tight and angry. "We did a thorough background check on you, and nowhere in it was there a hospital stay for an injury like that. Either your records are wrong or it was hidden from them. No matter which, it seems like you've got a lot of secrets."

I sighed, then shifted back enough to get Hayden's fingers off me. They reminded me of the scar, making it harder to force my brain to work, to come up with something plausible.

I'd known when Bray and Jarrod had set up my false identity that the scar was an issue. I couldn't exactly add 'shot by father' into my medical record and expect people wouldn't take notice. Something like that would draw too much attention, and since all gunshot wounds were reported, having it in my file would open us to scrutiny.

So instead, we'd left it off.

Leave it to these four to see through that lie.

"Does it really matter?" I asked.

"Of course it does." Hayden remained on his knees in front of me, and when I risked meeting his gaze, I regretted the choice immediately.

He was too close, his expression showing the volatile emotions inside him. He might be good at hiding them, at keeping them from boiling over, at behaving calmly, but I saw them deep in his eyes.

"You should have told me," he pressed. "It's my job to keep you safe, and a serious injury like this is the sort of thing I should be made aware of. What if you were hurt, and I had no idea that you had previous trauma there? What if you froze or panicked when faced with a gun because of that, and I was unable to predict it because I didn't know about this? Jesus, Kenz, do you really think none of us would care about something like this?"

"It's just a bullet wound," I argued, ignoring how incredibly stupid that statement was. "Let's be honest, here. At least half of you have probably been shot as well! Hayden, there's no way you haven't at least been grazed, and Tor? You think I didn't see the scar on your left arm? You all didn't tell me about that, so why do you think I had to disclose anything to you?"

"Because *we* are responsible for you, not the other way around," Hayden said before rising to his feet, his steps heavy and angry. "Besides, that sort of thing is expected in our line of work. For a civilian kid of your age to suffer through it is different. We expect boxers are going to get black eyes, but if I see one on a housewife, I'm going to have questions. So what happened?"

Him asking opened the flood gates, allowing the memory I'd tried to lock away to come back and roll over me, crushing me.

I recalled the way my father had swung the gun from Nem to me. It wasn't that I'd wanted him to shoot her, but realizing he cared so little for me?

It hurt. Kyler hadn't been the best father, but I'd still believed until the very end that he gave a damn about me, that he loved me. Maybe he'd been bad at showing it, but I'd still trusted that the love was there, that he did his best.

And with the squeezing of a trigger, he'd shattered that security.

My chest tightened to the point that an all-too-familiar dizziness came over me when I couldn't draw enough oxygen.

Great. A panic attack.

They happened from time to time. Less than right after it had happened, but leave it to these men to spark one. All those fears, those questions, that pain that I'd buried bubbled back up, like sewage coming up from broken pipes in a yard.

I leaned forward, trying to put my head between my knees like one of the therapists had taught me. My thoughts swirled, rough and too fast to come to terms with, to understand.

Mostly, it was a string of words, just hateful things that Kyler had tattooed on my psyche over the years. *Useless. Stupid. Naïve. A burden.*

I was only worth as much as someone could sell me for.

My head hurt, and it felt like the world dimmed around the edges. Even the sounds of the room felt far away, like I heard them from underwater.

Something touched my lips, forcing past them. A finger? Before I could make sense of it, cold water poured into my mouth, then a hand covered my mouth and tipped my head backward.

I swallowed, unable to resist, even my tight throat unable to stop the action. The cold water calmed the panic, and I found myself enveloped by warmth and strength.

Exhaustion made it impossible to fight. Hell, I didn't *want* to fight. I didn't want to hide or struggle or work so damned hard anymore. It all hurt too much.

So instead I let the strong body hold me, the world too heavy and his comfort too tempting for me to resist anymore.

Vance

Kenz was lighter than she should have been. In fact, I was pretty sure she was lighter than she had been when she'd first gotten here. It had only been a few weeks, but if I had to guess, she'd lost about ten pounds.

At least she was breathing, now.

The memory of her going pale, of those gasping, choking noises coming from her... I had no doubts they'd haunt my nightmares for a while yet.

"I guess we don't have to wonder why she has those anxiety meds," Char said, his tone unusually kind. Normally he snapped and insulted everyone unless he played one of his parts, yet that was oddly absent right now.

Maybe he was just as shaken as the rest of us.

It had taken a little time for the pill I'd forced into her mouth to take effect, but finally, she'd started to relax. Slowly, the muscles had unknitted and she'd breathed evenly.

She also cuddled against me tighter, nuzzling her cheek against my chest as though she couldn't get close enough.

In any other position, it would have been adorable.

"I'm thirsty," she whispered, my sweater muffling her words.

I caught her chin, tipping her face up toward me. She hid nothing as she stared back, her eyes impossibly wide. Hell, she reminded me of a cartoon fawn. "What was that?"

"I'm thirsty," she repeated. It surprised me, since in her time with us, she'd rarely asked for anything. Normally, she was so aware of others, of what they needed, but she never relied on any of us unless she had no other choice.

If she wasn't high off her ass from the sedative, she would have likely gotten up to get herself whatever she wanted before she'd ever ask for help.

"What do you want?"

She pursed her lips, as though I'd asked her a master level math question. "Hot chocolate."

"You sure that's a good idea? What about your blood sugar?"

She pouted, as though she'd just remembered and I had crushed her dreams by reminding her.

Tor clapped once, then gave me a thumbs-up, telling me he had it handled.

"Oh, whipped cream, too!" she called out, over my shoulder, toward the kitchen. She gasped, as though she'd just had an epiphany. "And sprinkles!" She crawled closer, moving into my lap like a cat seeking warmth. "Bray always added sprinkles. My dad told him he was spoiling me, so Bray would put the sprinkles in his pocket, then after he got to my room, he'd add the sprinkles just before he handed it to me."

"Who's Bray?"

"My bodyguard." She crawled off my lap, moving to the other side of the couch, her motions uncoordinated. It was only a quick grab from me that kept her from toppling right off the couch and onto the hard floor.

She'd passed the slightly out of it stage of drugs and was in the 'entirely fucked up' phase of it, now.

I looked past her to Hayden, a question in my eyes. We had quite the opportunity here, didn't we?

He pressed his lips together, but that didn't shock me. Hayden was surprisingly honorable given what we were doing.

Still, when would we get a chance like this again? The pill had loosened her tongue, and this might be our only chance to find out the truth about her. Sure, drugging someone to question them wasn't the noblest of choices, but wasn't that better than continuing to go into this blind?

Kenz let out a high-pitched sound that could have come from a six-year-old, making me jump. She clapped, and another quick save kept her from toppling off the couch.

And boy did Tor look strange with that smile on his lips. It seemed Kenz could tame even the surliest of men. He had a large green mug in his hands with a swirl of whipped cream on the top.

Kenz reached for the drink, and I wrapped my hands around hers because if I didn't, I was pretty sure the night would end with us trying to clean hot cocoa off…well, everything.

Tor reached into his pocket and pulled out an empty packet for sugar-free cocoa, showing it to Kenz and me.

I chuckled at the soft-hearted bastard. Since he'd known about it, I could only guess he'd been the one to get it.

"Thank you." Kenz smiled widely before leaning forward and taking a sip. I tipped the cup, ensuring she didn't pour it down her front. When she lifted her head, she had some whipped cream stuck to her top lip.

How was it that she could be even cuter than before?

Hayden spoke softly to Char, lowering his voice so Kenz didn't catch the words. "You're better at questioning. You do it."

Char showed no signs of hesitation as he nodded. Of course, he was one of the most morally ambiguous men between us, so the idea of questioning a drugged woman probably didn't bother him much.

Char came over and sat on the coffee table just in front of Kenz and me. He smiled, the false one that could charm anyone.

It was one reason I got along with Char better than Hayden or Tor. Char and I were similar, both more than willing to put on a mask to get what we wanted.

"Hey there, Kenz."

She frowned, as if she didn't care for something he'd said. She lifted her gaze from her drink to Char, giving him a glare. "I don't like you like this."

"Like what?"

"Nice."

Funny enough, he didn't seem bothered about the ethics of questioning her like this yet he was taken back by her words.

"What do you mean? I thought you said you didn't like when I was mean."

She removed one hand from the mug, and thankfully I held it or it would have spilled everywhere. She dragged her finger through the whipped cream then licked it off, the motion nowhere close to sensual. "I like when you're honest. Sure, it'd be nice if you *wanted* to be nice to me, but I'd rather you be mean than you be fake. I don't like when you call me Kenz, either."

"No? What do you want me to call you, then?"

"I like when you call me 'kitten'."

Char remained silent for a moment before he chuckled, this time the laugh sounding real as opposed to that fake one from before. "Okay then, kitten. Will you tell me what happened? How you got hurt?"

He didn't use the word shot, but that was probably on purpose. While the meds Kenz had taken would take the edge off her, they wouldn't entirely prevent another panic attack.

Some of that childish humor she'd had disappeared. She curled her shoulders in, seeming to want to make herself as small as possible. It broke my heart, which I didn't think I could even experience anymore.

"It hurt. I didn't think it would, because people always said getting shot didn't hurt right away. They said they were surprised and sometimes didn't notice at all." She sighed, then brought another finger covered in whipped cream to her mouth. "Maybe that just proves that I'm not as good as everyone else, because it hurt. Even though I was in shock, it hurt more than anything I've felt before. And healing wasn't much better."

Char tilted his head, his shrewd eyes taking in each detail. Then again, this was where he shone. He read people easily and knew exactly what to give them to get what he wanted. "How did it happen? Who did it?"

The pain in her eyes made me wish we could have not asked. I wanted to pull her back into my arms and call the whole thing off. It felt like when she'd seen my hand, when I'd wanted nothing more than to take it all back.

Except, as it turned out, she was a better person than me. Where she hadn't asked me any questions, hadn't pried even though I was certain she wanted to know about my hand, I was here forcing the answers from her.

Still, her being a better person than me wasn't something that was ever in question, so I let the question stand, waiting for Kenz to answer.

"My father," Kenz whispered.

The violence in the room skyrocketed. I wasn't a man who knew much about violence, hadn't been the sort to settle things with my fists, yet even I felt it in the air.

"What?" Hayden asked when no one seemed to know what to say.

Kenz nodded. "My dad did it."

"On accident?"

"No. He pointed it at me and pulled the trigger."

I'd had my share of issues with family, but this was on a whole different level. I couldn't imagine any parent willing to kill their own child, but knowing Kenz, it seemed even more impossible. How could anyone choose to hurt her? Especially someone who was supposed to take care of her?

Suddenly, Kenz's lack of self-esteem, her desire not to be a burden made more sense, given the person who should have looked out for her had failed to do so.

No one asked more questions, probably because what the fuck was a person supposed to say after something like that?

Kenz leaned against my arm, resting her head against my shoulder. "He never saw me as important. I didn't realize it, because he was my dad, and I wanted to see him how I wanted to. I wanted to be Daddy's Little Girl, I guess. He realized he wouldn't get to use me, that I couldn't benefit him, that he couldn't bend me to his will. Since I wasn't useful to him, I guess he didn't need me anymore."

"What happened after that?"

"He was killed."

"Why do the records show he died in a car crash?"

She blinked slowly. I would have normally guessed that was due to a lie, but she seemed too drugged to come up with one. Hell, she was a terrible liar even when sober—I doubted she had any chance right now. Instead, she must have reacted strangely because she was nearly out. "It's easier to fake a death than to face the truth."

She'd said he was killed, not that she'd killed him.

"Who killed him?" I asked.

She didn't respond, and I twisted to find her eyes closed, her breathing even. It seemed the meds had let her pass out.

At least that means she might get some good sleep for once.

I shifted, moving her head into my lap so she was more comfortable as I handed the rest of her drink to Char. Kenz wrapped an arm around my leg, grasping me as if afraid I'd get away.

"The bodyguards?" Hayden asked.

Char nodded. "That's my guess. She said they were like brothers. If her father shot her, I can't imagine that the men she talked about would just let it go."

"So they killed him, faked his death to ensure she got all the financial help. If the law got involved in the case, it would probably take a lot of that away from her. It'd be easier to just make it all go away," Hayden agreed. "I've never had a client that I've seen grow up like that, but when I've seen it with others? They become like family."

I stared down at Kenz and stroked my hand over her head. When I'd first seen her, I'd assumed a lot about her. I'd thought her a spoiled rich kid who had never suffered a day in her life. I'd figured she'd fall for me immediately, that I'd bed her for fun and we'd go our own way when it was all over.

How wrong I'd been...

She was kinder than I'd thought, tougher than I'd known, and she'd suffered in a way she appeared too fragile to survive.

And despite how badly I wanted my revenge, a competing desire grew inside me.

I wanted to ensure this girl never had to suffer again.

Chapter Seventeen

Kenz

I felt alive for the first time since this had all started. It was probably because I'd actually slept.

Not just an hour or two—I'd been out, sleeping deeply, for about thirteen hours. Those pills really did work wonders.

Other than how they loosen my tongue.

The meds made time feel as though it moved quicker, helping to settle my mind and panic attacks, but they also let me keep my memories.

"Are you all right?" Hayden asked from the driver's seat of his car, me seated in the passenger spot.

"Yep. I just miss alcohol."

He frowned but didn't remove his gaze from the road. I'd found he was overly careful when he drove me anywhere, as though I was precious cargo that he worried about. "What do you mean?"

"At least if I get blackout drunk, I don't have to remember what I did." I sank down in the seat, folding my arms across my chest and staring out the other way.

"I'm sorry you're feeling embarrassed, but I'm not sorry you were honest for once. I need to understand you to protect you properly."

"Yeah, well, when *you* display all your worst memories and moments to everyone else, I'll take your word on that. As far as I see it, you all aren't telling me much of anything, either. So until you start tearing off scabs, I'm going to go ahead and tell you that I don't need your advice." Sure, I knew my words were sharp, that I came across like a shrew, but my feelings were too bruised to soften my tone.

I'd grown used to others having the upper hand, but this time, it bothered me. I didn't like *these* men knowing that terrible part of my life, for them to know my own father hadn't loved me.

If he can't, how could anyone else?

Why did I care if they knew that? Why did that hurt so much more than I expected it to? Why were they suddenly that important to me? When I couldn't come up with an answer, I sighed.

Hayden said nothing else about the conversation. Then again, there was nothing else I wanted to hear about it. Each time I thought about it, that I recalled what happened, that I experienced that flash of pain from the worst moment of my life, if felt like Hayden dug a needle into the wound.

He turned the car down another road, the city passing by us as I tried to ignore where we were headed. I didn't want to think about what might happen, about what rested at the end of this trip.

Our meeting with Bradley about Lorien.

So far, I'd understood the danger, knew the risk against me, but it had been something without shape or form. It had been dark shadows reaching toward me, shifting and unknowable. After today, though, I'd at least have a voice to put with my own personal monster.

"I'll keep you safe." Hayden's voice came out strong as he pulled into the small faculty parking lot at the University. He said it with so much confidence that it was impossible not to believe him, not to trust that he could do so.

And I did trust him, but I knew better than most that it didn't matter how good a person's security was — there were always holes in it. The Quad had made sure to teach me that.

"I know," I told him as the car pulled to a stop.

"Then why do you look so nervous?"

"Shouldn't I be? I mean, this feels like such a culmination of what's going on. After everything that's happened, this is the first real step toward the end we've taken."

"Well, if we keep at it, you'll be able to get back to your real life soon."

"Real life, huh?" The words rested like bitterness on my tongue. I thought back to my days before them, when I'd worked on my art and gotten hassled by Nem and the Quad.

Was that real life? Avoiding anyone who might form a connection with me? Driving myself hard but with no real view of where I wanted to go or what I wanted to do?

I'd never felt bad about my life before, but it didn't look nearly as shiny right now. In fact, the very idea of leaving that house, of returning to my big empty apartment made my palms sweat. I didn't want to wake up to an empty place, to eat dinner alone.

Hayden got out of the car, but I waited as he'd instructed. He walked around, then opened my door for me. Given the higher risk factor involved here, he'd made sure to lecture me over breakfast about remaining right at his side. He'd even given me my gun—a surprise because I'd figured he wouldn't trust me enough for that.

Of course, he'd said the same thing the Quad always had, that if anything happened, if things went wrong, for me to run and not look back. No matter what, I was to escape, to go to our meeting point and wait. The one thing I was not to do was fight back unless it was to save my own life. Otherwise?

They wanted me to run.

I'd heard that my whole life. I recalled Colton's serious expression as he'd told me, when I'd been so small that I had to climb to get into my bed, that my job was to survive. Maybe a child that young shouldn't have had to worry about such things, but my life had never been normal. In our world, if we waited too long to tell people that, they might die in the meantime.

I'd been protected all my life, had others willing to use themselves as shields, all because of my name and my bloodline. Even Nem had done what she did not because of *me* but because she was my sister.

Had a single person given a damn about me because of me?

"Chin up," Hayden whispered. "Don't let people see you sweat."

I swallowed hard then followed his advice. He was right.

Even if I hated my name, my family, my blood, that didn't erase any of it. I came from some badass people, and though if I'd fallen far short of them, I could stand tall against anyone else.

We entered the large faculty building that housed offices for professors and staff at the school. In addition, they had conference rooms for meetings, which was the exact reason we'd come.

Given how the school wanted to keep Vance close, they'd been only too happy to offer him a room for a meeting when he asked. I didn't love bringing trouble here, but from a security point of view, it made sense.

We had campus police, which meant making a move here would be foolish. Plus, I knew every inch of this school, giving us the home field advantage. Tor and Char had watched over the building for a few hours before the meeting, to ensure nothing happened, and Vance called Bradley to give him the location just before the meeting time.

So far, everything had gone smoothly.

And boy does that make me suspicious.

I entered the room that Vance had given us the information for to find the man himself already there. Vance sat at the large table, his phone set on top, screen up as if to make sure he didn't miss anything.

His expression softened when he saw me.

It wasn't affection, I was sure. Rather, I was integral to their plan. I was necessary. If something happened to me, they'd have no leverage to draw Lorien out.

I dropped my gaze, unwilling to look at him. It was too uncomfortable, between the stress of the meeting and the memories of the night before. Plus, we hadn't really spoken much, not since I saw his hand. My gaze moved to that right hand of his, as though I could see beneath the gloves again.

He moved his hand down, to his lap, the action subtle as though not to draw attention to it.

I opened my mouth to apologize but shut it just as quickly. Sure, I'd been rude, but I had a feeling he'd hate me bringing it up — especially in front of Hayden — even more. It would only be for me, so I kept it to myself.

Hayden pulled the chair out beside Vance, then gestured for me to take it. I sat, and Hayden took the spot to my other side, closing me in between the two men.

It let me breathe more easily, their scents familiar and calming.

"He on his way?" Hayden asked.

"Yep. I gave him the location for the receptionist and left the room information there. Receptionist just called me to tell me he's on his way here. No word from Tor or Char, so he must be alone."

Everything was right on schedule, but that only made me tense. *Nothing* ever went entirely to plan, after all. When it seemed to, it was a sure sign things were going to go horribly wrong.

I tried to force that from my mind, since I couldn't do a thing about it.

After about ten more uncomfortable minutes, the door opened. Bradley came in, looking so much like he had when I'd been in that cage. It took me back, my breathing tight and uneven. When he'd come to the college before, I hadn't really seen him. Instead, I'd hidden behind Hayden's back, content to allow him to shield me from view and harm.

This time, however, I couldn't do that. I saw him, staring right at him, unable to shrink away and hide.

He took a seat at the far end of the table, leaving his security outside. Somehow, despite being alone, he still managed to look like the boss in a room of employees.

"You picked a strange place for this meeting," he said. "Though I can't fault you on the practical security of it. It feels as though you do not trust me."

"That's because we don't." Vance said that with a full smile, as though not trying to soften his comment at all.

Still, Bradley didn't react to the jab. "I trust you are ready for the conversation?"

Vance nodded, leaving Bradley to remove his phone from his pocket. A ringing came through the line, then he put it on speaker and placed the phone at the center of the table.

The ringing stopped before someone answered. "It's nice to speak to you, Mr. Moore." The voice was deep, and while something in it felt familiar, I couldn't place it. It took a moment to realize it sounded slightly off, just wrong enough to raise alarm bells.

"So you're using a voice changer?" Vance said with a laugh. "You are paranoid, aren't you?"

"Not all of us enjoy life in the spotlight as much as you do. I prefer my anonymity. You are one of the few who has even gotten to speak to me like this. You should be grateful."

"Should I? Last I checked, you have been seeking me out. I made a purchase and you are a sore loser."

The way the men spoke reminded me of dogs circling each other, trying to work out who was in charge, who was stronger.

A broken chuckle came from the other side of the line, distorted from the voice changer. "You are just as amusing in real life as you are in interviews. I dislike wasted time, though, so let's get to the point. Mackenzie Fox, are you there?"

I glanced at Hayden, who nodded. "Yes, I'm here."

"And you are unharmed?"

The question took me by surprise. We were talking about a man who had attempted to *buy* me. He was at fault for tearing my life apart. I didn't expect him to worry about my wellbeing. "I'm fine," I answered, my words clipped and suspicious.

"Good. Leaving you in their care was far from my first choice. I would have preferred to deal with this quicker, but your current companions have proven more elusive than I would have expected. Let me first say, to Vance, that should any harm come to her, you will pay the price."

"I'm not into hurting women, so you have nothing to worry about. Besides, since her picture is all over the news, if anything happened to her, it'd fall right on my shoulders."

"Yes, that was a rather clever little trick of yours, wasn't it? You ensured I couldn't make a move, because too many eyes were on Kenz. I have to admit, I never expected some crippled artist could make my life quite this difficult."

I sat up straight, ready to tell Lorien the hell off for daring to bring up Vance's hand.

A warmth on my own hand made me pause, and I looked down to find Hayden had taken mine in his beneath the table. He didn't look at me, didn't let on to what he'd done, but the meaning was clear.

He was telling me to stay quiet.

Which was the smart thing to do. Lorien was poking, trying to find wounds to exploit. If I said a word, I'd only give him ammunition.

I took a deep breath, then released it slowly to calm myself.

The fact that Lorien even *knew* about Vance's hand went to show just how well connected he was. It wasn't like Vance let that information wide.

"Most people are surprised by what a nuisance I can be," Vance acknowledged, showing none of the upset he had during the previous interview, when his work had gotten questioned.

"Let's not play games. I will pay you double what you paid for the girl."

"You're telling me you think she's worth twenty million to you? That's impressive, really."

"She's priceless to me. What are a few million dollars to someone like me? I would like to wrap this up as quickly as possible, so I have no problem handing over whatever makes this a quick and easy exchange."

"The thing is, I've grown rather fond of her. How do I know I'm handing her over somewhere she'll be safe?"

"For the price I'm paying, I don't believe that is your problem anymore."

I shifted in my seat. I didn't think they'd sell me off like that, but who knew for sure? Being talked about like property felt far too familiar.

For a moment, I was back at the table with my father and the man he'd tried to marry me off to. I recalled the way they'd planned out my future and the cost of the marriage like I was just a trophy to hand out.

Here I was, in the same position.

Things don't change that much, do they?

"I think you're overestimating your position," Vance said. "I don't like to give up what's mine. I bought her, I won the bid, I've put time and effort into training her to my taste. Starting over would be a hassle, and the idea of you chewing on my toy doesn't sit right."

"Gentlemen," Bradley said, breaking into the conversation. It was amazing that he could get the men to settle down, but they did, going silent. "I don't think that snapping at one another will get us anywhere, do you?"

"Tell them to sell her back to me," Lorien said. "This can be easily solved in such a way."

"I bought her—nothing he says changes that."

"Quiet," Bradley snapped, the demand loud enough to send a shot of fear straight through me. It was the tone of a man so over dealing with this. I'd heard it from Nem a time or two when the Quad bickered, and she'd hit her limit. "You *both* are at fault for this. Make no mistake—I am well aware that you both cheated my system. You both are at fault for this mess. I would love to simply take the merchandise back, but doing so would admit that we had a problem, and I can't do that. So instead, you will *both* settle down. You will not have fights and death in the streets, will not turn this petty fight over a *woman* into some public feud. Do I make myself clear?"

"And what do you suggest?" Lorien asked.

"Lorien, is there any way you are willing to give up the merchandise?"

"None," Lorien said without hesitation. "She is my soulmate. I can't turn my back on that."

"And you, Vance?"

"I have no need for money, so I see nothing he has that I might want. As far as I see it, I already won. Why would I surrender her?"

Bradley looked over at me, the first time he'd taken note of me since entering. Then again, he saw me as merchandise—nothing more. I was the least important part of this meeting in his eyes. He didn't have to say anything, his look said it all. *You really are a nuisance.*

"I had hoped to come to an understanding today," Bradley said. "But it seems neither of you are willing to budge yet."

"I have one last offer," Lorien said. "You bought her only to cause me trouble, to find me, right?"

His words caused a ripple through the room, the admittance that Lorien wasn't as unaware as we'd assumed.

Vance didn't react or respond.

Lorien chuckled softly. "Surprised? I've been aware of your pathetic designs on revenge for years—you've simply never caused me enough problems to do anything about it. This time, however, you've managed to actually annoy me. You now have my *full* attention."

Boy, does that sound like a threat.

"Call in Tor and Char," Lorien said. "If we are to discuss this, it should be all of us. They are just as involved, after all."

Bradley said nothing, sitting back and watching. No doubt he wanted to wait and see how it would all go.

Vance texted on his phone, and a minute later, the door opened and the two men walked in. They sat on the table, on each side of Hayden and Vance, further boxing me in.

"They're here," Bradley said.

"So we finally all get the chance to talk. You have trailed at my heels for years now — I'm sure you're glad to finally have me turn and face you." Lorien's voice came out unworried.

"Knowing it's us doesn't change anything," Hayden said. "We're still in the stronger position here."

"You think so? See, this is why you've never been a big enough problem before for me to bother with, because you have no real idea of the danger I pose."

Vance glanced down at his hand, and while I still didn't know exactly what had happened, it was clear Lorien was behind it. "I know *exactly* how dangerous you are."

"You really don't. Or perhaps it's more accurate to say that you don't recognize how dangerous I could be to you. You think that I have stolen everything from you that I can, but I feel as if you misunderstand what else you can lose. You think that your revenge is worth your life, but by this point, you should know that your life is not the only thing at risk."

I shuddered at his words, at the violence that filled them. I'd heard so many threats in my life, had seen those closest to me lobby them like ping-pong balls, that they rarely got to me. Something about Lorien's words were worse, though. Perhaps it was the seriousness in them, the absolute obsession, but it felt like a noose tightening and making it harder to breathe with each word.

"Save the posturing," Char said, his voice cheery, a matching false smile, the look not fitting the words at all. "It's beneath you to use such stupid tactics. Let's not think so little of one another."

"It's not a matter of posturing — it's the truth. You four have wasted five years of your life chasing me and for what? What do you have to show for it? No matter what you feel you lost that night, is it worth another five years? Is it worth your future?"

"If you have to ask that, you don't understand anything," Char said.

"What I understand is reality. I have the money, the backing and the skills to drag this out as long as I need to to get what I want. You lack anything to use against me beyond holding Kenz—no information, no leverage, nothing. The longer you allow this to continue, the greater the risk to those around you. I can be quite patient, but even I have my limits. I will have Kenz, and whatever I have to burn to get her doesn't really matter to me. That includes you, those you know, and those she knows."

"I thought I said there would be none of that," Bradley said.

"And if they do the wise thing, nothing will happen. You know as well as I do that eventually any problem will boil over. Give it enough time to build, and it will explode. I understand that you would prefer this to be dealt with quietly, and I have given them a way for that to happen. If they simply allow me to pay double the amount they did, this will resolve. They can go on with their lives, go back to whatever they want, and it will be over. It is best for you to press that issue. Best for both you and the auction house."

Bradley's expression stiffened. It seemed he didn't care for the very obvious threat. The way he stared at the phone made me want to take a step away from the table, to get away from the tension there. Even I knew better than to threaten a man like Bradley. Beyond the fact that he was willing to sell people like property, just the way he held himself showed his power. He wasn't the type to take it sitting down.

Still, Bradley didn't speak, didn't argue.

"I've got no intention of handing her over," Hayden said.

"Your revenge is worth that much?"

"It's worth everything." A haunted look in Hayden's eyes said he meant those words, that they were his real feelings, and the depth of them hurt. I still didn't know what Lorien had done, but it had left some deep wounds in these men.

It broke my heart, those chains that held the men so tight that they hardly lived at all. They'd devoted their every moment to their revenge, to making Lorien pay for what he'd done. They couldn't see past that.

But I'd seen what revenge could do to a person, how it twisted them, how it ate away at them until there was nothing left. Nem had given up a decade of her life to her revenge, had nearly died to get it, and why?

I didn't want these men to suffer the same, for it to take as long to recognize the damage it did.

"Well, it doesn't appear we'll come to an agreement today," Lorien said. "I'm willing to give you time to think it over. Hopefully you become less stubborn and recognize the best course of action for everyone involved. However, my willingness to wait comes at a rather small price. I want to speak to Kenz alone."

"Not a fucking chance," Char snapped.

"Put your claws away, conman. All I'm asking is for you and the others to step outside of the room. You've done your research, you know there is no other way in or out of this room. Leave the phone, so I can speak to her without prying ears."

"Why?" Hayden asked.

"I need to make sure she has not been mistreated."

"Like a murderer like you gives a damn about that," Hayden said.

"Even monsters have soulmates. Kenz is mine, and I cannot, in good conscience, leave her where she is if I find out that any of you have mistreated her. I also can't be sure she is free to speak unless she does so privately. This is non-negotiable. This is how you buy your time and my patience as you consider my offer."

I could tell from the expressions of the men they did not like this plan. However, I was also smart enough to know when to give. "It's okay. I'll do it."

Hayden flattened his lips into a severe line but nodded. Even if he didn't like it, he knew when we were backed against a wall. "Okay. You have five minutes. If anything happens, just yell. We'll be right outside." When he stood, I could tell he wanted to reach out, to set his hand on my shoulder, but he didn't.

They all filed out of the room, including Bradley, leaving me there with the phone. Despite the fact Lorien wasn't in the room with me, his presence was heavy. It felt like he sat across from me, staring at me.

"They're gone." I hated the way my voice cracked in fear. *What a coward.*

"Good. Now, I wasn't joking. Are you hurt? Have they mistreated you? Touched you in any way?" Threat vibrated through those words. It made me wonder, if I said yes, what he would do.

Nothing good. He seemed like the kind of man who would burn the world to get what he wanted.

"No, nothing like that. They've taken good care of me."

He let out a long sigh full of relief. "Good. I'm glad. Believe it or not, I have been worried."

I wanted to stay quiet. It was the old me, the one who had always bent to my father's will, who had given in because it was safer and easier. I'd have my tantrums, but in the end, I'd done as I was told.

Except, I couldn't do that, not now. "Why do you care?"

"Because we are meant to be."

"I don't even *know* you, so how can you say that?"

"You may not know me, but I know you. Not just who you pretend to be, but the truth."

My stomach clenched as my worst fears were made clear. Still, I tried to play it off, no matter how laughably pathetic and obvious the attempt was. "I don't know what you're talking about."

"Of course you do. We don't have much time, so let's not play games. I know exactly who you really are and your entire past. I know about your parents, about your sister, about what actually happened at your wedding, the part that wasn't made public."

"If you know who I am, then all you want is my last name. Don't sully that by calling us soulmates."

"You have no idea what you're worth, do you? I don't want you because of your family, because of your name. I want you because of *you.* Your name, your bloodline, and the things those can buy me are just the reasons that my family supports me having you. They are benefits, but not the reason."

"I've heard that before."

"Ah, yes, when your father tried to marry you off. You see, that man cared only about your name. He would have terrorized you had the marriage happened, making each day hell. He was just an old man excited to raise his position and sleep with a young girl. He deserved nothing more than the bullet he got—no different from your father."

"You don't know anything about my family."

"Don't I? I don't spend time on the West Coast, but information still travels, and stories about the Hester line, about the Williams girls, those are the sort of tales that spread far. Your sister has done well, especially for a dead woman."

"You shouldn't try to use my family as a threat. That's not a great way to get me to see you in a good light."

"I'm not threatening them. I have no desire to exert myself by tracking any of them down. Besides, they'd be difficult targets while at the center of their power in California. However, anyone in your position would be tempted to solve all your problems by calling up your sister. You haven't, and I'm curious as to why."

"I've been being watched every second. I don't have my phone or any way to contact them."

"Let's not start such a beautiful relationship with ugly lies, dear. If you wanted to, you could have gotten in touch. No matter what others see, you have more skills and strength than you let on, and if you wanted to get away from these men, you could have many times. So be honest with me. Why haven't you?"

"I don't want to put anyone else in danger," I whispered.

"Good girl. You see how easy things can be when you trust me? You're right, also. Nem is a hard target when in her territory, but if she came here? She'd find herself surrounded by enemies in a place where I am already entrenched. Even your precious Quad will be outnumbered and outgunned."

"She's too smart for you," I said. "Anyone who underestimates her ends up dead."

"Possibly," Lorien admitted. "However, everyone has a weakness. She was ready to die for you, Kenz, to take a bullet for you. Do you really think she'll care about risks if you call her? If you tell her you need her? Because I'm sure she'd rush into a burning building if you so much as whimpered. If you call her, if you tell her what's going on, you might as well sign her death warrant yourself."

I hated that he was right. Nem wouldn't think twice about coming, no matter how dangerous, no matter how much power Lorien had here. Even if it was an impossible situation, Nem would rush in headfirst if she thought I was in danger.

Which is why I haven't tried to get away or contact her.

She'd given up so much, risked so much to save me. I had to do the same for her. She finally had a real life after dedicating the last ten years to saving me. I couldn't let her throw that away now.

"So you just want to remind me of the dangers? Thanks."

"I want you to understand your position. The men you have been living with may still make foolish choices. They may let anger and pain rule their actions, may not listen to reason. You're smart enough to know where you stand. You went along with your father's wishes because you knew it was your only choice. You've always done what you needed to, no matter how difficult. Now that you see there is only one true choice, you'll do the right thing again."

It almost felt like he whispered in my ear, as if he stood just behind me, a monster I didn't care to turn around and face.

"No one has died yet, Kenz, and you can control if that continues or not. You're the only one who can, really. So when you're ready to end this, when you want to stop risking those around you, turn yourself into the hotel on Fifth and Main. Give them my name, and they'll take care of everything."

The door opened, with Hayden entering first, his face pinched in tight lines. Well, to be fair, all the men appeared at their limits. "Time's up," he said.

"Very well. We will be in touch soon." With that, the call ended, but Bradley didn't take the phone. Instead, he left it at the center of the table.

"That phone is yours to keep. I purchased two phones with the numbers programmed into them and delivered the other to Lorien. This way you can hopefully resolve this silly dispute without the need for me to get involved again. Now, I've wasted far too much time on this nonsense, so I'll be leaving." He didn't bother to even look my way before walking out of the room.

Char and Tor left after that, no doubt to make sure Bradley really left and that there were no signs of ambushes or attacks. Vance said nothing, and neither did Hayden.

I could only stare at the center of the table, where the phone was, and wonder just how I'd ended up in this helpless position yet again.

Maybe I was doomed to forever be a pawn in someone else's game.

Chapter Eighteen

Hayden

Talk about the last thing I wanted to do...

I'd faced off against some of the worst things without flinching. I'd jumped in front of attackers, breached doors knowing a gunman sat on the other side, walked into situations I knew I might not walk out of.

None of those had made me as nervous as the young woman seated on the swing in the backyard.

Kenz wore her favorite pajamas, the comfortable ones she seemed to always wear when she was especially nervous or upset. It was funny how, when she'd gotten here, I'd known so little about her. Now, however, I could tell just by her clothing or choice of food how she felt.

Did she think we were going to turn her over? That this little family meeting was to tell her we'd sell her off?

Judging from her expression, yeah, she probably did.

Her own father had tried to kill her.

I supposed I could understand why she might jump to that conclusion.

"Stop frowning," Vance said. "You'll give yourself wrinkles and who will want you if you do that?" His words were rude, but instead of snapping back, Kenz stared for a moment then laughed.

I might not understand her relationship with Vance—or with Tor or Char for that matter—but I couldn't deny that whatever strangeness existed between them eased her.

I took a seat in the empty chair across from the swing, putting us in a circle. It felt oddly private and personal, like we were a real family. The sun had set, but the heat and humidity still made my shirt cling to my back.

Or maybe that's just my nerves.

"So what's this about?" she asked as she brought her legs up and wrapped her arms around her knees, making herself into a ball. She set her chin on her knees. The worries were obvious on her face, but even then, she didn't try to hide, didn't run from the reality.

"You said something to me earlier. You said that until I told you the worst parts about my life, I didn't get to lecture you about your secrets. You're right. This doesn't just affect us anymore, so you have the right to understand what happened."

"You mean five years ago?" Her gaze moved around between us, pausing at Vance's hand.

Yeah, she's smarter than people give her credit for.

Vance sighed, then hooked the thumb of his left hand beneath the glove of his right hand. He paused for only a heartbeat before he pulled the fabric off, the first time I'd seen what he hid beneath it either.

In the dim light of the backyard, I could only see some mangled skin on the back of his hand. It didn't appear nearly as damaged as I'd have assumed, given how rarely he used it.

He wasn't done, though. He grasped his pointer finger and pulled, the action sliding off a prosthetic that had all the middle fingers. It left him with only his thumb and pinky.

"Five years ago, I was at the Kylotte Hotel here. It was just chance I was there, really. I'd met a girl in a bar, and we'd gotten a room there."

Kenz furrowed her brows. "The Kylotte Hotel..." she whispered.

Vance went quiet, so I picked up the conversation. "That's right. It was all over the news when it happened. You were a teen, but you probably heard about it."

"There was a bombing there. They found the culprit afterward, said it was because of a drug dispute."

I tilted my head, surprised she'd know so much. Few details were released about the drug connection, which meant she had information not known to the public. "Yes and no. Officially, they said it was because of contract disputes. Unofficially, they suspected the hotel was being used to sell drugs to high-end clients. That was true, but it wasn't the actual reason for the bombing."

She sighed, her guess easy. "Lorien did it?"

"That's right. He used the person they caught as a fall guy, but Lorien was behind it."

"You said Lorien is second in a crime family. Why would he do that? That sort of thing would be way too public, and I can't think they'd want that sort of attention on them." Her understanding of criminal organizations surprised me, but she was always doing that, wasn't she?

"He's a mad dog. He does what he wants, doesn't follow the rules other families do. Even his mother, who runs the family officially, can't rein him in. He leaves running the family to his mother and he prefers to take assassination contracts. One went out for a man who was trafficking women and had stolen money from the people he worked with. That man was in the hotel."

Horror washed across Kenz's face. "He bombed an entire hotel to get to one person?"

"Yeah, he did. Twelve people died in the bombing and twenty were seriously injured."

Kenz turned her gaze back to Vance's hand, understanding dawning on her features.

He nodded. "This happened that day. I was luckier than many others, but the rubble crushed my hand. They saved as much as they could, but, well, you've seen."

She turned her gaze back to me. "What about you?"

I sighed, hating going back to that day, to the thick, hot air, the smoke that I'd choked on. "I was protecting a man, a scientist working on an important breakthrough. I'd love to explain what it was exactly, but I'm not smart enough to understand it. He was a good man, though, and the company he worked for hired us because he'd become a target for religious extremists who didn't like his research. Lorien didn't target him—he just didn't care who he hurt."

I rubbed my palm over the top of my thigh. Admitting to one of my greatest failures wasn't something I enjoyed doing, after all. "We were in the dining room, which was one of the main targets. As soon as the room started to shake, I grabbed him and covered him. Parts of the ceiling fell, but I protected him from them. I knew where the emergency exit was, so I pulled him that way. I checked the hallway to see if it was safe, but when I did, the building shook again because of the damage to the basement. He had time to get through, but he didn't. Instead, he shoved a kid that was there through just before the doorway collapsed. He never made it out. He was the only client I ever lost, and he died for nothing—just because Lorien was having fun." Fire burned in my chest at the memory, at the life that had been cut short.

It wasn't just the loss that hurt, but the pointlessness of it.

My throat tightened and I couldn't bring myself to speak anymore.

Thankfully, Char took over. "I told you about Isla, my wife." He stopped there, just staring at Kenz.

Her eyes widened in understanding, which amazed me since he'd given all of nothing in terms of information.

"She was there?"

Char nodded. "We both were. It was an anniversary dinner and she'd wanted to see the place. She'd always wanted to go there, to stay in one of their nice rooms, to eat at the fancy restaurant. I gave her what she wanted, like I always did. I would have been with her, but she was in the lobby, waiting for me to come down for dinner. I was running late because I was dealing with a recent job, and she was used to having to wait for me, so she'd left the room and waited for me in the lobby."

He sighed and carded his fingers through his hair, brushing it back roughly. Had I ever seen him so undone?

"If I hadn't been working, she wouldn't have left early. She might have been in the room with me and survived. Or, if I'd gone and left her in the room, she'd have lived and I wouldn't have. Fuck, if I'd gone with her, we might have both perished but at least she wouldn't have died alone."

I'd never heard Char speak of his wife, of that day, but even five years hadn't seemed to ease his feelings about it. A glance at Kenz made me sigh.

I doubted any of us would have opened these wounds again for anyone else, would have gone down this memory trip without her.

She peered at Tor, a question in her gaze.

He took out his phone, and a moment later, a text came to us all. *The contract came to me, first, but I turned it down. I was busy with other jobs. Even if I had taken it, collateral damage is unforgivable. Lorien is a disease that needs to be cut out.*

He slid his phone back into his pocket, but didn't drop his gaze, staring at Kenz as if trying to explain something with that look.

It amazed me, in a way. We'd bought this girl, forced her to live with us.

When I'd first met her, I'd thought her dull. I'd seen her at the school, having gone to meet Vance, and figured her a rich spoiled brat who had attended in hopes of catching his eye.

When we bought her, when we brought her to the house, I'd still thought her a tool.

A tool I didn't want any harm to come to, but a tool nonetheless.

That had changed the longer I'd spent with her, the more I'd seen of her. She was smart and tough and sweet enough to burrow into the hardest of hearts. She had turned a cold empty house into a home.

When I returned here, I no longer simply showered and fell into bed. Now dinners happened at the table, and we'd even watched movies in the living room. Where the four of us had seemed frozen in time, trapped in the horrors of that day for five years, stuck in our anger and our loss and unable to move forward, that had only changed when Kenz had come to us.

She hadn't shoved us forward—she'd coaxed us. She'd been a kind person sitting outside the doghouse of a snarling beast, waiting until they felt comfortable enough to venture out. If she'd reached in, if she'd tried to haul us out, we'd have snapped.

Instead, she'd done the very Kenz thing and just waited, created a soft place, until we'd approached her.

And we had. We proved it here, sitting around her, bearing our wounds so she understood where we came from.

She remained silent for a long moment, her gaze on the ground between us. Was she working through all the information? It was the first time we'd so openly let her see who we were, where we'd not only shown her how we had gotten here, but our past without hiding it at all.

I expected her to speak up, to tell us she wanted to run. Perhaps she'd tell me that she didn't want to do this anymore, that she wanted us to help her escape?

None of that would have surprised me—they were the obvious responses. She'd gotten dragged into this by being in the wrong place at the wrong time, by somehow catching the attention of Lorien, then used as a pawn by the rest of us.

That made it all the more shocking when she did lift her gaze and speak, her words so unexpected that it took a long moment for my brain to wrap around her statement.

"You should hand me over."

Kenz

No one spoke again, as if I'd said something crazy.

It *wasn't* crazy, though.

It made perfect sense. If Lorien got what he was after—me—this was over. Nem and the Quad would be safe. No doubt he'd let me contact her, just to ensure she didn't come looking for me. We could fake a romance and marriage, and it would give him what he wanted. While these men wouldn't get their revenge, they *would* get their lives back, and I wanted that for them more than anything.

The only one to suffer would be me, and that sounded like a fair trade.

"Fuck no," Char snapped, the first to speak, and his sharp tone made me smile. While I might not have liked his attitude in the past, I appreciated it, now. It was the him that few saw, and for that reason, I cherished it.

"I don't like agreeing with Char, but I have to, here," Vance said. "There's no chance we're just handing you over."

I sighed, trying to use my best reasonable tone. "I know you want revenge, but what's the point if you lose everything else you have? Why keep at it if it only hurts you and those you care about?"

Vance looked the other way, a tightness in his jaw saying he understood what I said even if he didn't like it, but the stubborn man didn't respond.

Good. Let them just listen. "All Lorien wants is me. If you hand me over, you'll all go back to your lives and can get back the money you spent on me. It'll be like none of this ever happened."

"You think we'd just turn you over after all this?" Hayden asked.

"If you hadn't intervened, I'd have been in his hands anyway. You're not doing anything wrong—you're just putting things back the way they would have been."

"And you think that solution is okay with us?"

"I think it's better than the alternative. I know you want revenge, and you deserve it, but I don't want to see you all hurt anymore. There are things that are more important than revenge—"

"Kenz." The harsh voice took me by surprise, one I didn't recognize. I lifted my gaze to find Tor staring hard at me.

That was his voice? It had come out like a whisper, yet had managed to rise above my rambling and silence me.

"Tor?" Even though that had obviously been him, I couldn't quite believe it. He came closer, bending down to cup my cheek, his palm warm and large and comforting. His golden eyes bore into mine, anger flashing in them, before he shook his head and turned around, storming back into the house.

My cheek chilled without his hand, and I touched the spot with my fingers as my gaze followed him.

"That's Tor for 'fuck your stupid plan,'" Char offered before he stood. "And I'm going to second it.

Now, kindly shut the fuck up with that bullshit and go to bed." He didn't wait for a response before leaving, slamming the door behind him.

Vance laughed, shaking his head. "Way to piss everyone off at once. And to think I said you had no skills…" He stood as he reattached his prosthetic, then put his glove back on. "If you get lonely, feel free to stop by my room. Otherwise, guess I'll see you at breakfast." He left as well.

It left only Hayden and me outside. At least it left me with the nice one, the one most likely to be reasonable. "I know you want to get back at Lorien, but is it really worth risking this all?"

"You really are difficult, you know that?" Hayden's tone came out colder than I'd heard it before, at least when speaking to me.

It made me turn toward him to find a matching harsh expression on his face. The look silenced me. Disappointment tended to shut me right up.

"You really think this is *just* about revenge anymore?"

"That's why you bought me. That's what you wanted with me from the start."

"And things have changed. At least, they have for us. Jesus, Kenz, do you *really* think we could just hand you over to him?"

"But you want revenge—"

"But we won't sacrifice you for it!" Hayden raised his voice, his yell making my breath catch in my throat. For Char to yell or even Vance wouldn't have shocked me, but I'd basically been yelled at now by both Hayden and Tor.

I really did fuck up somewhere, didn't I?

Then Hayden's words soaked in, making little sense.

"It's not sacrificing me. I'm *offering*."

"You can offer anything you want—we won't take you up on it. I'm not here to trade one innocent for the life of another. I'm not about to lead you to slaughter just to get what I want. If you think I'm the sort of man who would be okay with that, then you sure don't think much of me."

The level of frustration and anger in his tone made me pull back, as if it burned me with each word.

"I'm trying to be smart," I whispered.

"What did he say when we were out of the room? Did he threaten you? Did he threaten someone you know? Maybe those bodyguards of yours? *Tell me*, and I'll help."

I shook my head. He hadn't threatened anyone, just warned me not to involve them. "It's not like that."

"Then what is it like? Because you've never mentioned this nonsense until right now. What changed? Do you think you'll have it better with him? Are you falling for his whole soulmate thing? Are you that desperate to be wanted that you'll do something that stupid?"

Normally, words like those would have shut me down. I'd have curled in on myself, licking my wounds and going quiet to not garner anymore anger.

Except, I'd spent too long with Hayden to do that. I sat up straight and met his dark eyes. "Are you kidding me? You think I *want* to be with that psychopath?"

"Then why are you suggesting that exact thing? Do you just not realize what he could do to you?"

"I'm not as stupid and sheltered as you seem to think I am. I know *exactly* what he could do to me. Do you really think he's the first man to try to buy me? To try to own me? My father, before he tried to kill me, had planned to marry me off to a man in his fifties. I wore a fucking *wedding dress* and walked down an aisle, knowing the absolute hell waiting for me at the end. So yes, I know what's waiting for me, probably better than you do. I saw so many women in that position all my life, women sold off to men for their name and giving them offspring with the right bloodlines, women who lost all their power. I know it's giving up my future. I know he'll do whatever he wants to me. Don't you dare treat me like some child who has no idea what the real world is like. Don't you speak down to me that way."

"So why, then?"

"Because I care about you! Because I care about *all* of you and I don't want to see you suffer anymore. I don't want Char to die for this, to run himself into the ground like he's doing now. I want him to move on, to show someone else the real him, to find *real* happiness. I want Vance to stop whoring around and respect himself, to realize he can still live a life, to find something he's passionate about. I want Tor to stop standing on the sidelines of his own life, for him to smile more, for him to find something he cares about. And you? You absolutely frustrating idiot! I want you to stop thinking you need to trade your life for someone else's, that you're worth so little that the only value you have is to die for someone else. I want you all to be happy, damn it, even if I don't much like any of you right now."

I took a deep breath, then swiped my thumb beneath my eye to remove the tears that threatened to fall. "I've lived my entire life knowing I was a product that would eventually get sold off. I got some time to live my own life, and that was nice, but ending up exactly where I thought I would all along doesn't change anything. But, hey, it's better this way. At first I thought I'd have to do it for my father or because that's just how it was done. At least this way, I'm doing it for a good reason. I think it's worth it if it saves you all, you know?"

Even as I spoke, my brain bounced between terror at my future and reassurance that the men would be okay. Doing just one good, useful thing in my life would validate all the sacrifices others made for me, right?

And I couldn't imagine trading my life so easily for anyone else. Somehow, these men mattered to me that much, and I needed them to be happy. I had to give them that chance.

Hayden said nothing, staring at me as though he couldn't make sense of my words.

He rose to his full height, then came to stand just before me. Where Tor had cupped my cheek gently, Hayden hooked a single finger beneath my chin and tipped my face up toward him.

It made our height difference—especially with me sitting—all the more obvious.

The point where his finger pressed into me took all my focus, the only place we touched, yet it felt like he had me entirely under his control.

Hell, I shuddered, because between the touch and his steady gaze, I felt entirely enveloped by him, like he'd embraced me.

No matter how much I enjoyed it, how much I wanted it, I knew this was it. They'd wake up tomorrow and realize I was right, that this was the best choice, and they'd do the smart thing.

Lorien had given us time to make a choice, but the longer I put it off, the harder it would be. I wanted to spend every second until that here. Fuck school, fuck classes, fuck everything except memorizing every last detail.

Char's sharp glares, Vance's shameless come-ons, Tor's calming presence and Hayden's constant worrying. I wanted them all, but that was selfish.

It would be better for us all to get it done as soon as possible.

So I wrapped my fingers around Hayden's wrist, asking him without words not to leave me alone, not tonight.

He blew out a harsh breath, as if fed up with me. "Go get some sleep."

"But…"

He shook his head, pulling his hand back. *Yet another rejection.* "We've all had a long day, and if we don't stop this now, we're going to say or do something we can't take back. We should sleep and come back to it tomorrow."

"Don't treat me like a kid," I whispered.

"You are a kid, sweetheart. Compared to me, you're a child. You're smart and you're tough and you're far too kind, but you're still a kid."

I blinked quickly, the burning in my eyes worsening. I had little I could give them, little I could do for them, but they kept rejecting what I had.

They saw me as useless, just like everyone else.

Just a burden.

I sniffled, unable to help it when it hurt too much.

"Kenz…" Hayden said, his voice softening. That made it worse, though. I didn't need pity, couldn't stand that was the only thing he would give me.

I rushed past him, flinging his arm off when he tried to grab me. I didn't stop until I reached my room and locked the door for the first time.

I sank to my knees in front of the closed door, then leaned my forehead against the wood.

A knock came a moment later, but I didn't answer it.

"Open the door, Kenz." Hayden's voice floated through the door, and it squeezed at my heart. I wanted to open it, but what was the point?

It would be no different than before. He'd followed me because he felt bad about having upset me, not because he'd changed his mind. Hair of the dog wouldn't make me feel any better in the long run.

"Go away," I whispered.

"I don't want you to cry alone."

I wished I were stronger, that I could have said I wasn't crying, but we both knew the truth. Lying would have been pointless. "Just leave me alone. I've gone along with everything you all want, haven't fought you on anything, so please, just this once, let me have this. Let me have my pride and just let me be."

His breath was heavy, and a soft thud echoed against the door, then a sliding sound. "I won't make you open this door," he said, "but I'll stay right here in case you change your mind."

I shifted, placing my back against the door, mirroring his position. The tears fell until exhaustion pulled me under, until I couldn't keep my eyes open.

And through it all, I knew he was there, that he wouldn't leave. That was why no matter what they said, what they wanted, I had to make things right. I'd been protected my whole life, had others throw themselves between me and any threat, and I'd just obeyed. I'd followed what they said, let them protect me, but no more. I wouldn't let anyone else suffer for me.

I couldn't let these men who had become such a big part of my life get hurt because I was too afraid to do what was right.

For once, I'd do whatever it took to protect the people I loved.

* * * *

Kenz

My eyes ached but crying all night did that to a person. No doubt I looked like 'fresh hell warmed over,' as Rune would have said.

A pair of dark sunglasses helped keep me from squinting at the bright sun.

Getting out of the house hadn't been that difficult. It might have been for a normal person, but I hadn't grown up normal. I didn't know what normal was, even if I'd tried to live like it the last year.

All those lessons I'd gotten had repeated in my head as I'd disconnected the alarms on the windows, as I'd picked the locks. I'd packed a bag with my insulin, my glucose reader and some clothing. I'd left the phone back at the house, since I had no doubt they could track it, that they would the moment they found me missing. I'd left my sketchbook behind, because somehow I couldn't imagine wanting to draw when I got where I was headed.

I forced one foot in front of the other, heading toward the hotel Lorien had told me about.

I just wish I could have had a little more time.

I scolded myself at the thought. I'd gone through this after losing my mother and sister. There was never enough time with those we care about. It didn't matter how much more we got, it was never enough. If I had another night or another week with them, I'd still want more.

Just be happy you had it at all.

I could have ended up in this same place without having met Tor, Char, Vance and Hayden, without having felt the fluttering in my stomach when one smiled, the reassuring warmth as I leaned against them, the way I laughed when they said something unexpected.

I treasured those memories, held them close, and they'd have to keep because it was all I'd had.

I sighed and walked faster. With the sun having risen, I'd guess the men would find me missing soon. They'd let me sleep in, probably feeling bad that I'd had a rough night. They'd only intrude to make sure I ate something, and when they did?

They were smart enough to guess my plan. I needed to get to the hotel before that happened, before they could find me.

I passed by another alleyway, my thoughts swirling in my head so fast, I failed to check it this time.

Someone grabbed my arm and yanked me into the alleyway, then covered my mouth with their hand.

Will my luck ever turn around?

Chapter Nineteen

Kenz

I was so close to doing the right thing, and somehow, life kept screwing it up. The person who grabbed me might work for Lorien, or maybe they weren't connected at all.

Maybe they were just a creep grabbing me off the street? Wouldn't that be a hilarious change of events?

I reacted the way I should, though, since I had no idea who held me. I swung my elbow back, aiming for their side to knock the breath from them.

They shifted, narrowly avoiding the strike, and when I took advantage by balling my fist and swinging back on the other side — now exposed — aiming for their groin, they caught that hand as though they expected it.

"Who do you think taught your sister to always go for the family jewels?" Jarrod's voice in my ear forced the strength from my legs, and I sagged forward.

How long had it been since I'd heard a truly friendly voice? Since I'd heard someone from my family?

Jarrod released my mouth but didn't take away the arm wrapped around me, using it to keep me upright. He didn't laugh at me, didn't mock me for the reaction.

But *damn* had I missed this feeling of safety. I didn't spend as much time with Jarrod as I would have liked, didn't have as close a relationship as would have been nice, but he'd somehow ended up in that father spot for me despite us sharing no blood.

Sometimes I wondered if it wasn't because I looked just like my mother, because he saw her in me?

Whatever the reason, he'd saved me many times when he'd had no reason to.

After a moment to gather myself, I forced my legs to work on their own and pulled away from Jarrod, turning to look up and into his face.

Damn, I'd missed him. I missed his sighs, the way he fought against smiling because he worried that it would convince me to do whatever he didn't approve of more.

I even missed the way he'd rented romantic movies and watched them while I'd recovered, even if the main reason was just so I'd be quiet and stop trying to draw him into conversation.

"You are wilier than a stray cat," he said before he caught my chin and tilted my head, staring down like he was checking for injuries.

I waved his hand off as I stepped backward. "What does that make you? Animal control?"

He let out a soft huff that only those who knew him well would call a laugh. "Do you have any idea how worried your sister's been?"

"She's always worried."

"Yeah, but most people pace and eat too much junk food when they're worried. Nem shoots people."

"Nem shoots people all the time."

"True enough." He released a long breath slowly. Was he that worried about me?

It warmed me that he'd come all this way, that he'd found me like this. Jarrod was a busy man, had enough of his own work, but he'd dropped it all and gotten on a plane to come look for me?

Look at that, I'm making things difficult for everyone still.

He took his phone out, and I didn't need to ask his plan. It wasn't all that hard to guess. Sure enough, after him putting on speakerphone, a familiar voice came on. "Did you find her?"

"Yeah, I did." Jarrod nodded at me, telling me to answer.

"Hey, Nem."

"Kenz." Nem breathed the name out like I were some mirage she didn't quite trust was really there. "Where have you been? It's been three weeks since we've been able to get ahold of you!"

"I've been busy," I said.

"Busy? You think *busy* is going to work as an excuse? You haven't had your phone for these weeks. It was turned off entirely, and even when Bray tried to hack into it, to force it on, he couldn't. That means it was destroyed. There has been only one entrance into your apartment in all this time, so you haven't been sleeping there. Where the fuck have you been?"

"I've just been living my life," I hedged, a desperation sinking into me.

I was *so* close to making this all right, to freeing everyone. I couldn't give Nem any reason to worry, to chase after me. If she thought I was in trouble, I had no doubt she'd arrive by morning, that she'd drop everything and ride in like some dark hero.

And she might just ride into something too big for her to deal with out here.

I couldn't allow that. I couldn't have any more deaths on my head.

"And so just disappearing is okay?"

"Maybe I did that *because* you were watching me," I said.

Nem paused before answering, and boy did it feel like a dangerous pause. "What?"

"You and the Quad are always calling me, always in my business. I can't even go to the doctor without you getting the results like I'm a child!"

"We do that because we worry. You have people who care about you, who want the best for you. Can you really blame any of us for going a little overboard? You're the youngest in the family, and we just want what's best for you."

"Shouldn't I get to decide what that is?" It was strange how I spoke.

My words were part of a lie to get out of here, to make Jarrod leave, to buy me time and reassure Nem, but that didn't make them untrue. They were my feelings and frustration that I'd experienced over the past year — no, longer than that, since I'd felt this same stifling, suffocating isolation from life with my father.

Nem wasn't my father, and I knew that. Nem and the others did what they did for my good, for my benefit and not their own, but their methods felt so similar that they created the same reaction in me.

Maybe that was why I kept talking, why my words came out so earnest. I didn't want to hurt Nem, but I couldn't stop blurting out my true feelings, even if I'd twisted them into the story I had to tell.

"I moved away because I wanted to live my own life for once. I wanted to make my own choices."

"But you get to do that. You chose your college, your major, what you want to do. All you have to say is what you want and when have I ever not made it happen?"

I pushed away my guilt and kept going. "You have, but it's still always been *your* way. I wanted to stay at the dorm, but you said we couldn't have the right security there. I wanted to rent a cute, small little studio, but Colton decided I needed the penthouse. You are always stepping in and changing my life to the way you think it should go. I mean, what do you want from me?"

"I just want you safe and happy." Nem's words came out a small whisper, the voice so unlike the woman most people saw of her.

She was bigger than life, more terrifying than any monster, willing and able to destroy *anything* around her, but here she was like a scolded dog, tail tucked between her legs after just a few words from me.

This is the last time I'll ever hurt her.

"I know you do," I offered, to soothe that wound. "But I felt like this when Dad was still around. He never listened to me, never heard what I said. He just did what he wanted and forced me to go along with it. I lived my whole life under his thumb, and sometimes I wonder if that's changed at all. Sometimes, I still feel like I have that same collar on, that the only thing that's changed is who's holding the leash."

Nem let out a low curse, telling me the blow had landed exactly where I'd meant it to. Any comparison between my father and Nem wouldn't sit well, not for her.

Just a little more. "Just give me a little time. I want to date if I want, to pick where I live, to succeed and fail on my own. I want to fall in love, to make mistakes, to experience things, but how is any of that possible if I just walk the safe path you've prepared for me?"

"So what are you asking for? Do you want me out of your life entirely?"

"No, nothing like that. I love you, Nem, and I know how much you've done for me. I just need space. I need time to work things out myself."

"How much time?"

"I don't know. I'll contact you, okay? I promise, I'll keep in touch, but *wait* for me to reach out. Don't send Jarrod, don't send the Quad, don't come yourself. Let me make my decisions on my own and trust that I'm capable, that I can do it myself."

It took a long time for her to speak again, and I nearly cracked in the meantime. "Okay," she whispered. "I'll do as you ask, so long as you swear you will contact me the moment you need anything. I don't care what it is, how big or little an issue—I'll be there the second you need me."

This might be the last time I ever spoke to her, so I had to make it count. I had no idea what the future would hold for me, how much freedom I'd have with Lorien. The pain of all the things left unsaid with my mother, with my father, they haunted me. I didn't want that with Nem.

"I know that. I don't think I've really thanked you, not enough. You've always been looking out for me, even when I didn't even know you lived. You never turned your back on me, even when it would have been so much safer and easier for you to do so. I can't thank you enough for that, can't make that up to you, can't repay that debt. I love you, Nem, you and the Quad. You all taught me so much, and you made it so I could live my own life. You all" —I lifted my gaze to Jarrod— "even a very grumpy fox, are all my family. So, I promise, the moment I need something from you, I'll reach out."

"Okay," Nem said softly. "Then I'll hang up now. You be careful, Kenz, and check in occasionally, please. If you don't, the Quad will be all over my ass with worry."

I laughed even through the tightness in my chest. "I promise."

Jarrod ended the call and slid the phone into his pocket. He didn't speak at first, and something in his gaze made me suspect he didn't *quite* believe me.

Then again, leave it to Jarrod to see through my bullshit.

"Who are those men?"

"What men?"

He tilted his head as though to scold me for lying so poorly. He wouldn't be mad about my lying, just about doing it badly. "Finding you wasn't easy. I've been here a few days, and I spotted you at the college a few times. You always have one of four men around you. I would have followed you from there, but the one who wears a suit clearly has training and would have spotted a tail."

I swallowed hard, not wanting to put them in any danger. "They're friends."

"Friends? Is that what kids are calling it nowadays?"

My cheeks heated, but I tried to play that off as though I hadn't noticed. "Aren't I allowed to have friends like that? I *am* an adult, after all."

Jarrod remained silent until I looked into his eyes. "Are they forcing you into anything?"

"Of course not."

"You're lying to me. You're easy to read, and I know all your tells. You want us to leave you alone, but you stand here and lie to me about something so basic and important."

Jarrod was far too good for me to hope to get anything over on him. So, instead, I steeled my courage and told him the truth — at least, a part of it.

"I'm not afraid of them. They haven't hurt me or caused me any harm."

"Truth," Jarrod said softly.

"I don't need you to do anything, to rescue me, to intervene at all. I know what I'm going to do and how to do it."

"Also true." He frowned softly, as though coming to an idea that he'd never considered. "Do you love them?"

I went to tell him no, to tell him of *course* I didn't love them. I barely knew them, and during that short time, we'd lied to each other more than seemed possible. They frustrated me and we argued and we had no future. In what world could *that* be love.

Except, I couldn't say that.

I thought about my time with each of them. I recalled how Tor bought sugar-free treats to ensure I always had them available. Vance's smirk as he teased me, the way he always stood just a bit too close, the fluttering inside me when I reacted to it. The way Hayden made me feel impossibly safe, as though the rest of the world slid away when I was by his side. Even Char, with this sharp tongue, had made me feel valued, had made me want to see a real smile from him. I cherished those memories, and they made the truth dangerously clear to me.

Those could only mean one thing, right? "Yeah, I do."

Jarrod shook his head. "Well, they'd better be pretty damned tough if they're going to survive in this family."

They won't have to worry about that.

I forced a smile to keep myself from crying. "Thank you for coming, but I really have to get going."

"We'll see each other soon, right? Sasha wants you to come home for Christmas, again. She says it's a tradition now. Maybe you could bring these men home and introduce them, then?"

"Yeah, sure."

He pressed his lips together. No doubt he'd heard that lie loud and clear.

"Bye," I said, and turned my back before he could see the fear on my face, the pain of losing people so important to me.

"Kid." His one word stopped me, but I didn't turn back toward him. "Don't think you're fooling me one bit. Dane taught you how to answer the question you want instead of the one you're asked, so don't think you've pulled the wool over my eyes here. You're in trouble all right—big trouble."

"Are you going to stop me, then?"

"No. I've learned my lesson about that. You can't stop people who are determined, and even if Nem doesn't see it, even if no one else in the world sees it, I know you're damned tough. You're a lot like your mom, you know. Strong, stubborn, tough as nails. I trust that you can take care of yourself, that you can deal with anything that comes your way."

"You're the only one who thinks that," I whispered back.

"Maybe. Just remember that no matter what, you aren't ever alone. If anyone fucks with you, you show them who they're dealing with. At the end of the day, no matter what else happens, you keep your chin up because you are Mackenzie Williams, and may the devil have mercy on anyone who forgets it, because they'll be meeting him soon."

I spun around, but found myself alone in the alleyway. Jarrod's words weren't ones I'd ever thought I'd hear. They felt like ones meant for someone like Nem, for someone strong, for some badass who others feared.

That had never been me, but he'd still said it with complete confidence. Maybe he saw something in me that I didn't, something I couldn't.

And now it would all end. No matter how nice it had been to hear, what did it matter?

I'd hand myself over to Lorien and that was it. The end of my life as I knew it. Whatever Jarrod thought me capable of didn't matter anymore, did it?

My hands shook, but I balled them into fists. Fear didn't matter in the face of what had to happen. I could tremble and cry and shake but I'd do what I had to.

Maybe that was true courage, to face the end, to walk toward it no matter how it terrified me.

When I couldn't wait any longer, I exited the alleyway and looked toward the large hotel. There it was — the end.

Of my life.

My freedom.

My time with the men I finally realized I loved.

I walked along the sidewalk, dazed. Where before this, I'd been afraid of each person, each alleyway, I didn't even notice them anymore. Everything was hazy, like I walked through deep waters, my gaze locked only on the building.

A rumble to my side broke through my thoughts, but even it didn't feel important. At least, it didn't until someone grabbed my arm and yanked me to the side, into the open door of the back seat of a car.

Apparently getting abducted is just my thing.

I twisted to find myself beside a familiar face—Char.

And *boy* did he look pissed. He reached across me and slammed the door shut. "Got her—let's go," he called into the front seat.

"Let me go!" I shouted and reached for the handle.

"Not a chance, kitten." Char grasped my hands and pinned them together, holding them tightly enough that my thrashing did nothing.

"I have to go. This is for the best."

"For the best?" Hayden's voice growled from the front seat, his voice dark and angry. "You sneak out like this, and you say it's for the *best*?"

"I'd suggest you just stay quiet, Kenz," Vance said from the passenger seat. "Anything you say now will just be digging you deeper into a hole that your pretty little ass is going to have to climb out of."

"How did you even know where I was? I left my phone behind so you couldn't follow me!"

Char reached into my bag and pulled out my glucose reader, the one they'd given me on that first day. He lifted it, then lifted his own phone. "This is how."

The voice echoed out from his phone, the meaning becoming clear. They'd bugged my glucose reader, which meant they'd heard...

Hayden met my gaze through the rear-view mirror, his expression serious. "It seems we have some things to discuss, Mackenzie Williams."

And here I'd thought my day couldn't get any worse.

Want to see more from this author? Here's a taster for you to enjoy!

Black Heart Auctions: Buying Time
Jayce Carter

Excerpt

Kenz

Well, I'm fucked.

If only I meant it in a more literal way. Instead of me getting to finally ditch my virgin status, however, I was just in trouble.

Again.

Hayden, Tor, Char and Vance hadn't said anything else to me on the ride home, but had they really needed to? Hayden had uttered my most tightly guarded secret, calling me by my *real* name, Mackenzie Williams.

The silence in the car crushed me. I struggled to breathe deeply, as if the air had thickened until it became too heavy to draw in. Despite that, even when the car pulled to a stop in front of the house, I didn't move.

I didn't reach for the door, didn't make any attempt to exit. Even when the others got out, I sat there, frozen, staring down at my own lap because I couldn't bring myself to look anywhere else.

Was this it? They knew who I was, knew how they could use that. If only I'd moved faster, avoided Jarrod, left that damn bugged reader behind, I wouldn't be here. Now I'd potentially put Nem and the others in danger because I hadn't been smart enough.

Here I am again, screwing up everyone else's life.

The door opened, and I expected to find Hayden there. He was usually the one who escorted me, who watched out for me.

Instead, a dark hand appeared in front of me, waiting. I glanced up to find Tor staring down at me, his expression unreadable.

I'd caused enough trouble, so I set my hand in his and got out of the car. The slamming of the door felt like a warning shot.

We went inside, and I knew damn well I wouldn't be allowed to go to bed. No matter how tired I felt, how much I wanted to lie down and sleep, it wasn't possible.

Interrogations are better done when the subject is tired. I recalled Dane telling me that once, when he'd been trying to find out where I'd hidden some candy I'd stolen from the kitchen.

The memory made me smile, even as my eyes stung.

Tor released my hand and gestured at the couch. I'd done enough to piss them off, so I did as he asked, sitting like a good girl.

Why do I keep failing at that? Even when I want to do well, I still don't measure up.

It seemed my path in life.

A mug was set on the table before me, the wonderful scent of coffee streaming from the top. Char pushed it toward me on the table with a single finger.

"Thanks," I whispered and picked it up. The warmth seeped through the ceramic and into my palms, easing that tightness in my chest.

The others filtered in from the kitchen, one at a time, each with a cup of their own. It seemed we *all* needed the caffeine. Then again, I had no idea when they'd realized I was gone, so I didn't know if they'd slept at all.

When they sat, however, the juxtaposition struck me. How many times had we done this?

"What are you smiling about?" Char asked, an edge to his voice.

"I was just thinking about how we've sat here just like this so many times. It's weird to think it's only been a few weeks."

"And we almost never did it again," Vance muttered, a simmering anger in his tone.

"Getting right to it." I took a sip of the coffee, the taste of the sugar substitute familiar and welcome. "So you know who I really am?"

Hayden nodded, his face an already familiar one. He had the expression he wore when he was trying to stay calm, to be the adult in the room. "Yeah, we know."

"How much do you know?"

"Enough," Char snapped. "Even this far away, the Williams family is well known. Of course, as far as anyone knew, Mackenzie Williams, the last legitimate heir, was killed about a year ago."

Tor's gaze dropped to my stomach as he narrowed his eyes until the gold just barely peeked out.

"Yeah," I nodded and touched the scar through my shirt. "I wasn't lying about that. This is where my father shot me."

"Why fake your death?" Hayden asked.

"Because it was the only way for me to have a life. Otherwise, people would try to use me. I wouldn't be able to go to school, to have a real life, because people would constantly be trying to make use of my name and my bloodline. My father was Kyler Williams and my mother Caroline Hester."

Hayden cursed beneath his breath, the word vulgar enough to take me by surprise, given he didn't typically say such words. "So you're essentially a mafia princess, huh?"

"So you see why I lied? If anyone knew who I was, I'd never be free, I'd never get to live my life how I wanted. My father used me all my life, caring only about how he could sell me off to benefit himself. I didn't want that future."

"There are rumors that the girl who took over Kyler's spot was related to him, but it's not easy to get anything specific."

I couldn't stop myself from seeing Nem's face then, from seeing the way she scowled, or better the way her expression softened whenever she looked at me. "Nem. She's my sister—well, half-sister. We share a mother, but her father wasn't Kyler."

"Fucking hell," Char whispered. "You're telling me that your sister is *Nemesis*? The psycho bitch who runs the west coast?" He paused, then let out another string of curses. "Which means those bodyguards you talked about, you're saying they're the Quad?"

I laughed softly at his tone. It was far from the first time people had reacted in such a way when they figured out I knew the Quad. Normally, it amused me. A flash of fear when the recognition hit.

This time, my laughter felt hollow.

"Yeah," I admitted. "They're like brothers to me."

"And who were you talking to in that alley? I didn't recognize the voice and it doesn't seem from the conversation that he was one of the Quad," Hayden asked, his tone barely contained anger.

In for a penny. I had no reason not to tell them, did I?

"He's a fixer. He goes by the Fox."

"Jesus," Vance growled out. "Even I know about him."

"I guess this explains why getting attacked didn't freak you out," Hayden said. "Why would it when you were raised as a mafia princess surrounded by the worst of the worst, when your family has the most dangerous killers in it?"

"It's not like that," I said.

"Not like what?" Char asked. "Because I've worked in the shadows long enough to hear plenty of stories. Are you going to tell me they're killers with a heart of gold or something?"

I shook my head. "It's not that. I know how dangerous they are, but that's not who they are *to me.* To me, they're family. To me, Nem is the woman who could have left me to my fate, to get sold off by my father and killed, but she didn't. She risked everything and came back to rescue me. The Quad are my brothers, men who put themselves between me and danger time and time again. They're overbearing and annoying, but they care about and look out for me and gave me stability in life when I didn't have any. Even the Fox—he stepped in like a father for me when he had no reason to. I'm not stupid. I know people fear them, but to me? They're just my family."

Hayden let out a sigh that implied he thought me stupid. "You're naïve, Kenz."

"I'm really not. I didn't grow up nearly as sheltered as you seem to think. I've seen my share of terrible things, I've seen people killed, I've been targeted, I even know what it's like to feel my blood leaking away and think…this is it. It was the Fox who carried me to help, who saved me, and it was Nem who took over for my father to ensure I could leave and get away from that life. I know exactly who and what they all are."

Silence descended on the room, but it held less tension than before. It seemed like they each thought hard, like they worked through the pieces I gave them.

"Does Lorien know who you really are?" Char asked.

I nodded. "He does. He said it on the phone when we spoke alone."

"So that's why he wants you?"

I shuddered as I remembered the way he'd called us soulmates. "He said he loves me. When you were out of the room, he said that my real identity was why his family supported him going after me, but that he wanted me because we're soulmates."

A strange chill crept over my skin, and when I looked toward Tor, a darkness in his gaze made me want to curl in on myself. He blinked quickly and ripped his gaze from mine, as though shielding me from it.

"Doesn't that mean you've met him?" Vance asked. At my look, he shrugged. "If he claims he loves you, he must have met you. He came back specifically for this auction, for the one where you were set to be sold. He had to have met you somehow then, or he wouldn't have had any reason to target you."

"He used a voice changer on the phone," Char pointed out. "Even if she knew him, she wouldn't recognize his voice."

Hayden set his coffee down, most of the drink gone. "His family here is almost as big as the Williams family on the West Coast. It's possible he met you at an event sometime. Maybe he became obsessed then? While his family is important, it's too far for him to have had a hope of getting you from your father, but once you weren't protected? If he figured out your death had been faked, he might have just kept searching until he found you."

"Maybe," I said, unable to deny it. "My father knew a lot of people, after all, and I met more than I could hope to remember from parties." I rubbed my eyes, the coffee not doing nearly enough to keep me awake.

Then again, I'd snuck out the night before, which meant I hadn't managed any shut-eye. The idea of going to class today felt wholly impossible. How could I force myself to get up, put on a fake smile and see anyone?

"You should sleep," Hayden said.

"No, I'm fine."

"You aren't fine. You're going to pass out on the spot." Hayden took my mostly untouched drink from my hands. "You can miss your classes today and rest. You won't be any good in them anyway."

"I'm supposed to meet up with my advisor," I said.

"That's at four this afternoon. If you sleep now, you'll get a few hours before you have to go."

"So I can still go?" Hope sprang inside me. I'd thought after this fiasco he'd end up locking me down. I figured they wouldn't let me do anything after this whole mess.

"Yes," Hayden said, but the harshness in his tone said he I was far from being off the hook. "And tonight, after you're back, we will have a *very* thorough conversation on exactly what you did wrong, Kenz."

And here I thought I'd gotten off lightly…

* * * *

Hayden

"She asleep?" Vance asked when I got back to the living room.

"Yeah. I didn't know if she'd fall asleep, so I sat there for a few minutes, but she was out fast."

Char let out a long sigh, annoyance tinging the sound. "Well this sure all went to shit, didn't it?"

I couldn't argue with that. We'd thought we had some rich spoiled brat in our custody, but come to find out, we'd been really damn wrong. Who knew we'd had the pup of an entire wolf pack?

I sure don't want to tangle with that pack if they come looking...

I drew my hand into a fist as I thought about how close we'd come to serious danger without even realizing it. If the Quad had found out we'd all but abducted their little sister...

I shuddered to think about the hell they'd rain down on us.

Not that we couldn't handle it, but if we hadn't even known? It could have easily turned into a bloodbath.

"She didn't rat us out," Vance said. "When the Fox asked her about us, she could have told him what we'd done, could have asked for help, but she didn't. She lied to him and said we hadn't done anything to her."

Which brought up the *other* thing she'd said, the part none of us had mentioned.

Her words still echoed in my head, the ones that had come through our bug. *I love them.*

She loved us? I shook my head at the foolish idea. She didn't love us—she didn't even know what love was. Even if she did, she was far too young and trusting to be making such claims.

"It's just more proof that she's too innocent," Char said. "She should know better than to fall for people like us. She stupidly protected us instead of herself."

"And she was turning herself over to Lorien for us, too," I pointed out. "She was headed for that hotel just to keep us safe, to make sure Lorien didn't target us."

Just saying that made my temper sour, and I was glad she slept soundly in the other room instead of seeing my expression. Just the *thought* of her handing herself over made me feel as if I'd lose my sanity. What would that piece of shit do to her if he got his hands on her?

I won't let that happen.

But how was I supposed to deal with a girl so ready to sacrifice herself? How was I supposed to protect someone who didn't seem to give a damn about her own life?

My clients hired me because they wanted to live, typically, and they did as I said because they valued their lives. Did she not care about hers?

No, that wasn't it. That was my frustration speaking. I knew she valued her life, but she valued ours more. Maybe she understood love better than I did, then?

"So what now?" Vance asked. "We know who she is, have a better understanding of why Lorien is after her, but what does it change?"

"Not much," I admitted. "It doesn't give us any real leverage. If we expose what we know about her, it'd only put her in more danger. Instead of one psycho after her, she'd have countless ones."

"Kyler William's fucking daughter," Char muttered to himself as if he'd yet to fully come to terms with that revelation.

"He's not much like her, is he?" I said.

"You knew him?" Vance asked.

"Not much. I'd met him before, on a few jobs. I've done security work on the West Coast, and some of my clients weren't the best people. I ran into him from time to time. He was a serious man with cold, calculating eyes. I've heard plenty about him, though, and none of it's been good."

"Yeah, well, he's nothing compared to Nem who took over," Char said. "Maybe the apple didn't fall far from that crazy tree. I wasn't kidding when I called her a psycho. Her territory is peaceful, but that peace comes at a steep price. Anyone who causes trouble is dealt with in a very bloody way. I heard about someone who got into trafficking young girls, and my understanding is that they're *still* finding pieces of him all over that city."

I tried to picture Kenz surviving among people like that. I thought about her sweet smile, about the way she seemed entirely defenseless, and that didn't fit at all with the people I knew about. How could she keep being the person she was after living with and being raised by monsters like that?

How had she not turned into the same?

"Nothing changes," I finally said. "Her history helps us understand why Lorien wants her, or at least why he's targeted her. We've got to buy time and make sure Kenz doesn't do anything as stupid as this stunt again."

"Then what?" Vance asked. "Delaying only pushes the risk down the line. We still have no way to draw him out since he wants to make the exchange at a hotel. He's too smart to fall for the bug or tracker trick, either, so it's not like we can use her as bait and just follow her."

We are not using her as bait. The words scrolled across my screen from Tor after my phone chimed.

"I'm not planning to use her as bait. I don't think any of us are okay with that idea anymore."

Except Kenz. No doubt that girl would have done it in a heartbeat if we asked her to, which was the exact reason we had to keep her away from this.

"So what else?"

Give him what he wants.

The words on the screen had me turning my gaze on Tor. "Excuse me? I thought you just said we wouldn't use her like that."

He shook his head, his fingers moving quickly across his screen. *He thinks they're soulmates, right? People say that when they want to believe in love and romance. Give him the chance at that.*

The point remained lost on me.

Vance chuckled softly. "That's not bad, Tor. Never would have figured you for one to play that sort of sneaky game." He turned his gaze on me, his lips pulled into a smirk. "Lorien wants to believe they're going to fall in love. He seems to care what happens to her and what she thinks of him, right? What if we tell him that she wants to talk to him? That she's afraid of him right now, but if they talk, she might change her mind."

The pieces came together. It wasn't the worst idea I'd ever heard…

"So you think he'll agree to that, and he might let something slip?"

"He's arrogant and in love — at least, he thinks he is. That's a recipe for loose lips. Give Kenz the chance to talk to him and we might just find something to use against him."

"What if he gets his claws into her? She's already willing to sacrifice herself for us—clearly she doesn't make great choices when it comes to men. What if he tricks her and she decides life with him might not be so bad? What if she betrays us?" Even as I said that, I didn't quite believe it possible. Kenz was sweet and trusting, but I didn't think betrayal was in her nature.

However, that trusting nature could lure her into confusion, into making a choice because she thought it the right one.

She's smarter than that, Tor texted. *She can do this.*

When I couldn't come up with a better plan, I nodded. I didn't love putting Kenz in the line of fire, but I had to trust we could keep her safe.

All our lives were on the line, after all.

"And what about the other thing?" Char asked.

I love them. Those words echoed in my head again, precious and frustrating and proof of all the reasons we needed to be careful.

"What about it?" Vance asked. "She's young. It isn't shocking that she'd confuse reliance with love. Lock up men and women together and eventually they'll think they're in love. Just basic human instinct."

I hated Vance's words, but he wasn't wrong. It wasn't like we could indulge in anything. Our time was limited.

We knew it, had made our choice five years ago, knew that our lives were over one way or another when we finished this.

If we gave in to Kenz, if we let her think for even a moment that a future was possible, she'd be the one to ultimately pay the price. At the end of it all, she'd be the one to remain, to live on with that pain, and that wasn't fair.

"So we all agree, right? No one touches her." I checked, my gaze hard.

These men were almost brothers to me — with just as many complicated feelings between us — but I had no problem putting a bullet in any of them who dared to make a move on Kenz.

They each nodded in agreement, though the same shadow rested in each of their eyes. It was a desire for what she offered, for the fantasy that we could have some happily ever after with a girl like her.

But that wasn't possible.

We were broken, just moving along a path to finish this, and at the end?

No matter what happened, we couldn't hurt Kenz by leaving her to pick up the bloody pieces. It meant no matter how hard it was, how much I wanted to taste what she offered, I couldn't.

I had to focus on the task and nothing more, and that might just be the hardest thing I'd ever do in my life.

About the Author

Jayce Carter lives in Southern California with her husband and two spawns. She originally wanted to take over the world but realized that would require wearing pants. This led her to choosing writing, a completely pants-free occupation. She has a fear of heights yet rock climbs for fun and enjoys making up excuses for not going out and socializing.

Jayce loves to hear from readers. You can find her contact information, website details and author profile page at https://www.totallybound.com

Home of Erotic Romance

Sign up for our newsletter and find out about all our romance book releases, eBook sales and promotions, sneak peeks and FREE romance books!